# Courting Trouble

LIZZIE SHANE

## DEDICATION

For Kim Law, who helped me figure out how much I wanted to write Elena's story.

# CHAPTER ONE

"Oh my God, you're *her*, aren't you?"

*Oh, hell, not today.* Elena suppressed a groan as a woman in head-to-toe pink yoga couture stepped into her path on the sidewalk. The fuzzy pink roadblock clutched a rolled hot-pink yoga mat to her chest, her eyes wide and eager as she reached out with her other hand to clasp Elena's arm as if they were old friends bumping into one another on the street rather than complete strangers.

The move also locked Elena in place in case she'd been considering dodging around her new friend and making a run for it. Not that she'd considered running. Much.

Elena had long since learned there was no point denying it once she'd been recognized—especially when she was wearing a dress she'd worn to one of the cocktail parties on the show. Unfortunately, buying a new outfit for Caitlyn's wedding wasn't in the budget right now so the slinky blue wrap dress was getting another appearance—and making Elena stick out like a bright blue beacon on the Santa Monica sidewalk. She could already see other shoppers pausing and glancing her way.

Best to give the fans their thirty-second thrill and get back to her life.

LIZZIE SHANE

Elena curved her lips into a catlike smile, winked and admitted, "I might be."

"You are!" her hot pink barricade crowed gleefully. "Oh my God, I just *love* you. Can I get a picture with you? Just one? No one will believe I met you for real. Heather!" She flapped a hand at another woman exiting the yoga studio inconveniently situated midway between Elena and her car. "Heather, come here! It's the Slutty Suitorette!"

And there it was. The all-too-familiar kick in the stomach.

*You get topless with* one *guy on national television and suddenly you have a hashtag nickname you can never escape. Thank you, social media.*

Her super-fan turned away to frantically wave her friend over, momentarily releasing Elena—whose smile didn't so much as waver even as she mentally punched more pins into her imaginary Twitter Voodoo doll.

Heather joined Elena's new best friend, adding a chorus of "No *way*" to the "Oh my God" anthem. The two of them kept up a running commentary of "You are *so* much hotter in person" and "Is Samantha going to be the next Miss Right?" and "Was Daniel as big a dick as he seemed on television?" and "Do you just *hate* Caitlyn now?" even as they aimed and fired their camera-phones.

Elena concentrated on her smile and the perfect pose. Sunglasses off, chin down, eyes up, shoulders back, hand-on-hip—the motions were automatic now. She may not be able to control what the tabloids were saying about her or stop people—even people who claimed to *love* her—from using that goddamn nickname, but she could damn sure guarantee that she looked hot every time she stepped out of her apartment and took a phenomenal photograph whenever she was ambushed with a camera-phone.

She graciously accepted their compliments, protested she did not know who the next Miss Right would be, and confirmed that Daniel was, indeed, the douchebag to end all douchebags, before explaining that she and Caitlyn were actually quite good friends and she had to be running along because she was on her way to Caitlyn's wedding—to a man who deserved her a thousand times more than Daniel-the-dipshit ever could.

That last bit of news sent her new friends into paroxysms of delight—and had the desired effect of extracting her from their clutches. They shooed her off, mortified by the very idea that they would make her late for Sainted Caitlyn's wedding, and called good wishes for the bride and groom after her as she moved quickly down the sidewalk.

Elena kept her gaze straight ahead and distant behind her sunglasses, avoiding eye-contact with her fellow pedestrians in the hope that no one else would be tempted to waylay her now that Heather and Michelle had broken the seal. She'd learned in the last few months that after the first person accosted her, everyone else in the vicinity thought they had automatic permission to do the same, becoming more and more insistent as they gained in numbers.

And if she tried to turn them away that insistence could quickly turn belligerent. She had chosen to go on national television and make a spectacle of herself, after all. What right did she have to privacy? Or personal space?

She'd reveled in the attention at first—the whole idea of going on the show had been to get famous. To stop being invisible and become notorious enough that she could at least get an audition for a real part rather than just being another pretty face in a sea of unknown hopefuls.

Well, she'd gotten what she wished for. She was notorious and the offers were rolling in, but they were the wrong kind of offers. Doing a shoot for Playboy online wasn't going to help her escape the Slutty Suitorette appellate. And a porno was hardly going to be the break-out film that would land her a Golden Globe nomination.

She'd given up her day job to go on the show—and she hadn't worried about it for a second because *Marrying Mister Perfect* was supposed to be her big break. But now her savings were getting lower every month and prospective employers didn't want the kind of attention she brought with her. Elena Suarez was a walking fiasco and all of Southern California seemed to know it.

Though if she ever decided she wanted to take up stripping, she'd have her choice of poles.

And unfortunately if things didn't turn around soon, she may find herself trying on G-strings before long.

She'd hoped the initial frenzy would die down—and it had, somewhat. At least the paparazzi weren't camped outside her apartment anymore, like they had been when the worst of the episodes were airing. She was still a sideshow act, but being stopped by fans of the show who called her the Slutty Suitorette without ever seeming to realize they were insulting her wasn't so bad.

It wasn't the worst thing that had been said about her online. Or to her face. America's Sweetheart she was not.

She'd learned never to give out her email address and had gotten a lot of practice at changing her cell phone number after it was posted on a message board once and hacked twice—but that was just the price of fame. She could handle it. She'd wanted this. Been desperate for it.

Now if only she'd had one or two of the perks of fame to go with it.

From the corner of her eye, she saw several phones being lifted for stealthy pictures as she walked past, but she made it the rest of the way back to her car unmolested. She unlocked her little Beetle and slid inside, setting the bag from the stationary store which contained Caitlyn's wedding present on the passenger seat.

They were still watching her. She didn't need to look back down the sidewalk to feel the stares. How many of them would sell those cell phone pictures? She didn't fool herself for a second that the captions would be as innocuous as *Slutty Suitorette Goes Shopping!* The gossip rags would probably have her buying crotch-less lingerie for an affair with a married septuagenarian by this time next week.

Elena threw her car into first and pulled out of the parking spot, enjoying the feeling of revving her little yellow Bug through the gears as she zipped north toward the Pacific Coast Highway.

Caitlyn's wedding was being held at a private beachfront mansion in Malibu—thanks to some help from the deep pockets of the *Marrying Mister Perfect* franchise who were filming a Making-the-Wedding Special. The ceremony wasn't scheduled to start until much closer to sunset, but Caitlyn had invited Elena and a couple of the other former Suitorettes to join her for a private champagne toast at the mansion before she needed to start making herself bridal.

Elena checked the time and floored it up the

highway, digging one-handed in her bag for the little scrap of paper on which she'd scribbled the directions.

She found it, wadded in a corner of her bag, and smoothed the scrap against the steering wheel, frowning as she tried to make out her own handwriting. The name of the street was clear enough, but the number had been smudged.

Catching sight of the street, she turned sharply across traffic—and almost had to slam on the brakes to avoid running over a paparazzo. Not that it would have been much of a loss, but it would have been hard to explain to a judge. Plausible deniability and all that.

She needn't have worried about figuring out which house was the right one—a small pack of paparazzi swarmed around the gate at the second driveway on the street. It wasn't a Kardashian level feeding frenzy, but it was a bigger group than she'd expected. Especially this early in the afternoon, before any of the guests would normally be expected to arrive.

The fence was high, the foliage thick and the driveway long, so she could only see the roofline of the mansion as she pulled up at the gate. The paparazzi swarmed closer, shouting, "Elena! Elena, over here!"

She smiled and tossed them a wave—resisting the urge to add a middle-fingered salute. One of the security guards at the gate shouted something that made the ravening hordes fall back and she rolled down her window at his approach.

There were two guards, neither of which she recognized from the show, but she vaguely remembered Caitlyn telling her something about hiring additional muscle—and these two both had muscular down to an art.

Unlike the show's security guards who tended to

wear t-shirts and jeans and look more like bouncers than bodyguards, these two wore dark, tailored suits that looked like they cost more than her car. Both were jaw-droppingly handsome in very different ways—more like actors hired to pretend to be security than actual security, though they carried themselves like they knew they were the biggest badass on the block. The bigger of the two was built like a professional football player—a giant hulking mass of muscle, his shaved head gleaming darkly in the sunshine.

The one who approached the car, on the other hand, was all lean grace—more quarterback than linebacker. His light brown hair was cut short, which only seemed to accentuate the classically handsome lines of his face.

*Hello, gorgeous.*

Stud Muffin here was exactly the kind of guy she would lose her impulse-control for, if she hadn't sworn off men. And anything else that negatively impacted her impulse-control. She was New Elena now. And New Elena did not cause scandals. She was too busy trying to live down all the ones she was already saddled with thanks to Old Elena.

Stud Muffin carried a tablet, which he lifted as he stopped at her open window, all business. "Name?"

She arched a brow over her sunglasses, waving toward their paparazzi audience. "Didn't you hear? I'm Elena-Elena-look-over-here."

"Is that under L for 'look over' or H for 'here'?" he deadpanned.

Elena grinned, tempted to like this guy. He hadn't even missed a beat. "Suarez. Elena Suarez. Caitlyn's expecting me."

He hummed acknowledgment and tapped his tablet to flick through his list, while she occupied herself with admiring his profile. The man really was entirely too handsome for her self-restraint. The urge to flirt had her reaching up and tipping her sunglasses to the top of her head so she could make eye contact. Daniel—useless douchebag though he may be—had always told her that she could make him lose his train of thought with just a look.

She cranked The Look up to full volume.

Stud Muffin didn't even notice.

His attention was wholly focused on the tablet. She cleared her throat softly. He flicked another page.

She looked down at his left hand, but there was no ring on his finger.

Elena hadn't been invisible in so long she'd forgotten how *annoying* it was. All too soon he found her name on his list. Tapping it once, he snapped a crisp nod to his partner, who moved to open the gate.

"Have a nice evening, Ms. Suarez." He patted the roof of her car, stepping back.

"Thanks." Elena flipped her sunglasses back down over her eyes, resisting the urge to pout. She shouldn't have been flirting in the first place, but she was irrationally irritated that her target hadn't even *noticed* the do-me eyes she was giving him. That was premium grade sex appeal she'd wasted on him.

She rolled through the gate, one elbow resting on her open window. Another guard—this one even more disgustingly handsome and whom she *swore* she recognized from a cologne ad—passed out of the gate as she was driving in, calling out, "Hey, Dylan, the boss man wants to see you in the command center. I'm supposed to relieve you of duty."

Stud Muffin—Dylan, apparently—passed over the tablet and started moving toward the open gate before

Elena's car rounded a curve in the drive and the Studs on Parade at the gate vanished from her rearview. She forced her attention forward. She was New Elena now. New Elena did not ogle. New Elena was chaste and pure if it killed her. *And it just might.*

The long driveway switched back and forth a few times before the mansion came into view. "Wow," she whispered to herself, grateful she was alone so no one could see the greed—or intimidation—in her eyes. It was magnificent—everything Elena expected from a seventeen million dollar beachfront Malibu dream home. And totally out of her league.

She parked her car next to a small cluster of vehicles off to one side and climbed out, retrieving the gift bag from the passenger seat along with her purse.

"Elena!"

She'd taken only two steps toward the front door when it burst open and revealed Sidney, looking as perfectly put together as ever. The wedding planner and fellow former-Suitorette could have been the poster girl for California blondes—everything about her expensive and flawless. She looked right at home in the doorway of the gorgeous mansion, even as Elena's heels wobbled on the cobblestones of the driveway, her stilettos finding every hole.

The Suitorette mansion in Beverly Hills had been posh, but she'd known her role there. She'd had a part to play, taking the luxurious accommodations as her due, but now she just felt out of place—so she hid it behind her most confident smile. "Hello, Quitter."

Sidney laughed. "Hello, Trouble. It's so good to see you." She tucked her tablet under one arm as she rushed to greet Elena. "Samantha's already inside with Caitlyn. Come on. I'll show you to the bridal suite." Sidney hooked their arms together and Elena found herself carried along into the house. "How was your drive? You're still living in LA, aren't you?"

"Yep. Hopelessly addicted to Tinseltown," Elena confirmed.

They made small talk as Sidney guided her through the stunning foyer and up the *Gone With the Wind* staircase to the sprawling master suite where Caitlyn and Samantha waited.

Elena spread her arms wide as they crossed the threshold. "Fear not, ladies, the party has arrived."

"Elena!" Sam and Caitlyn squealed and leapt up for hugs—and Elena's discomfort melted away.

She hadn't gone on *Marrying Mister Perfect* to make friends—and there were several dozen sound bites of her saying exactly that to prove it.

She hadn't cared about being kind to the other girls—initially she'd only wanted to be memorable and that meant screen time and *that* meant being outrageous and saying the things no one else would say.

Then, as the show had progressed, she'd just wanted Daniel. The things he'd said to her, the way she'd felt about him, she'd been certain the other girls were fooling themselves by sticking around and had felt no compunction whatsoever about telling them that in the bluntest possible terms. It was *her* love story and they were the parasites on her happily-ever-after.

No, she hadn't made friends.

But then the unthinkable had happened.

He'd chosen Caitlyn.

She'd been blindsided. She *loved* him and all of his promises had proved to be lies. Everything she'd done had been because she was positive they would end up together. The ends justified the means. Nothing made sense if they didn't.

The world could have started spinning in reverse and she would have been less shocked.

Then the show had begun to air.

America hated her. The editing was brutal—but she couldn't entirely blame the editing. She'd said and done everything they showed on television, even if it was often shown out of context.

Trashy Elena. Bitchy Elena. The Slutty Suitorette. The show's viewers became an online lynch mob.

And Daniel was giving interviews, going on daytime talk shows, lining up to pass out the tar and feathers.

Strangely enough, the only people who didn't judge her for what she'd done on the show were the women who had been on it with her. Even her family had stopped speaking to her, but Samantha had reached out to her, becoming her lifeline as they spoke on the phone for hours every week.

She hadn't reconnected with Caitlyn until the reunion special—by then both of them had realized what a slime bag Daniel really was—and in the months since they'd formed a surprising sort of friendship.

She hadn't gone on the show to make friends—but some days it felt like the friends she'd made were the only good thing to come out of it.

She, Caitlyn and Sam had been the last three—the ones in the trenches the longest—while Sidney had chosen to remove herself from the show several weeks before the end of the season, stating that she just didn't feel a connection with Daniel.

*Smart girl.*

Samantha was a small-town Midwestern blonde—the show loved blondes—while Caitlyn had fiery red curls at odds with her quiet, sweet demeanor. They were all beautiful—*Marrying Mister Perfect* didn't pick unattractive Suitorettes—but as different as the Studs on Parade at the front gate.

Sidney and Caitlyn had bonded early—having quieter personalities and silver spoon backgrounds in common.

They both looked right at home at the mansion they'd chosen for the wedding venue, but Samantha made her eyes huge as she hugged Elena and mumbled, "Crazy digs, eh?"

"Oh, you mean you weren't planning to rent out a seventeen million dollar mansion for your wedding day?" Elena teased.

"No, thank you." After leaving the show, Samantha had gotten back together with her ex and now had a ring on her finger as well. "We're keeping it small—and cheap."

Sidney chimed in with tips for wedding planning on a budget as they migrated to the suite's private balcony overlooking the patio below where the reception would be held after the beach wedding. Plush white chairs formed a cozy seating area with killer views of the Pacific.

This was the life. The one Elena had always wanted that had always been tantalizingly out of reach. Luxury and beauty and all the comforts money could buy. And she was no closer to it than she'd ever been.

"Champagne!" Caitlyn declared, reaching for the bottle that had been left chilling for them. "My maid of honor and Will's sisters took me out for a bachelorette thingy in Tuller Springs, but after all the toasts to true love we had to do on the show with Daniel, it wouldn't feel right getting married without toasting *real* love with my Suitorette ladies."

The cork popped off and Caitlyn yelped as champagne overflowed. She filled three glasses and passed them out. Then she reached back into the ice bucket and pulled out a can of ginger ale, popping the top and filling her own champagne glass.

"Holy shit," Elena said without thinking. "How did you keep it out of the tabloids?"

"Keep what out?" Samantha asked, having been distracted by the view and missed the ginger ale sleight of hand.

"Congratulations," Elena offered, eyeing Caitlyn's waistband to try to judge how far along she was...and who the daddy might be based on the timeline.

"I'm pregnant," Caitlyn explained, when Sam continued to look confused.

Sam squealed, issuing her own congratulations, but Sidney didn't even blink—obviously the wedding planner had been in on the secret.

"Is Will excited?" Sam asked—much more tactful than Elena's silent question: *Is it Will's?*

"He's thrilled. We both are. And terrified. And anyone who says pregnancy is a wonderful glowing experience should be shot. I've been throwing up for three months straight."

"Yet another reason I will never breed," Elena said, raising her glass in a mocking toast. Apparently the baby wasn't a legacy of Caitlyn's brief engagement to Dickhead Daniel. Thank God.

"It's a minor miracle it hasn't leaked," Caitlyn went on, "but I think we're in the clear now. The press around us has been dying down lately. I think the only reason the wedding is a story is because it's happening so soon after the show ended and because they haven't announced the next Miss Right yet." She waved a hand to wipe away the topic. "Enough talk of *Marrying Mister Perfect*, let's toast before all the bubbles evaporate."

Elena obligingly extended her own glass as Caitlyn lifted hers high.

"I know there are going to be a lot of toasts tonight, but this one is just for us. The show was insane—no one knows that like we do—but if I never went on the show, who knows if I would have met Will, or if Sam would have gotten back together with Jase, and Sidney wouldn't have met Josh—"

Elena tried to keep her surprise off her face at the mention of Sidney and *Marrying Mister Perfect*'s recently divorced host. That was one bit of gossip that hadn't hit the tabloids.

"That isn't anything—" Sidney started to protest, but Caitlyn waved away her protests.

"Maybe. Maybe not. But you're still planning the wedding of the year and Elena is going to be the next big star. So I want to propose a toast. To real love and dreams coming true. To us."

Elena's smile was natural and easy—Academy Award worthy—as she clinked her glass against the others.

Caitlyn and Sam were both getting married, Sidney was planning the wedding of the year on a televised special that would launch her business into the stratosphere, and what was Elena doing? Running around taking fan photos in her fruitless career as the Slutty Suitorette and contemplating her future as a stripper named Cinnamon.

*Dreams coming true, indeed.*

Elena reached down and lifted the gift bag she'd brought with her to the balcony. "I also got you the traditional gift from your registry, but this is a little something extra from me and the girls."

Caitlyn made a soft sound of delight and accepted the bag. Reaching inside, she pulled out the album Elena'd had made from mementos from each of the Suitorettes from their season.

"It's us!" Caitlyn flipped through the pages of candid shots that had never made it on the air, exclaiming over each memory. "Oh my goodness, Madrid. The homemade sangria was such a bad idea—"

"Alcohol is always a bad idea on *Marrying Mister Perfect*," Sidney intoned dryly.

Elena had to agree—alcohol had figured strongly in the infamous Jacuzzi Incident to which she would forever be linked—but she held her tongue as Caitlyn kept exploring her gift. The Bahamas, Tahiti, Spain—they'd gone around the world in a hundred and eighty dates. A whirlwind trip on the quest for love.

A love the others had now found, just not on the show.

"Elena, this is beautiful," Caitlyn said finally, when she turned the last page. "And so thoughtful. Thank you."

Elena shrugged. "I figured you could use a reminder that it wasn't all Dreadful Daniel. As tempting as it can be to want to wipe those three months from our collective memories, there were good times too."

"There were," Caitlyn agreed.

"Absolutely," Sam said, "but thank God I never have to do it again."

Sidney raised her champagne. "Here here. I'm so glad I said no when they asked me to be Miss Right."

"Me too," Samantha chimed in. "Of course I was already secretly engaged to Jase at the time so he might have objected. Did they ask you, Cait?"

"Yes, but I was already head over heels for Will." She turned to Elena. "They probably asked you first."

Elena smiled her most mysterious smile. "I'm still weighing my options. There are so many opportunities to consider."

If she implied that the opportunities were good ones, or that the executives at *Marrying Mister Perfect* had actually asked her to be the star of the spin-off show, *Romancing Miss Right*, it was a harmless lie.

She certainly wasn't going to admit that she was the only one the producers hadn't asked. America may not care about the hopes and dreams of the Slutty Suitorette, but Elena had become a master at saving face. If only that were a marketable skill.

Caitlyn fell back in her chair, smiling dopily as she gazed toward the beach where the ceremony would take place, one hand resting lightly on the barely visible swell of her abdomen. "I'm getting married in four hours."

Everyone else's dreams were coming true. Elena smiled, sinking back into the plush chair on the perfect California afternoon, and pretended her life was going perfectly too.

And she planned.

The executive producer and host of *Marrying Mister Perfect* would both be at the reception tonight. Sure, they hadn't asked her to be Miss Right, but they also hadn't announced who it would be. Which meant nothing was official yet. Nice girls might wait to be asked, but Elena had never been the kind of girl to wait for things to come to her. If she wanted something, she had to go after it. So she would ask Miranda and Josh tonight.

She'd shot herself in the foot the first time, getting lost in the moment with Daniel, but this would be different.

She might be a reality television cautionary tale now, but *Romancing Miss Right* could be her redemption. She would be the New Elena and America would fall in love with her. It had happened before. This was her second chance. She wasn't going to screw it up. And she sure as hell wasn't going to let it pass her by.

# CHAPTER TWO

Adam Dylan knocked on his boss's door, ready to get his ass chewed for doing the right thing. It wouldn't be the first time, but at least this time there was a shadow of a chance his boss might listen to him.

Maybe.

A distracted voice called out for him to enter and he pushed open the door to the room that Elite Protection had commandeered as their command center during the wedding detail. The space was a decent sized home office, but was too small for all the equipment crammed into it, leaving little room for the room's two occupants.

Max Dewitt, owner of Elite Protection, stood leaning over the shoulder of the company's tech expert, Candy Raines, as she pointed out something on a laptop screen. Today Candy was all sleek black skirt-suit and a slicked down bun—like a high-end lawyer in a legal thriller—but in the six months since Adam started with Elite Protection, he'd seen her in everything from a Japanese school girl outfit to biker leathers.

When he'd asked her—one afternoon when she'd shown up for work in Daisy Dukes and a flannel crop-top—why she went to such varied fashion extremes, she'd told him she was conducting an informal sociology experiment to see what kind of assumptions people made about her based on her appearance. And then winked and told him she just liked to mess with people's heads.

She was a wizard with electronics, and as far as Adam was concerned she could wear whatever the hell she wanted. Which today was lawyer chic.

Max had shrugged off his suit jacket and tossed it over an empty equipment bin. The tableau could have been intimate, but the vibe in the air was off. All business.

"There! See? Someone is clearly piggy-backing the signal." Candy tapped something on the screen as Adam clicked the door shut behind him and she spoke without taking her gaze away from the computer. "Hey, Dylan. One sec and Max is all yours."

Adam wasn't surprised she knew who had knocked—the wall of video monitors in front of her linked to all the cameras she'd set up in the house. There was nowhere to sit, so he found a patch of wall that wasn't supporting a tower of equipment and leaned against it, folding his arms.

Max straightened, frowning down at the screen. "We don't have enough of our ear-buds to outfit all of the show's regular security with them. Can you do something to their comms to upgrade their encryption so whoever is listening in can't do it anymore?"

Candy lifted an ancient looking headset, disgust plain on her face. "I'll see what I can do. If they weren't such bargain basement Radio Shack crap I could do more, but MMP obviously wasn't spending the big bucks on their security gear."

"Do what you can," Max instructed. "We have to play nice with their security on this one."

"Even if they don't know what the hell they're doing," Candy muttered, her attention already diverted by the problem in front of her.

Max turned to Adam, snagging his suit jacket and shrugging into it. "Come on. Let's find somewhere we can talk where we won't disturb Candy."

Adam silently trailed his boss up the stairs and down a long hallway. Max was only a year older than Adam himself, but he'd already built from scratch and sold-off one multi-million dollar company before deciding to launch Elite Protection, a personal bodyguard service for the crème-de-la-crème of Hollywood. The celebs at this event were more D-list than Elite's usual carefully cultivated clientele, but Adam had heard that the pretty blonde wedding planner running around the mansion was Max's sister.

Like everything in this town, it all came down to who you knew.

Max opened a door and waved Adam into the upstairs study before following and shutting the door behind him. Adam looked around the lavishly appointed room, seeing none of it as he wondered whether he would still have a job when he walked out of it.

Max cut right to the chase. "Would you care to explain to me why I got yelled at by Sandy Newton this morning?"

Cassandra Newton. Box Office Gold. Top of the A-List for over a decade. The rare movie star who had transitioned fifteen years ago from being America's rom-com sweetheart to perennial Oscar nominee without missing a step.

And bane of his existence.

"I turned down a job," Adam said simply. When getting his ass chewed, he'd learned from experience that simplicity was best.

"So I gathered," Max said dryly, taking a seat on the couch and waving him toward one of the large armchairs. "Apparently you also informed one of the biggest stars in Hollywood that you were booked solid for the next month and would not be able to take any job she had for you for the foreseeable future."

Adam sat, rigid with tension. "It wasn't for her—"

"It was for her daughter. I'm aware."

"She wanted me on the red carpet with her at the premiere of some big summer blockbuster. That's not security. It's a publicity stunt."

"Of course it is," Max said, without turning a hair. "You saved little Cassie's life and now she wants to show off her hero."

"My job is to protect people. Not to be a show pony."

"Your job is both," Max said, blunt and unsympathetic. "Clients come to us—and pay our astronomical fees—because we're more than just security. We're image enhancement. Our clients want Tank and Cross because they want to be guarded by former Pro-Bowl athletes. They want Pretty Boy because he's not just a black-belt, he's a model, and in this town there's status in having the most handsome bodyguard in the room. And they want *you*, because you're the All-American hero."

"The Secret Service asked me to avoid unnecessary publicity." Right before they asked him to resign.

"Which is idiotic. You're the best PR they'd had in years."

"I failed to do my job," Adam argued, feeling a certain vicious satisfaction in voicing the truth that few people knew and even fewer would acknowledge out loud. "Very publicly." Thanks to cell phone videos and the magic of YouTube, his dereliction of duty had gone viral.

"And in the process you saved a girl from a burning building. A very *famous* girl. The truth may be that you left your detail to do it, potentially endangering the life of the son of a vice-presidential candidate in the process, but the optics are all the media care about. And the optics right now are that you don't want to be seen with the first family of Hollywood in public after you saved precious Cassie Newton from certain death. Which is pissing off her mother, who feels the need to call me at seven in the morning and yell at me. I don't like it when my clients yell at me. And I like it even less when I'm blindsided by it because one of my guys is turning down jobs without telling me."

"I should have told you about it," Adam acknowledged.

"You should have. Especially since I'm supposedly the asshole who booked you solid for a month so you couldn't work for the Newtons again."

"Understood." He braced himself for whatever came next. The ultimatum. The line in the sand.

This had been a good job. He would miss it. Guarding celebrities wasn't exactly serving his country, but the jobs could be interesting and his coworkers were nice enough, though he'd never really bothered to get chummy with anyone because he'd known this was just a temporary measure. Just something to pay the bills until he figured out what he was going to do with the rest of his life now that his career had gone up in flames. Literally.

He'd sure as hell miss the money.

Max grimaced and rocked back on the couch, scrubbing a hand over his face. "Look, I don't want to be a dick about this—"

"But you will if it gets you what you want." No point bullshitting about it.

Max released a short laugh. He'd always appreciated the direct approach. Something Adam had liked about him. Especially after the politics and double talk of government work.

"Exactly. I want to have your back, but I'm a businessman. Sandy Newton is offering me triple fees and you're asking me to turn them down because you don't want your photo taken with a beautiful young girl who hero worships you."

"It isn't like that." *At least not entirely.*

"It's exactly like that. You saved her life. You are her hero. Forever. So don't be a dick about it just because it ended your Secret Service career."

Adam ground his teeth, still waiting for that ultimatum. "I won't do the job."

Max sighed. "You can have a pass on this one, but if you won't take jobs that put you in the public eye, you might want to think about another line of work."

And there it was. "Are you firing me?"

"Hell, no," Max said, lazy and completely at ease, not rising to match his aggressive tone. "You're great for business. And believe it or not, I like you. But you have to be willing to actually *work* for me. And all my clients want publicity. They want flash. And they pay us very well to get what they want." Max met his gaze, calm and unflappable. "Right now they want you. So you need to decide if you want to keep working for me, because that involves jobs where you are on display."

"I can do that. Just not for the Newtons."

"It would help if you would tell me why I'm turning down triple fees."

Adam shifted uneasily, resisting the words before

finally admitting, "Cassie… *likes* me." He ground his molars. "It felt like being asked to Prom."

Cassie had shown up unannounced at his beach house—which her mother had insisted on giving him as a thank you for saving Cassie's life, so it wasn't like he could refuse to let her in—wearing a skimpy little sundress and too much make-up. She'd batted her eyes and licked her lips, asking him to be her bodyguard like she was asking him to go steady. Considering she was seventeen, it had been unbearably awkward and the only thing he'd been able to think of was the booked-solid excuse.

He braced himself to have to explain more, but Max just nodded. "Fair enough." When Adam blinked in surprise, Max went on, "I like to give my clients what they want—within reason. She's got a crush on you because you're her savior and the tabloids are already all over any story with the two of you because it's like something out of a movie—completely ignoring the fact that she's underage and that shit's just creepy. You want to stay far away from that, I get it. I'm not running a gigolo service. Any of the clients try to treat you that way, you let me know about that shit pronto. Or if you don't want to bring it to me, Tank's wife is especially good at laying out what is and isn't considered sexual harassment for any clients who might be a little confused. Some people have seen *The Bodyguard* too many times."

He couldn't quite make Max's words compute. After the way his Secret Service partner had thrown him under the bus after the fire fiasco, Adam had gotten out of the habit of expecting anyone to back him up. "So I don't have to work for the Newtons."

"Nope. Plenty of other clients are requesting you—

though I'm not sure I can keep you booked solid for the next month, I can probably come close if you want to work that much."

"That'd be great." The property taxes alone on the beach house were kicking his ass. He needed all the work he could get.

"Good. Now get back to work."

He didn't wait to be told twice.

He still had a job. That was good. And his boss had no intention of pimping him out to the highest bidder. Also good.

So why didn't he feel good?

That was the story of his life these days. Ever since that damn fire.

Life should be good. He'd saved a life. No one was hurt in the process. A movie star *gave* him a fancy house on the beach. He lost his job and his reputation as the Secret Service golden boy, but a much more lucrative job in private security landed in his lap and he became *America's* golden boy. Whenever things started to go bad, they turned around and got ten times better.

And it just felt *wrong*.

Everything felt off. Like he didn't know what the hell he was doing anymore.

First world problems.

A door popped open in front of him, spilling feminine laughter into the hall. Adam stopped so he wouldn't run into the two women who stumbled out. Laughing, they hung onto each other and an open bottle of champagne, the blonde spinning awkwardly to shut the door as the brunette's eyes fell on him.

The same brunette from the dented yellow Beetle, with the Selma Hayek body and the Marilyn Monroe attitude—whom he'd recognized instantly from the one episode of *Marrying Mister Perfect* that would be forever emblazoned on his memory.

"Well, hello," she said appreciatively, dark eyes glinting. "I would say we really should stop meeting like this, but I'm so glad we do."

The force of her personality seemed to pulse around her like a heat wave, all sensuality and daring. The woman was hot enough to make not flirting with her a crime, but he was on the clock, so he gave her a crisp nod and a polite, "Ms. Suarez."

"Please. Call me Elena," she said, somehow managing to make the request sound decadently suggestive.

"Who's your friend, E?" the blonde asked, momentarily tugging his attention away from the supernova of sexual charisma that was Elena Suarez.

"How rude of me! Introductions. Samantha, this is Stud Muffin. Stud Muffin, Samantha."

He found himself wondering the same thing he had while watching her on that one episode of *Marrying Mister Perfect*—was she drunk, tipsy or just naturally that brash?

Whatever the answer, he had no business wondering about her.

"Nice to meet you, Stud Muffin."

"Adam Dylan," he corrected, extending his hand to shake her friend's. "I'm part of the security team for the wedding and I really should be getting back to my post. Ladies." He nodded, intending to move around them, but Elena pivoted neatly, hooking his arm and falling into step beside him.

"You can walk us down. The bridesmaids evicted us so we're on our way down to dip our toes in the sand until it's time for the I-Dos."

"You'll have a long wait." The rest of the guests weren't due to arrive for hours.

Her smile turned impish. "Yes, but if you had the chance to kill an afternoon playing around here at the lifestyles of the rich and famous, would you pass it up?" She didn't wait for him to reply. "If you get a break, you're welcome to join us down on the beach. Maybe a little pre-wedding skinny-dipping?"

"Elena," her friend scolded.

"Fine, Sam's fiancé might object to her skinny-dipping." Her eyes glinted wickedly. "But I'm not engaged."

They reached the bottom of the stairs then and Adam took her hand, detaching it from his arm. "As tempting as that is—" And tempting didn't even begin to cover it. "—I'm afraid I'm on duty. Enjoy your afternoon, ladies."

He ignored her pout, forcing himself to stride out the front door without looking back. Even in six months of working in Hollywood, he'd never met anyone quite like Elena Suarez. She was sexual quicksand—he'd get lost in her if he wasn't careful. And Adam Dylan was always careful.

# CHAPTER THREE

Stars glittered overhead. Love songs floated through the warm spring air. Smiles passed from face to face. The reception was perfect.

And Elena was officially having a deeply shitty night.

The network had dropped the *Marrying Mister Perfect* franchise—and with it her chance at redemption.

The ratings had been solid in the last few years, but apparently the new president of the network wanted to move away from what she felt were exploitative reality television shows.

Elena had heard all of this from the show's former executive-producer, Miranda, when she'd begun to pitch herself as the next Miss Right only to learn that Miranda had already moved on to a position at *American Dance Star*.

There were rumors that the show would be rebooted on one of the basic cable channels, but with all the people Elena knew at the show jumping ship, she'd have to approach the new producers through her agent. Unfortunately Dale was unlikely to do so willingly since he was convinced Elena would never make the transition to acting if she didn't get far away from reality television now that she'd gotten some name recognition out of it.

Not that Playboy was a better gateway to Oscar

nominations.

The ceremony had been lovely. Caitlyn looked gorgeous—and euphoric. The toasts had been heartfelt—everyone going on and on about how no one deserved love more than Caitlyn and Will. As if there was some measure of deservedness and they topped the list.

Elena tried not to feel a stab of bitterness that no one had ever said the same of her. Even as she tried not to let her disappointment show that she wouldn't be able to redeem herself in the eyes of the American public.

There wouldn't even be another season starting soon to take the attention off of her with another villain for America to hate. And even if there was another season on another channel somewhere down the road, who knew when that would be, or if it would be sensational enough to dethrone her as the reigning bitch of reality television?

Frustration welled, but she swallowed it all down— in part because she didn't want to infringe on the happiness of Caitlyn's big day, but also because she was a firm believer in never showing weakness. *Never* let them see you cry.

Old Elena would have grabbed a cocktail and a handy groomsman and slipped off to one of the mansion's many bedrooms to make herself feel better, but she was New Elena now. New Elena was drinking seltzer water and determined to be the freaking Virgin Mary if it was the last thing she did.

Surprisingly, the alternative wasn't even tempting. One drunken man in a purple tie had gotten a little too handsy on the dance floor earlier and she'd walked away without a backward glance, completely uninterested.

Now she sipped her seltzer and watched the dancers from the fringes, trying to fade into the crowd for possibly the first time in her life.

"*Bellissima* Elena." Dickhead Daniel lurched up to her side, reeking of gin and beaming at her in a way she couldn't believe she'd once found charming.

She'd never bothered explaining to him that *bellissima* was Italian the way he pronounced it, not Spanish, finding his effort at the time endearing. Of course, that was before he threw her under the bus of public opinion, back when he'd actually seemed like he deserved the title Mr. Perfect.

She couldn't believe Caitlyn had actually invited the asshat to her wedding, but maybe that was part of why Caitlyn was so much more deserving of love than Elena was. She could forgive and forget.

Elena tried forgiveness on for size by deigning to acknowledge his presence. "Daniel."

"Wanna dance?" he slurred, waving his glass toward the dance floor so the ice rattled.

Forgiveness didn't stretch that far. "No."

Daniel pouted, swaying like a drunken pendulum. "No one wants to dance with me tonight. Did you know Samantha's engaged?"

"Yes."

"*Engaged*," he reiterated, as if she'd missed the significance. "Thought I had a shot there. But no. Engaged."

Realization rose up in an unwelcome tide. Daniel was making his way through his exes, seeing if any of the Suitorettes would give him a second go. And Elena—the one he'd strung along the longest—hadn't even been his first stop. *Dickface*.

"I screwed up," Daniel admitted.

Elena turned to look at him, shocked by the words, by the startling hint of self-awareness in them. "Yes, you did."

He wasn't looking at her, watching the happy couple on the dance floor instead. "Could've been me," he slurred morosely. "Caitlyn's wife material."

"Which is why you proposed to her if I recall." *And not me, you drunken dipshit.*

"She said yes."

"Yes, she did. And then she changed her mind."

"I think I loved her."

*Was that before or after you told me I made you feel like the luckiest man in the world, you slimy excuse for a human?* Elena wondered if she kneed Daniel in the balls if it would make the papers as the high or low point of the wedding. Probably both.

The song ended and the dancers left the floor. Daniel swayed, pivoting toward her, and grinned, "*Bellissima* Elena," he said again, seeming to recall who he was talking to. "Always the sexiest Suitorette."

"Thank you," she said without enthusiasm.

"What do you say? You and me? Old time's sake? There're bedrooms upstairs."

Revulsion must have shown on her face. "You can't be serious."

"You're not still mad about the show, are you? You know why I couldn't pick you. America would have hated me if I'd picked you over Caitlyn."

There were so many insults in that one sentence she couldn't seem to process them all. Her hand tightened on her glass of seltzer, the urge to throw it in his face almost overpowering.

*New Elena. Be calm. You're New Elena.*

"Did it even occur to you that maybe you shouldn't

have told me repeatedly that you were going to pick me if you knew all along you were going to propose to Caitlyn?"

He frowned, visibly confused. "I didn't tell you that."

"You told me you didn't want anyone else the way you wanted me. You told me that you forgot the other women existed when I looked at you. You told me that nothing you felt for anyone else would ever compare to our chemistry."

"Well, yeah. Our *chemistry*," he said as if she was the idiot. "Of course I wanted you. You're the hottest thing I've ever seen. I never thought I'd have the chance to sleep with someone like you in my life."

"The show isn't called *Fucking Mister Perfect*; it's called *Marrying Mister Perfect*. Did it ever occur to you that I might have had a different idea about your intentions?"

Daniel held up his hands. "Hey, I never made you do anything you didn't want to do."

"Because I thought you were in love with me!"

The words burst out of her, louder than she'd intended. A quick glance around showed that no one was staring, but if she kept shouting at Daniel that wasn't going to last.

*New Elena. Be Zen.*

"I have to go." At her words, he perked up with a look she recognized all too well and she snapped, "And no, you are *not* coming with me."

She turned, moving rapidly away from the dance floor, along the edge of the patio. She deserved a freaking medal for not making a scene, if she did say so herself.

Her steps were quick, fueled by the sharp burn of anger and something she didn't want to acknowledge.

Hurt.

She hated that he still had the ability to hurt her. She wanted to be impervious to it all, immune to feeling like she was somehow less when he told her he wanted to marry Caitlyn and Sam, but he'd only ever wanted to fuck her.

He was the asshole. *He* was the one America should hate.

But he was Mr. Perfect and she was the Slutty Suitorette.

Heat burned behind her eyes and she veered toward the house. Bathroom. In instinct born out of reality television, she needed to get somewhere no one could see her before her cracks started to show.

Up the stairs, she ducked into the bridal prep suite where she'd toasted dreams coming true with Caitlyn only hours earlier. And dreams were coming true. They just weren't hers. She was the Slutty Suitorette. She didn't *deserve* her dreams.

The en suite bathroom was unlocked and Elena stepped inside, her heels clicking sharply on the tiles. Facing herself in the mirror, she was surprised to see her face looked almost normal. Which was good. She couldn't hide up here forever.

Not that she was hiding. She just needed a few minutes to regroup. Even the Slutty Suitorette was allowed to be rattled when the man she'd thought she would marry told her he'd only ever seen her as a sex toy.

A high-end sex toy he hadn't expected to ever get, but a sex toy nonetheless.

"*Elaaaaay-nuh.*"

The call came from inside the bridal prep suite. A lilting male voice she didn't recognize.

"Oh Christ. What now?" she muttered, reaching for the bathroom door right as the knob began to turn.

The door swung open and a man lurched in. The man in a purple tie. She didn't know him—hadn't even gotten his name when they were dancing—but she knew he was a wedding guest with wandering hands. Someone's embarrassing cousin or frat brother, no doubt. Some idiot who had a little too much to drink and decided he had carte blanche to pat every bottom in the room.

"There you are." He grinned sloppily. From the bleary look in his eyes, he hadn't sobered up any in the last hour.

"Here I am." She waved toward the toilet at the back of the expansive master bath. "It's all yours."

She made to move around him, but he sidestepped, blocking her path. "How's about a kiss?"

She almost rolled her eyes. "Sorry. I don't kiss men in purple ties."

He leered, yanking at his collar. "If you wanted me to take my clothes off, all you had to do was ask."

*Nice try, Casanova.* She tried to move past him, but he barred her way with one arm and her patience with drunk leches evaporated. "What if I want you to piss off and get out of my way?"

"Is that any way for a lady to talk? But then, you aren't a lady, are you?" He grinned, sloppy drunk and obviously suggestive, his long arms caging her between him and the counter. "I think that's my favorite thing about you, E-*lay*-nuh."

"Gee, thanks."

She tried to duck under his arm, but he moved faster than she would have given his drunken limbs credit for. "Hey. Where do you think you're going?" He wrapped both of his arms around her waist from behind, turning her so they were facing the mirror.

She glared up at his reflection, huffing a lock of hair out of her eyes. "Back downstairs. My boyfriend will be looking for me."

She hated that ploy. Hated that dangling an imaginary boyfriend over the head of a drunken asshole would often get him to let her go when telling him to piss off and die failed, but it had a remarkable success rate.

Not tonight though.

Purple Tie laughed. "You don't have a boyfriend, but I could be your boyfriend for the night." He rubbed his crotch against her ass. "What do you say, E-*lay*-nuh?"

She pushed against his hold. He wasn't huge, but she was on the petite side and he had a good ten inches and eighty pounds on her. "Sorry. Not interested."

"Now, that I don't believe. I know you. You're always interested." The hands that held her tight against him began to move over her hips, her waist, her ribs.

She caught his wrists, trying to yank his hands away from her body without success. "You don't know shit about me."

"Sure I do. I watched every episode." He leaned in close to her ear. "Twice."

*That fucking show.* She twisted, trying to wriggle free, but he used her movement to spin her until they were face to face. He pivoted and pinned her against the wall with his body. *Fuck.* She needed to get out of here. Now.

She brought up her hands to scratch his face off, but he caught her wrists, slapping them against the pretty filigreed wallpaper. "Come on," he crooned encouragingly, grinding his pelvis into hers. "Where's the Elena from the show? Let me see what got you all the way to the top two."

His lips mashed down on hers, along with the sickening awareness that no one knew where she was.

# CHAPTER FOUR

"Does anyone have eyes on Elena Suarez?"

Adam came alert as the call went out over the comms. He'd seen her at the edge of the dance floor earlier, talking with that douche from the reality TV show, but when he scanned that area now they were both gone. She hadn't looked happy.

"Nothing on the monitors," Candy's voice sounded in his ear, responding to Max's initial query. "She must be in a bathroom."

"She could have left already," Tank suggested. The bride and groom hadn't made their big exit yet, but one or two guests had already slipped out discretely.

"I'm watching all the exit points to make sure no one unauthorized slips in," Candy argued. "She didn't go out."

Adam frowned, remembering the way the reality show asshole had leered at her. He scanned the patio until he found Mr. Perfect Daniel—about to get a face full of knuckles if he didn't stop hitting on a very married bridesmaid—but Elena was nowhere in sight.

Unease whispered in the back of his mind, calling up a recent memory—the man on the dance floor with Elena getting a little too familiar with her ass as she repeatedly replaced his hands on neutral territory. That same man heading toward the side entrance, looking entirely too anticipatory for a man who was just wandering off to find a bathroom.

Shit.

He wouldn't be able to relax until he checked. "I may have seen her head toward the side door a few minutes ago," he lied into his mic.

After his last detail at a party had gone wrong because he'd been paying attention to the wrong female, he wasn't eager to admit his primary evidence right now was the fact that he didn't like the way some jerk on the dance floor had grabbed Elena's ass.

"Dylan, can you check on her? Sidney's worried."

"On it." He'd already been moving toward the side door before Max's request.

He took the stairs two at a time. There were a dozen bedrooms, each with its own bathroom, and she could be in any of them. He started with the door he'd seen her come out of this afternoon.

The bedroom was empty and the bathroom door was partially open, but some rustle of sound made him move closer to investigate.

"Ms. Suarez?"

The couple stopped kissing as he appeared in the doorway.

"You're interrupting, buddy," the man complained, but something about the tableau struck him as off even before he heard the heated crack of Elena's temper in her sharp, "No, you aren't."

He couldn't see her face. The man was blocking her— intentionally? But he didn't like the way she seemed to be pinned against the wall.

"Sounds like there's a difference of opinion." He stepped into the bathroom, trying to get to an angle where he could see Elena's face, make sure she was all right. "Do you want this guy here?"

"Of course she does."

She looked small, dwarfed by the man's larger frame, but there was nothing timid or petite about the anger in her eyes when he finally managed to meet her eyes over the man's shoulder.

"*No,*" she bit out, crisp and clear.

"That's good enough for me."

Half a second later he had an arm around the man's throat, his other arm looping under his armpit to put him in a half-Nelson and physically lift him away from Elena.

"Hey!" The asshole flapped his arms uselessly, instantly releasing the hold Adam now realized he'd had on Elena. Adam wished the asshole would struggle more, give him an excuse to kick the ever-loving shit out of him, but he just flailed helplessly and Adam held the drunk bully easily immobilized.

"Are you all right?" He sought out Elena's dark gaze. She hadn't moved from the wall, watching him manhandle her attacker with wide-eyed silence, but at his words she visibly pulled herself together, spine straightening, chin going up as something hard and strong entered her eyes to match the angry fire there. Her clothes weren't torn and he didn't see any visible bruises, but he knew the external didn't always tell the whole story.

"I'm fine."

"See?" the asshole in his grip was stupid enough to squeal, "I didn't do anything she didn't want me to."

Adam tightened his hold until the man gagged. "Right now the best thing you can do is to shut the fuck up." He met Elena's eyes over the man's shoulder. "Do you want to press charges?"

"I didn't do anything!"

Elena's eyes widened as if she was surprised by the question before she slowly shook her head. "He's drunk."

That was no excuse and they both knew it, but Adam wasn't going to argue with her over the pig's squeals at the idea of being arrested.

"I need to escort him downstairs. Are you okay to—"

"I'll come with you," she said, before he could suggest she wait here. He nodded. Right now, the lady could have whatever the hell she wanted as far as he was concerned. Especially if what she wanted involved kicking her attacker in the balls hard enough to seriously threaten his ability to procreate.

Shifting his grip, Adam twisted the man's arms around behind him and pulled out a zip tie to bind his hands. It was the first time he'd actually had to use them in the line of duty, so he gave them an extra tug until they dug into the asshole's skin, just to make sure they were on securely.

He marched the jerk in front of him, through the bedroom and down the stairs, more tempted than he cared to admit to give him a little shove and watch him tumble headfirst to the marble tiles below. Elena followed like a shadow, watching him, unnervingly silent.

At the foot of the stairs, he nodded her toward an armchair. "I'll be right back. Why don't you wait here?"

"Elena," the bastard whined. "This is ridiculous. You know I didn't do anything."

Adam shoved him toward the command center. "Don't talk to her."

As soon as he was out of earshot, he called in the situation, keeping it simple, knowing the rest of the team would fill in the blanks when he said he'd located Elena and there was a drunken guest who needed to be helped off the property.

Tank met him at the door to the command room, his massive arms folded across his chest in a pose that was designed to make lesser men piss themselves. "Who's this?" his deep basso voice rumbled.

"Don't know and don't care." In fact it was probably best he never learn the man's name. That ignorance was the only thing that would stop him from hunting him down and making him bleed. "All I know is he was bothering one of our guests and needs a lesson in how to treat women who say no. I'd love to be the one to teach him, but I need to get back." Elena had seemed surprisingly okay—more pissed off than traumatized—but he didn't want to leave her alone right now.

"I didn't *do* anything," the man whined.

Tank reached out and dropped one heavy hand on the weasel's shoulder. "I'll take care of this."

Adam nodded his thanks, leaving punishment in Tank's large, capable hands. He treated his wife like a princess and didn't appreciate men who did anything less.

Adam left the whimpering behind, heading back to the woman who was his top priority.

\* \* \* \* \*

He'd just kissed her.

She told herself that, over and over again, but her nerves refused to settle, buzzing like angry bees.

It could have been so much worse. Maybe nothing would have happened if Stud Muffin hadn't appeared like a knight in shining armor. Maybe Purple Tie would have realized she wasn't feeling it and done the gentlemanly thing.

And maybe pigs were sprouting wings all across America.

Her hands were shaking, so she fisted them, trying to squeeze away the tell-tale weakness.

There had been a moment—just a fraction of a second—when she'd first seen that it was Stud Muffin who'd come to her rescue that she'd wondered if he would just walk away. It was a he-said-she-said, after all. And hadn't she flirted with him that afternoon? Invited him skinny-dipping? What reason did he have to think that she didn't do that with every guy she met? Wasn't she asking for it? Wasn't that what they all thought of her now?

Then he'd lifted Purple Tie away from her, the feat of strength shocking her and sending a jolt of something like awe straight into her chest. He was one of the good guys. The ones who didn't care that she was Slut Elena. Who believed even she had the right to say no.

Her relief had been so acute she'd been embarrassed by it.

She didn't want to think she needed a man to save her. She wanted to believe that she could have clawed and scratched and bit and fought her way free—and maybe she would have. She should have bitten him. Made him bleed. But he was bigger than she was. Stronger. Drunker. If he didn't want to stop, could she make him?

Stud Muffin appeared then, crouching down in front of her with a sealed water bottle in his hands. "We can get you something stronger, but I figured this is a start," he said, holding out the bottle.

She took it automatically, twisting off the top and

taking a sip. She didn't like the way he was looking at her. As if she might fall apart. *Just a kiss*.

"That was very caveman of you," she said, nodding up the stairs to indicate his display of muscle upstairs. "Pretty hot stuff, Stud Muffin."

He ignored her attempt at flirtation. "Is there someone I can get for you?"

"No, I'm good." She took another sip. The water seemed to actually be helping.

His expression called that into doubt. "Are you sure you don't want to press charges?"

Visions of the press getting their hands on this story danced in her head. They'd have a field day with it. She could see the headlines now. *Slut Elena Cries Rape!* And did she really know that things would have gone in that direction? It was just a kiss, he would say. And was he wrong? Did she know what his intentions had been?

And Caitlyn's wedding day would forever be the day Elena accused another of her guests of attacking her.

"No. Thanks. But no." She stood, pleased with her composure. "I should get back to the reception. Don't want to miss the bouquet toss." She patted his arm, rock hard with clenched muscle. "Thanks for your help, Stud Muffin. I'll make sure those muscles get a bonus."

"Elena." Her name on his lips startled her and she realized it was the first time he'd called her anything other than Ms. Suarez. He frowned. "Are you sure you're okay to be alone?"

"Of course." No other answer was acceptable. Elena was always okay. "I'm great."

# CHAPTER FIVE

She wasn't okay. And she sure as hell wasn't great.

Adam kept an eye on Elena as the night went on, watching as she put herself in the middle of everything, sticking close to her fellow Suitorettes and their dates and avoiding Daniel, who eventually staggered off to pass out in the bushes before being escorted off the property and poured into a cab. She surrounded herself with friends and none of them seemed to notice anything amiss, but Adam could see it—the way her smile flickered and died when she thought no one was looking, the invisible barrier she'd erected around herself keeping the world at bay.

She was rattled and he hated it. Hated that she had reason to be.

She didn't want to press charges, so there was nothing more he could do. That was her call and he would respect it—even if he kept wishing he'd "accidentally" smashed his fist into the guy's face once or twice for the satisfaction of it.

The wedding continued as if nothing had happened—just like Elena wanted it to—and his gaze kept finding her to make sure she was okay, through the bouquet toss and the final dance, again and again after the bride and groom drove away and the guests began to trickle out. Some members of the wedding party were staying at the mansion overnight and they started heading upstairs as the celebration wound down, the dance floor slowly emptying.

The band stopped playing and the caterers did a final sweep to collect stray cake plates. Elena was on the edge of the dance floor hugging her fellow Suitorettes goodbye when Adam headed to the command center to hand his comm over to Candy.

Off the clock, he headed back outside one last time to make sure she got to her car okay, but when her friends went toward the driveway where the valets waited with the last of the cars, Elena drifted toward the path that led down to the beach where the ceremony had been held that afternoon. He caught up to her when she paused at the edge of the sand to remove her heels.

"You shouldn't be wandering around alone."

She looked over at him, obviously unsurprised by the sound of his voice. "I know." She took a few more steps in the squishy sand, moving into the darkness until he could barely see her, and her voice drifted over her shoulder. "Aren't you coming?"

\* \* \* \* \*

He followed. She'd known he would. For the last two hours she'd felt him watching over her, felt the weight of his protective gaze. Surrounded by people, feeling him watching her, it should have made her feel safe, but instead she was edgy, and his eyes on her gave her an awareness of him that felt almost sexual.

She didn't know what she was doing, leading him down the path to the beach. She couldn't trust her instincts anymore—they'd led her to be Slut Elena. She had been trying so hard to check her impulsiveness—

and look where that had gotten her.

She didn't know what this feeling was—only that everything seemed sharper and more acute in this moment. Part of her wanted to hang onto the crisp purity of sensation. To remember it. To use it in her acting.

What was it? Helplessness? It wasn't rage. She wished it was rage. Rage would have been easier. Acceptable. This felt too much like weakness. Like blame. Like all the shadows that had crept into her life lately, blocking out the sunshine of pure, wild feeling. She wanted that sunshine back.

Adam didn't speak as he followed her, respecting her silence. Respecting *her*.

She couldn't think of him as Stud Muffin anymore. Earlier the nickname had kept him at a safe distance, kept her from feeling crushed under the weight of her gratitude, but now it felt wrong. Dismissive in a way that dishonored what he had done.

How did you thank someone for something like that?

She sank down on the sand, setting her shoes next to her hip. Adam waved to the patch of sand at her side. "May I?"

"Of course."

He sat, somehow knowing the exact distance to make her feel comforted by his presence without being crowded by it.

They lapsed into silence, listening to the surf. She'd chosen a spot close enough to hear the water and just see the edge of the dark waves through the night, but all of her attention was consumed by the man at her side.

"Thank you," she said finally, knowing it was inadequate to encapsulate everything he'd done.

He grunted, as if he had no better idea how to accept

her gratitude than she did to offer it, and they were silent again, until the need to explain rose up and began to push against the inside of her throat.

"I've always been a flirt," she admitted. He didn't react, but she could feel him listening, the slight incline of his body toward hers inviting her to go on. "It was my super power. The ability to turn men into blithering idiots. Most guys were intimidated by me. Like I was too good for mere mortals. Look, but don't touch unless the goddess Elena gives you permission. But now, because of the show, they feel like they know me, like they have permission to put their hands on me, like I gave up my right to say no to anyone when I said yes to him."

"They're assholes."

She released a soft laugh. "No argument here."

"You okay?"

"I'm always okay."

He waited, letting his silence call her a liar when it would have been too rude to say the words out loud. Such a gentleman, her Galahad.

"I thought it would be different tonight," she confessed. "These people, the show people, they're the only ones who know there's more to the story than what people saw on TV. Whether they like me or hate me, at least they know that."

"I don't think anyone hates you."

"Oh, trust me, there are people who hate me." And she had the Twitter hashtag to prove it.

"All you did was make some guy's fantasies come true, but you did it on national television with a guy who used you and made you feel like trash when he should have respected you and protected you. You weren't wrong. He was."

"Yeah, but our society never blames the guy. I was

the seductress. The slut. He was the stud." She kicked the sand. "He was a shitty lay."

Adam coughed to cover a startled laugh and Elena felt a little surge of victorious pleasure at having wrung that sound out of her stoic, contained hero.

"He wasn't even a good kisser," she went on extolling Daniel's lack of virtues. "Do you know how long it's been since I've had a really good kiss? Two *years*."

She turned her head, eyeing the man beside her. He was probably a terrible kisser. The hot ones tended to be the worst—as if they thought the more attractive they were, the less they had to try. You'd think they'd be good because they would have gotten more practice, but no. The hot ones were useless.

"I'm not going to kiss you," he said, obviously feeling her speculative gaze, though he didn't turn toward her, gazing out over the water.

"Of course not. Because you're a gentleman. And the nice guys never want to kiss me because they think I'm trashy. So I get kissed by guys who kiss me like I'm Super Slut."

"Hey." He did turn toward her then, frowning. "Knock it off."

Her hero, who never let anyone say anything bad about her—not even her. "Sorry. Just having a little pity party. Don't mind me."

"You didn't strike me as the self-pitying type on the show."

"*You* watched the show." The words were drenched in disbelief. "No. You will not convince me that you're addicted to *Marrying Mister Perfect*."

"Actually, I just saw the one episode. I was in the hospital for a day—emergency appendectomy—and as I was recovering from the surgery my roommate's wife wanted to watch it. Half of the nurses on the floor came in to gossip about it. I had no idea what a big deal those shows were."

"Yeah, the fans can be pretty opinionated." *Understatement of the year.* "Which episode did you see?"

He gave her a look, like certain scenes had been burned into his memory.

Elena groaned. "Of course you saw that one. Awesome. My knight in shining armor knows I'm the Slutty Suitorette. There went that fantasy."

"What fantasy?"

"That you had no idea who I was and we could run away together to Greenland where you would never find out."

"It's awfully cold in Greenland, but I think they still have televisions. And Google."

"God, I hate Google. And YouTube."

"No argument here."

"Did you know I have a greatest hits montage set to porno music on YouTube? It's classy stuff."

"Look on the bright side, another season will start soon and then the internet will forget about you because they'll have someone new to torment."

"They cancelled the show."

"You're kidding. The nurses seemed obsessed with it."

"Apparently it was bringing down the moral tone of the network. But whether there's another season or not, I don't want to be forgotten. I don't want to be the Slutty Suitorette anymore, but I didn't come to LA to be invisible."

"Actress?"

"Can you think of a better reason to go on a reality

dating show?" Admittedly, she'd thought it was love with Daniel, but she'd also thought the two of them would stay in LA and make careers in Showbiz. "Unfortunately, my agent is so busy fielding offers from Playboy and soft core pornography, he doesn't have time to get me any real auditions. Not that I have anything against Playboy. Marilyn Monroe did Playboy. I just don't want that to be all I am."

She dug her feet into the sand. The heat of the day had faded, but it was still warm enough that the cool sand felt good against her toes. Adam was quiet beside her, but she could feel the subtle weight of his full attention on her. He tipped his head toward her, his silence inviting her to go on. There was no judgement emanating from him. Only a kind of waiting, accepting quiet that tempted her to fill the stillness with her innermost thoughts because he was the kind of man she could trust with them. And suddenly she *had* to speak.

"I was sort of hoping a turn on *Marrying Mister Perfect* would land me a spot on *Dancing with the Semi-Famous People*, but apparently I'm just not wholesome enough for them. They only want the good girls. Who they then dress up in skimpy sequins and hyper-sexualize every week for the viewing pleasure of the American public. If you're overcoming your embarrassment over being seen as a sex object, everyone loves you. But if you actually embrace your sexual power and *enjoy* being hot, then everyone has to shame you for being the whore of Babylon. It's that whole Madonna/whore thing. Because only men are allowed to enjoy sex. Women are the ones responsible for saying no. The guardians of morality. That's our job and God forbid we forget it for a second and actually have an orgasm we don't feel ashamed of."

She fisted her hands in the sand, all the frustration of the last several months pouring out of her, the words pushing their way up the back of her throat. She couldn't stop. Not now that it felt like someone was actually *listening*.

"Have you noticed that there are no roles for attractive women that don't objectify them? Even our most badass role models wear skin tight lycra or skimpy little bikinis. But God forbid a woman dress that way in her real life. Then she's *asking for it* and you don't have to treat her like a human if she's a sex object. Take Daniel." Daniel, who didn't see anything wrong with leading her on. "Daniel wanted to fuck me, but Caitlyn was pure." She held up one hand. "Madonna." Her other hand popped up like the scales of justice. "Whore. Who do you ask to marry you on national television? And what kind of idiot doesn't see that coming?" She'd been angry with Daniel. So angry she couldn't see straight, but she'd also been beating herself up because she hadn't seen the writing on the wall. "Men look at me and they want to use me. They see a walking, talking sex toy. And if I want to be treated with respect, I need to dial back my sexuality. It's my own fault, right? I'm asking for it."

"That's bullshit."

"Right?!" she exclaimed. "But those are the rules. If you don't act like a nun, you're fair game. Because if you don't treat your pussy like Fort Knox you aren't *respecting* yourself and you can't expect men to treat you like a human being if you demean yourself by having *sex*. But maybe I don't want to have to play hard to get or change who I am just to get a man to want me for more than my tits—spectacular though they may be."

She shook her head, digging her hands back into the

sand. "The Slutty Suitorette. I bet whoever came up with that one is proud of himself. But you want to know the kicker? The ironic little tidbit that makes this all that much more of a ridiculous farce?" She glanced at Adam to make sure he was still with her and found him watching her, intent and focused. "The infamous Jacuzzi scene? I didn't even take off my own top."

He frowned. "It looked like—"

She almost grimaced. Figured he would have seen *that* episode if he only caught one. Fate was that kind of bitch lately. "Of course it did. The editors know what they're doing. They made it look like we hopped in and suddenly my clothes were flying, but the truth is I played with my bikini strings, teasing Daniel, but it was almost an hour of flirting and three glasses of champagne later before *he* untied my top and sent it floating away in that infamous shot. But that doesn't fire up the viewing public. That's not as good a story."

"Assholes."

She laughed, soft and startled. "Yep. But what are you going to do? Argue that yes you took your clothes off on national television but there were *nuances* that got lost on the editing room floor?"

"You could have."

"I shouldn't *have* to. And it's not like anyone would have believed me. Why should anyone care about the little shades of truth when what they already believe is so much juicier? It's not like I wasn't willing. I went along. Even if it was always Daniel pushing down the accelerator, I wasn't exactly pumping the brakes. And I'm still kind of pissed off that America thought I should. Like it was my job as the woman to be the moral compass of the relationship."

·   "Fuck them."

56

She laughed again, louder this time. "You don't talk much, do you?"

"I say what I need to say."

"A man of few words." Which was fine because she had more than enough words to fill up the silence. "I guess I have a lot to say." But that wasn't new. She'd never been good at keeping her opinions to herself. It was just the topics that had changed. She'd never seen herself as a vigilante for feminine justice, but then she'd never thought she'd be slut shamed by America at large, either.

She studied the man beside her, marveling that he didn't see anything trashy when he looked at her. The last good man.

"Are you gay?"

# CHAPTER SIX

Adam choked on a startled laugh. "What makes you ask?"

"You haven't made a pass at me."

"And only gay men don't try to get you into bed?"

She shrugged, the movement a confirmation.

Adam wanted to apply his fists to every man who had ever treated her like she was only good for sex, but he simply said, "I'm on the clock."

It was a lie, but a convenient one.

"Ah. No mixing business and pleasure."

He nodded and she mirrored the gesture, seeming relieved to have an explanation that made sense.

She turned her attention back to the waves, drawing up her knees and resting her chin on them with her arms looped around her legs. "I don't know what to do if I can't be an actress," she mused. "No one will hire Slut Elena for a regular job. Morality clauses. Who knew? Maybe I *should* do porn."

"You were so much hotter when you weren't feeling sorry for yourself."

She shot him a flirty glance. "I thought you were gay."

He just looked at her, letting the silence speak. She was gorgeous, almost so beautiful it hurt his chest when he let himself really see her. Black hair moving against her shoulders in the slight breeze, full, kissable lips and dark, challenging eyes. And then there were her curves, which were—as she'd said—fucking spectacular. His body reacted, tension and heat gathering as blood rushed away from his brain, but still he held her gaze.

She was temptation and sin, but she was more than that. She was a dare from the universe. A wild, brilliant flame.

"I should go."

Horny hope died a painful death, but it was the right call and they both knew it. He stood before she had a chance to change her mind, offering her his hand to help her up. "I'll walk you to your car."

She gathered her shoes and took his hand. They walked up the beach in silence and back to the house, which was silent and dark now. The bridal party guests were asleep upstairs, but the patio was quiet and empty, lit only by moonlight.

He stood sentry as she collected her purse from the room where she'd stashed it, and then watched as she slipped the heels back onto her feet. He put a hand under her elbow when she wobbled on the cobblestone walk, applying barely enough pressure to keep her steady without indulging his senses by touching her more.

Her car was parked where she'd left it this afternoon, among the row of cars of those who were staying overnight. He stood with her as she dug into her purse for her keys.

"Are you okay to drive?"

"I was never that tipsy and I haven't had a drink in hours."

"That isn't what I meant."

She lifted her head, coming up with the keys. "Are

you worried about me?" A smile played around her lips. "Careful, Galahad. You'll spoil me."

She unlocked the car and he held her door as she slipped into the driver's seat. One of the business cards from his inside jacket pocket was in his hand before he formed a conscious decision to give it to her. He extended it through the open door. "In case you ever need a bodyguard."

She took the card from him, studying it for a moment before looking up at him with another of her guarded smiles. "I can't afford you."

Impulse and the need to see her again made him add, "Or we could go out sometime."

Her smile widened and something bright kindled in her eyes, but she was already shaking her head. "Honey, I'm trouble. You can't afford me either."

Then she was tugging the door out of his hands to close it and he didn't fight it, allowing her the exit line. Watching her drive out of his life. Kept company by the certainty that he'd missed out on something incredible.

\* \* \* \* \*

His business card taunted her.

She should have thrown it away—gotten rid of temptation—but instead she'd tossed it into her purse and now every time she dove into the messy jumble for something it seemed to be the first thing to touch her fingertips.

She could call him back and accept his date. She'd certainly replayed the moment when he'd asked her out enough times in her head. She'd almost said yes. It had been so long since she'd been asked out by a quality man and the way he'd asked her—as if there were no expectations behind it, just an honest interest to see more of her—he'd made it so damn hard to do the right thing and say no.

She liked him. Liked him way too much, if she was honest with herself. And she *trusted* him, which was even more dangerous.

Trust was not to be trusted. So she would keep her distance.

But she also kept the card, running it absently through her fingers as she waited for one of the self checkout stands to open up at the grocery store on Monday afternoon. People left you alone in the self-check lines and she didn't have the energy today to deal with the excitement or censure or feigned nonchalance that came with being recognized by the sales clerk.

And the absolute last thing she needed was some enterprising store employee selling her shopping list to the tabloids. She might be living off of Ramen noodles and cereal, but she didn't need all of America to hear about it, thank you very much.

She scanned the glossy magazines as she waited for her turn, automatically checking for her face, her name. Her hashtag.

Nothing. The issues with bootleg pictures from Caitlyn's wedding would no doubt hit newsstands in a few days, but right now they would only be online.

There was an odd sort of relief to not being on the cover of some scandal mag. Odd, because she'd always wanted to be there. Always wanted to be one of the glamorous people living their glamorous lives on the covers of glossy magazines. When she'd first started appearing on them, Elena hadn't minded that the coverage was negative. It had been a thrill. Her picture had been bigger than Jennifer Aniston's one week. Who cared if they were using that damn hashtag? She certainly hadn't.

Not at first.

But it was a funny thing, publicity. Like being slowly buried in sand, a handful at a time. It's all fun and games…. Until suddenly you can't breathe and the sand doesn't stop. It just keeps coming, burying you deeper and deeper.

It was a relief to see no one was piling on this week. At least not yet.

A register opened up and Elena moved to it quickly. She was wearing the cliché celebrity disguise—baseball cap, sunglasses, hair in a sloppy ponytail—and no one gave her a second glance, everyone absorbed in their own lives, thank goodness. Some days it was nice to just buy her Ramen noodles without a production number.

She quickly tucked her groceries into her canvas tote—god forbid Elena be seen to be environmentally insensitive—and swiped her debit card, wondering exactly how long she could live on Ramen and cereal before even that exceeded her budget. She hadn't been this broke since college, but that was the price you paid for living your dreams, right? She was just in her starving artist phase. So what if it seemed to be lasting longer than a single phase ought to? That would make the vindication of pulling herself out of it that much sweeter.

She'd have an excellent story to tell Barbara Walters. The Year I Lived on Ramen, she would call it. Provided Barbara Walters was still doing that sort of thing by the time Elena dragged herself out of the Starving Artist Pit of Despair. But of course Barbara would be—even if she had to come out of retirement to do it. Barbara was the Methuselah of Hollywood. Barbara was forever.

Elena was preoccupied envisioning her triumphant Barbara Walters interview as she stepped out of the elevator on the third floor of her apartment building, so she barely registered the envelope taped over the peep hole on the door to 303. Her door. When she did notice it, her brain shuffled through the logical explanations—change in building policy, misdirected mail, neighborly complaint, invitation to a roof party. It wasn't until she got closer that she could read the writing on the front.

The big block letters. The bright red pen. The pair of words slashed across the front of the envelope that stopped her in her tracks.

*DIE WHORE.*

# CHAPTER SEVEN

He'd hoped Elena would call, but not like this.

Adam hadn't planned to spend his afternoon off hauling ass down the freeway, his hands tight on the steering wheel and his heart in his throat as he remembered how shaken she'd sounded. *Turns out I could use a bodyguard after all. Someone was in my building. They got inside.*

He took the exit ramp too fast, weaving his Jeep through traffic and accelerating through a yellow light. How long had she been being harassed? Was it just notes or was there more to the stalking? He told himself he was only concerned because he felt a sense of responsibility for her after Saturday night, but he was more worried about her than he had any right to be.

He got to her apartment building in half the time it should have taken him and lucked into a parking space less than a block away. Elena waited on the sidewalk outside, a re-useable canvas grocery bag slung over the same shoulder as her purse, making her look lopsided. He took in the cap and sunglasses as well as the flip-flops, snug jeans, and half-zipped hoodie over a plain white tank top. Her arms were wrapped tightly around her middle and she was pacing—two steps north, two steps south—until she caught sight of him and moved to meet him halfway.

"I didn't know who to call," she said, apology dusting the words.

"Are you okay?" He hated how often he seemed to have to ask her that question.

"I didn't touch anything," she said, instead of answering. "You aren't supposed to touch anything, right? In case there are fingerprints?"

He nodded, even though forensics had never been his specialty. "Show me."

She waved him toward her building. "I couldn't wait inside," she said as he watched her unlock the exterior door.

He studied the security, realizing it was fairly decent. A CCTV camera was aimed at the door, which had reasonably new looking locks.

"I couldn't have been gone more than an hour," she said as she led the way to the elevator. "Just to the grocery and back. Do you think they were watching me? Did they know when I left?" She didn't seem to expect an answer, which was good because all he had was directionless anger at the bastard who'd frightened her.

The elevator opened and she preceded him inside, hitting the button for three. The building was five floors, with a handful of apartments on each floor. Not big enough or ritzy enough for a doorman, but the kind of place a single woman shouldn't have to worry about feeling safe.

"I'm used to getting them online," she said, speaking more to herself than to him, as she had been since he arrived. "The insults, the threats…"

"*Jesus,*" Adam mumbled, appalled by her reality.

"But this is different," she went on, as the elevator doors opened. "Someone was here. Where I live."

She waved toward a door with an envelope taped at

eye level. He read the words scrawled there and the buzz of worry for her in the back of his brain escalated to full on rage. His hands fisted, but there was no one to punch.

"You need to call the police."

"I can't," Elena protested. "It'll get out. The press. They'll spin it. Total fiasco."

"Fuck the press. This is your safety."

But she was shaking her head.

"Elena…"

"Don't you know anyone? You do all that bodyguard stuff. Don't your clients have problems like this? Problems they want handled quietly? This is what you do, isn't it? This sort of thing… it's normal for Hollywood, right?"

He wanted to argue that stalkers shouldn't be normal for anyone, but he forced himself to focus on the problem at hand. "Max will know who to call."

Elena nodded eagerly. "Right. Good. We'll call Max."

Max, unsurprisingly, knew a guy. Within the hour they had Max's detective friend and a very discrete team of police investigators at her apartment. The pros confirmed that it didn't look like anyone had been inside her place—and Elena agreed that nothing had been touched that she could discern—but they were taking the envelope on her door very seriously, especially after the threatening letter inside was revealed to contain some "concerning phrases" and disturbingly graphic details.

They asked Elena about previous incidents and he was relieved to hear this was the first time something had happened at her house, even as she put the cops in touch with her agent who was keeping a file on her "most concerning anti-fans."

Adam hovered, feeling useless, wishing for a battle to fight. He told the police about the incident on Saturday night, but they agreed that it was probably unrelated—which did nothing to make him feel better about the current situation.

After the detectives had gathered their evidence and left, Elena stood in the middle of her kitchen, her arms still wrapped around herself, not even leaning against the counter as if she was afraid to touch anything. It had gotten dark out and even with the lights on, the apartment seemed to be filled with shadows.

"Do you have somewhere you can stay tonight?" he asked, hating the idea of leaving her alone when she looked so fragile.

"A suite at the Beverly Hilton would be the Hollywood answer, but I can't really afford that at the moment," she admitted dryly—unbreakable Elena holding herself together by sheer force of will.

He couldn't just leave her.

"I have a guest room. You're welcome to it, if you like." He trailed off, because she was already shaking her head.

"No," she said, and he wasn't in the least surprised. He may not have known Elena long, but he'd learned she was not the kind of girl who accepted help readily. "Thank you, though. It was nice of you to offer."

"Who's being nice? You'd be doing me a favor. I'm not going to be able to sleep if I leave you alone here. It's either you crash in my cozy guest room or I camp out on your lumpy old couch—and that thing does not look comfortable."

Her lips twitched, but a smile didn't break the surface. "Has anyone ever told you that your savior complex is a little over-developed?"

"Once or twice." He thrust his hands into his pockets so he wouldn't reach for her. "It's okay to say yes. We'll both sleep better," he coaxed, fully expecting her to refuse again.

It was a sign of how rattled she must be that she said softly, "You don't mind?"

"Not exactly what I'd envisioned for our second date, but I'll take what I can get."

She lifted one eyebrow. "We had a first date?"

"I'm counting the beach."

"Ah." Her smile was small, but real. "I don't really want to spend the night here by myself," she admitted. "But I'm not sure I'm up to driving either."

He kept his expression neutral, knowing how difficult that confession must have been for someone as fiercely independent as Elena. "We can take my car and come back for yours some other time."

"If you're sure?"

"Positive."

He didn't question his jolt of relief when she moved toward the bedroom. "I'll just get a few things."

While she vanished to pack, Adam pulled out his phone and checked in with Max, taking the opportunity to request his schedule be lightened for the next few days. He was optimistic the surveillance tapes from the front door would reveal Elena's stalker and he'd be behind bars in the next twenty-four hours, but until he knew for sure she was safe, he wasn't going to take any chances. And he wasn't going to evaluate when she had become such a high priority.

She stepped out of the bedroom pulling a small hot pink leopard print roller bag. Manners drilled into him by his mother urged him to get it for her, but his training had pounded that instinct into submission.

"Can you manage that? I want to keep my hands free."

Elena nodded, understanding without needing to be told why she couldn't pull a diva act. Not that she would have. In spite of her reputation as the Queen Bitch of Reality Television, he'd never seen any hint that she was the kind of woman to put on airs and make ridiculous demands.

He was hyperaware of his surroundings, taking note of every detail as he led her down to where his Jeep was parked, Elena his silent shadow. She didn't speak as he drove them north toward his place, maneuvering through pockets of heavy traffic on his way to the freeway—which gave him plenty of time to think. And to kick himself.

Tonight had been an education.

He'd known about the show, of course, had known the paparazzi went into a frenzy when she drove by at the gate, but when she was complaining the other night on the beach he hadn't realized the extent of it. When he'd been trying to coax her out of her funk, he hadn't suspected how much she was dealing with. He hadn't understood.

The hashtag. The online threats. Email accounts hacked. Cell phones hacked. Losing her job. Months of harassment. All for a single impulsive moment caught on camera.

The frantic coverage around his moment of heroism had been one hundred percent positive and he'd found it hard to handle. He couldn't imagine what it would feel like if the media firestorm was negative.

"I'm sorry," he said finally, as they finally found a stretch of open road and he could accelerate. "About the other night. On the beach, I didn't know you had every right to bitch—"

A soft laugh from the passenger seat cut him off. "So now my life is pathetic enough that I have the right to a pity party? What was the tipping point? The *whore* on the door?" She snickered. "God, it even rhymes."

He frowned, trying to study her without taking his eyes off the road for too long.

"What? Why are you suddenly checking my straightjacket size?"

"You're laughing about it?"

"Too soon?" She shrugged and slipped out of her flip-flops, propping her bare feet on the dash so her sky blue nail polish caught the light of passing streetlights. "Some days it's laugh or cry and I do *not* cry."

"I'm sor—"

"Stop it. You're one of the few people in this country who doesn't owe me an apology right now. Save it for when you need it."

"Can I apologize on behalf of America?"

"No. Trust me, you don't want to take on the blame for that crap." She looked out the side window. She'd lost the hat and the sunglasses, but she still looked softer somehow. Vulnerable.

He hated that this day had done that to her. That her *life* had done that to her. But she was right. He couldn't take responsibility for every asshole with an internet connection—no more than he could pummel sense into each and every one of them.

"I look them up sometimes," she said conversationally, her head turned to watch the lights flow past the passenger window. "It's amazing how few people make any effort to hide their identity when they're insulting you from the safety of their home computer. And sometimes it sort of helps to know who is screaming the invective. When you can't ignore them. When they feel too real. So I make them all the way real. Like imagining the audience with no clothes to get over stage fright. Make the mob human. It doesn't make me feel better about it—sometimes it feels worse, but it takes away the fear."

The simple truth of her reality made his stomach churn.

"This was different," she said softly. "Today. It's one thing for some asshole online to tell you that you're a slut who doesn't deserve to live, but something else for someone to come to your house and write it on your door. Funny, I never thought that would be a distinction I would have a reason to think about."

"We're going to find whoever left that note," he said, instilling confidence into his tone. "And you can stay at my place as long as you like. I have plenty of space."

"My hero," she murmured, but the sarcasm she'd tried to lace into the words didn't quite make it.

"I'm not a hero." He'd never liked that word. It was a pedestal he didn't deserve.

"That just confirms it. The ones who protest they aren't anyone's hero are the really heroic ones."

His driveway saved him from having to respond. He hit the button to open the gate. The security lights—tastefully concealed in the landscaping—illuminated the beach house as he spun the wheel and pulled into the drive, the gate sliding silently closed behind them. "Here we are."

The cottage, Sandy had called it when she gave it to him, proving that movie stars had very different definitions when it came to real estate.

Elena dropped her feet from the dash, her jaw dropping as well. "You're kidding. You live *here*?"

Adam's neck heated. "It was a gift."

# CHAPTER EIGHT

Elena was busy gawking, so it took a moment for his meaning to register.

It wasn't huge, maybe two thousand square feet, and there wasn't much in the way of land between the high, solid walls separating it from the neighboring mansions—but she hadn't missed the fact that they were right off the Pacific Coast Highway in Malibu. On the beach side, no less.

This little patch of real estate had to be worth several million—and that was without counting the house, with its subtle touches of elegance that screamed money. The excessive kind of money. The charming little oasis of calm sat amid multi-colored cacti and other artful drought-friendly landscaping, overlooking what she was fairly certain would be a spectacular, unimpeded view of the Pacific when the sun rose the next morning. It looked like heaven. And it was his.

"Wait." She turned to look at Adam as he parked in the driveway and cut the engine. "Someone gave you a house as a gift?"

She was fairly certain he was blushing. "You really don't know who I am, do you?"

"When I saw this place I was thinking Tony Stark, but if people are giving you houses my best guesses are Scientology leader or gigolo. Either way, I have grossly underestimated you."

"Where were you last October?"

"Sequestered in the *Marrying Mister Perfect* bubble with the other Suitorettes. Who gave you a house?"

He hesitated for a moment, as if he would lie, then answered, "Cassandra Newton."

Elena's eyebrows took a trip toward her hairline. "And why is the most famous actress in America giving you houses? Are you the secret love child she gave up for adoption when she was fifteen or something?"

He didn't laugh. "Google me." The words were steeped in resignation.

"What?"

"Google my name."

"Ooo-kay." She pulled her phone out of her purse, feeling his eyes on her. He'd said it casually, almost tossing out the request to Google him as a challenge, but there was nothing casual about the intense way he watched her. This was a Big Deal in Adam's world. Whatever it was.

"Dylan with a Y, like Bob Dylan not Matt Dillon," he corrected, when she would have spelled his last name like the movie star's.

The most popular result was a link to a YouTube video. *Agent Adam Dylan Saves Newton Princess.*

"That's the one."

She tapped the link and moments later the video filled her screen. It was jerky and unfocused at first, obviously shot from the cell phone of someone who was running. For a few seconds all she could tell was that it was night, and then the running stopped and the camera spun dizzily until a house came into view. A beach house—larger and more opulent than the one they were parked in front of—and consumed with fire.

"Whoa," she murmured.

"Entire place went up like kindling, thanks to the drought," Adam narrated, his tone deceptively mild. "Entitled celebu-brat idiots decided to try setting off fireworks in the basement while a party was going on upstairs."

She looked up at him, but he pointed to the screen. "There. The side porch."

She directed her attention to the side of the burning house right as a man sprinted out with a large bundle in his arms. The figure ran directly at the camera, until it became obvious the man was carrying a limp teenage girl in his arms. In the background, Elena heard the other party goers who had become spectators on the beach gasping about how someone had been left inside and she knew who the hero would be long before the man came close enough to identify.

"Cassie Newton," Adam commented, as detached as if it had happened halfway around the world, rather than to him. "Sandy's one and only baby girl."

"No wonder she gave you a house."

Adam came into focus, Cassie Newton stirring feebly in his arms as he gently lowered her to the ground. She gazed up at her savior with undiluted hero-worship before someone jostled the cameraman and the cell phone video abruptly stopped.

Elena lowered her own phone to her lap, looking at the man beside her with new eyes. "You really are a hero."

"That's what they say," he admitted, the words coated in a startling layer of bitterness. "Only problem is I was supposed to be protecting someone else." He turned away, opening the driver's side door. "Come on. Let's get inside."

Elena scrambled after him, no longer nearly as interested in the house as she was in the man who owned it. "Hang on. Don't I get to hear the rest of the story?"

He already had her bag out of the luggage compartment, rolling it toward the house.

"Adam! Come on. You have to tell me the rest."

"I screwed up." He stopped next to the front door, turning to face her. "That's the rest of the story." He typed a code into the number pad on the front door until she heard the locks click open. He swung open the door and reached inside to flick the lights on in the entry before waving her inside.

"What? Were you the fireworks supplier or something?" she asked as she turned sideways to slip past him.

He brought in her bag and shut the door, typing into another keypad inside to reset the security system. "I was in the Secret Service," he said to the wall as he punched in numbers. "I'd worked my way up and finally gotten on my first protective detail. Sylas Walsh."

"The Vice President's kid?"

"He was just the son of the Governor of California and Vice Presidential candidate at the time, but yeah. And he wanted to go to that party." He was still facing the wall, but she didn't think he was seeing the security panel anymore. "When the house went up, our one priority was to get Sylas to safety. You aren't supposed to notice that there's a girl unconscious behind the couch and you sure as hell aren't supposed to leave your detail to go back to make sure she got out okay."

"Was Sylas hurt?"

"No. My partner got him out. But I walked away from the kid who was supposed to be my top priority. I

76

was the Secret Service golden boy. They were grooming me for a presidential detail and everyone knew it—but you can't guard the President of the United States if you can't be relied upon to put your subject's safety above all other concerns."

He turned to face her then, but he still wasn't seeing her. "My partner was only too happy to tell our bosses that their golden boy had fucked up. Knock me down a few pegs. Not like I could have hidden it. The damn video went viral. It might have anyway, but Cassandra Newton's only child? There was no way the press was going to ignore that."

"You saved a life."

"I did. And the Service couldn't publicly censure me without implying I should have let Cassie burn, but my career was over. I was told I could ride a desk for the rest of my career or I could quietly resign and look for work in the private sector."

"So you resigned."

"From the only job I ever wanted to have. And Sandy Newton gave me a house and Max gave me a job and the media hailed me as the greatest thing since Captain America—and it all feels like a lie because I can't tell anyone my big moment of heroism was also the moment I screwed up my life."

"Would you do it differently, if you could go back?"

His eyes focused on hers finally. "Of course not."

"Then own it." She glanced around the foyer—light, airy and filled with beachy charm. "As consolation prizes go, this house is pretty sweet."

"If only I could afford it."

"I thought it was a gift?"

"It was. And an offer I couldn't refuse. But just the property taxes on a place like this are more than I can afford. And that's before you consider maintenance and insurance and utilities…" He waved her farther into the house and she preceded him into the state-of-the-art kitchen, which looked down over a sunken living room ringed by floor-to-ceiling windows for panoramic ocean views in the daylight. Right now they revealed only the Adirondack chairs and outdoor couches scattered across the curving back deck. "Celebrities don't always think of the logistics behind their big romantic gestures of gratitude when they're declaring on national television that you *have* to let them show their appreciation."

"Not the worst problem you could have."

"No," he agreed.

*At least no one was taping notes to his door.*

The memory of why she was here seeped in. She'd been doing a good job of avoiding thinking about her Whore-on-the-Door friend, but reality could only be ignored for so long.

She wandered down into the sunken living room, staring out into the darkness beyond. Focusing on the house was much more pleasant than her reality. It was a calm, contemporary beach casual oasis of wealth. Like something out of a magazine. "So this is your style, huh?" She picked up a decorative seashell sculpture.

"More like Sandy Newton's style. Or Sandy's decorator's style. I haven't changed much since I moved in."

That explained the complete absence of anything that felt like him in the house. It felt like a vacation rental rather than a home. Somewhere he hadn't bothered to make his own because he knew he wouldn't be staying. "It's nice. I used to dream about places like this. I would read about the beautiful people with their beautiful lives and dream about the day when I was going to be a famous actress."

"Don't believe the hype. It isn't all it's cracked up to be."

She laughed dryly. "Sure it isn't."

Adam descended to the sunken living room with her. "You forget. I do private security for celebrities. I've seen way too much of their lives to call them beautiful. It's hard to keep the illusion that money buys happiness when you see it firsthand."

"Have you ever noticed that the people who say money doesn't buy happiness always have money? It may not buy happiness, but it sure as hell buys ease and comfort—and something to eat besides Ramen and cereal."

"I'm not saying money doesn't make life easier," he agreed. "I just meant that it's easy—especially in this town—to get so focused on getting rich and famous, and staying rich and famous, that you forget that what you're ultimately shooting for is *happiness*, not fame and fortune."

She shrugged. "Fame and fortune are easier to measure. I'll worry about happiness when I'm holding my first Oscar."

He looked at her and she could see the memory of the note she'd found today shadow his face. "Are you sure it's worth it? From what I've seen, the rest of it doesn't suddenly get easier or less invasive when you're winning Oscars."

"It'll be worth it." It had to be.

She hadn't come this far only to give up. She hadn't torpedoed her relationship with her family and smiled through being labeled the Slutty Suitorette only to walk away. She'd never wanted anything the way she wanted to be a star. She *loved* acting, loved it with the piece of her soul that would always be hungry. If she could give up the dream, she would have. This was what she was meant to do. The second she stopped believing that was when she felt like she lost herself.

This would be her success story. She was just at the noble failure part of the tale. It would turn around. It had to.

"Let me show you the guest room."

# CHAPTER NINE

The guest suite was small, but as elegant and tasteful as the rest of the house. It occupied a quarter of the second floor, facing toward the street side. Adam jerked his chin toward the other door on the street side of the upstairs landing and identified it as his office, before waving vaguely toward the single door on the beach half of the house and mumbling something about the master.

He seemed slightly embarrassed to have her in his space, but after the day they'd had she didn't have the energy to tease him about it. Instead she followed him into the guest suite and tried not to gawk.

Heavy patterned cream curtains were drawn over the windows, blocking out almost all the road noise. Every item in the room looked like it had been picked out by a decorator—with the glaring exception of the bargain-brand bookcase wedged into the corner to the left of the windows. The books were obviously not there for show—well-worn paperbacks rather than stylish leather-bound classics—and she wanted to move closer and investigate, but Adam's obvious discomfort stopped her.

He set her bag inside the door and pointed toward the en suite bathroom. "There should be fresh towels and stuff in there. Sandy sends over a housekeeper every few weeks to make sure everything is freshened up."

Elena set her bulky purse on the bed, turning to take in the entire room. "It's gorgeous. Like one of the fancy hotels *Marrying Mister Perfect* put us up in. And I don't even have to share it with five other girls who are dating the same guy. Bonus."

"I can't imagine…"

She shrugged. "Most people can't."

Her reality was a wild and surreal place, but she wouldn't complain. Especially not since it had landed her here. In this gorgeous room, with this gorgeous man.

Suddenly it was crucially important that she understand *why*.

She turned to Adam where he hovered near the door. "Why are you helping me?"

He didn't have the smug self-righteousness she saw in people who helped others so they could brag about their godliness. He wasn't trying to call attention to his good deeds. If anything, he seemed uncomfortable being confronted by them.

He frowned. "I need a reason?"

"You have one. I just can't figure out what it is. Most guys would only be helping me because they're hoping to get laid, but here I am, all vulnerable and susceptible to seduction and you won't come within ten feet of me. And you're acting like if I laid down on this bed right now you would run in the other direction. You said you aren't gay. Are you just not attracted to me? Not your type?" *Too trashy? Too slutty?* Why hadn't he made a move?

"You know you're a beautiful woman."

The *but* was loud for an unspoken word.

Was it possible he didn't want her and yet he still wanted to help her? She couldn't make sense of it. Men wanting to use her for her body might get old, but at least she understood it. She could work with it. His nebulous motivations made her nervous.

"But?" she supplied when he didn't seem likely to go on without help.

"You've been through a lot."

"So you feel sorry for me?"

His expression screamed yes, even as he stumbled over his words, trying to find an argument that didn't scream pity. "It isn't—I only—I want to make things better for you. Not be another of the things making your life worse."

"You're that bad in bed?"

He blushed. The man really was too adorable when he blushed. "You seem like you could use a friend. I'm trying to be one."

The man really was a saint. A freaking hero. He wanted to help her and he didn't expect any payment. He just wanted to.

She didn't know what to do with that. But it felt…

Amazing.

She couldn't remember the last time she'd been with someone who wasn't trying to use her—or who she wasn't trying to manipulate. But with him, she could just be. Somehow he had become a friend—and she realized that was what she wanted from him as well.

"Thank you."

He nodded to accept her thanks. "Are you hungry? I thought I'd make us something to eat. Why don't you get settled and join me in the kitchen when you're ready?"

He'd slipped out of the room and down the stairs before Elena could respond, leaving her in the Lifestyles of the Rich and Famous guest room, and fleeing like she was contagious. Didn't it just figure that the one good man she met in her life was the one man who didn't want her?

* * * * *

Adam wasn't in the habit of running away when things got dicey—which was part of why leaving the Secret Service didn't sit well with him—but standing in that bedroom with Elena, with her looking like a physical manifestation of temptation, he'd turned tail and run.

He moved around his kitchen on auto-pilot, trying to pretend he wasn't supernaturally attuned to every whisper of sound trickling down from above—and trying to forget the conversation from upstairs.

She thought he wasn't attracted to her, did she? His palms had itched with the urge to touch her the entire time he'd been standing in that room with her, hyperaware of the bed only inches away. If he'd stayed in that room two seconds longer, he would have kissed her. He'd had to escape.

He was such a hypocrite. Telling her he only wanted to be her friend, when he was just as bad as all the others. Just as desperate for her.

Though that wasn't why he was helping her. He hadn't lied about that. He didn't want her as payment. He just wanted her because… damn. How could he not?

She was sexy as hell, but it wasn't her insane body that made her the hottest thing he'd ever seen. Well. Not just her body. It was the wry glint of amusement in her eyes. That little edge of knowing cynicism. She was smarter than he'd ever imagined. And stronger. He'd seen seasoned celebrities have hysterics when a paparazzo got too close, while Elena had someone leaving notes at her apartment threatening her life and she simply reached down deep inside her into her reserves of calm and handled it.

She was incredibly contained—which was probably something no one else would ever say about wild, impulsive Elena, but then he had a feeling very few people knew her at all. He was beginning to think she was an incredible actress, capable of putting on any face she wanted the world to see, but somehow he felt like the face he had seen—the fear she'd let him see—was real.

And that reality was sexier than any façade.

Not that the façade wasn't sexy. The way she looked at him—the overt invitation in the curve of her full lips and the wicked flash of her eyes—God, her *eyes.* Black as sin and twice as tempting. Half-veiled by her lashes most of the time. They'd fall closed with a sigh if he reached for her, her face already tipping up for a kiss. He could practically feel her back arching under his touch, pressing ever closer.

"Shit!" A sharp jab of pain brought him back to reality. The reality that he'd just cut his index finger.

Adam swore again, holding it up so he didn't bleed all over the vegetables he'd been chopping as he flipped on the faucet and rinsed away the first rush of blood. The cut was shallow—thank God. He wouldn't need stitches. The wound slashed across the fleshy pad of his trigger finger, but it wasn't his dominant shooting hand so it shouldn't impact his job. He cleaned it quickly, wrapping it tightly in a paper towel as he rummaged for band-aids.

The house had come fully furnished and stocked and in the six months he'd lived here he'd avoided moving things—preferring instead to learn where Sandy had kept them and keep her house the way she liked it—but it did make finding what he needed in a hurry more of a challenge.

He knew Sandy kept a first aid kit somewhere in the kitchen; he'd seen it a dozen times, but where?

He heard Elena moving around at the top of the stairs, the slap of her bare feet on the hanging risers, and redoubled his efforts to find a freaking band-aid. He could just see explaining the cut to her.

*What happened? Oh, I just sliced open my hand fantasizing about how responsive you would be if I bent you over the bed upstairs and took advantage of you while you're feeling vulnerable. How's that for friendship, pal?*

Giving up on the drawers, he yanked open the cupboard beneath the sink—and there it was. A shiny white box with a shiny red cross. Adam crouched, popping it open on the floor in front of the sink, and grabbed the first band-aid of the right approximate size. He fumbled with the packaging as Elena's bare feet hit the hardwood floors of the lower level.

Sticking on the bandage, he snapped the first aid box closed and shoved it under the sink, shoving the band-aid wrapper into his pocket and straightening as if nothing had happened as Elena stepped into the kitchen.

"I forgot to ask. Any allergies? Things you don't eat?"

"I'm omnivorous." She took in the scene at a glance—the vegetables on the cutting board, the pans on the stove. "And you're full of surprises, Adam Dylan. I expected bachelor cooking—frozen pizza or noodles with canned pasta sauce. You actually know what you're doing," she said, sounding almost accusatory.

He returned to his post at the cutting board, picking

up the knife and getting back to work. "I've always enjoyed cooking," he admitted. "It relaxes me." *When I'm not fantasizing about Latina goddesses in bedrooms.* "You don't like to cook?"

She shrugged. "I like the end result. What's this going to be?" She leaned a hip against the counter a few feet away from him. Friendly distance. Because they were *friends*. And friends didn't fantasize about friends naked.

Much.

"Chicken Madeira with Sautéed Vegetables. Specialty of the house. You want to help?" He lifted the knife.

She held up her hands stick-em-up style. "I'd probably chop off my finger."

*You and me both.*

"Better to leave things to the experts," she went on. "Though if you need milk poured over cereal, I'm your girl." She snagged a slice of carrot from the cutting board, crunching into it. "Did your parents teach you to cook?"

"They showed me the basics, but I didn't really know what I was doing until I started working in restaurant kitchens for extra cash when I was in college." He moved around her to check on the pans on the stove, giving her a wide berth. "I even had a moment of rebellion during my junior year when I told my parents I was going to drop out and become a chef. But that ambition lasted about a week—much to their relief."

"They wanted you to take a bullet for the president?"

"Not a fatal one. But they probably wouldn't have minded a nice flesh wound." At her incredulous expression, he explained, "My father is career military and my mother is a nurse. Doing something honorable, doing your part to provide a service for your country and your fellow man is one of the core principles I grew up with."

"We've all gotta eat. Feeding people isn't helpful enough?"

"Not when I could be more." Gauging the time before the chicken would be done, he grabbed the cutting board and slid the vegetables into the sauté pan. "My parents were so proud when I got into the Secret Service. It was my only goal for so long—they can't understand why I left. And I haven't been able to bring myself to admit to them that it wasn't my choice." He grabbed a spatula, shifting the vegetables so they cooked evenly.

"Would you go back? If you had the chance?"

"Of course." The answer was automatic, ingrained.

"Because of your parents?"

"Because it's who I am." Even if it hadn't always fit like a glove.

"So you loved it? Your dream job was everything you dreamed it would be and more?"

"Life isn't that simple. When you work so hard to achieve something, of course the day-to-day business of the job isn't going to live up to the dream."

"So you didn't love it."

"No. Of course I did." He frowned. "How did we get on this topic?"

She ignored the question. "Are you still hoping to get back into the Service? Is that why you haven't told your parents you were asked to leave?"

He shrugged, poking the vegetables with the spatula. "Maybe. In part. I hate the idea of disappointing them, so I lie to them instead. And then I feel like an asshole for lying. Son of the year."

"I'm not exactly the poster child for good daughters,"

Elena said dryly.

"Your parents were upset about the show?" He grasped the chance to change the topic, though by the tone of her voice he had a feeling he already knew the answer to his question.

"You didn't see the Meet-the-In-Laws episode, did you?"

He shook his head. "Just the one."

"The infamous Jacuzzi." Elena groaned at the memory—and Adam very nearly did as well, for his own reasons. "It feels like the whole world knows every tiny detail of my life, but then I have to remind myself that's just reality television hubris. If you *had* seen the Meet-the-In-Laws date, you would know—along with the rest of America—that my father is very stern. Very traditional. And *very* religious. He made it quite clear when he was interrogating Daniel that he believed his precious baby was still a virgin and expected me to remain one after we spent the night together on the two-day dates. Suffice it to say watching the show was something of a shock to my father."

Adam frowned, reaching past her for plates. "I know he's your father, but…"

"How could he miss the fact that I'm not chaste and pure?"

"I didn't mean—"

"No, I'm not offended. I've asked myself the same thing for years. Silverware?" He pointed her toward the drawer and she began setting the breakfast bar with two places. "I'm twenty-six years old. I've been living on my own in LA since I was eighteen and I haven't been a virgin since I was sixteen, but to my father there are two kinds of people—good people and sinners. He knew I was good, so his precious baby could not possibly be a sinner. Now that he knows I'm a sinner, he's having a hard time adjusting. His world is very black and white. He's never been particularly comfortable with grey—but I've known since I was fifteen that grey was where all the fun is."

Adam had met more black and white thinkers when he was in the Secret Service than he'd expected. It had to be either yes or no. But the truth was so often more complicated.

She paused in the act of putting out wine glasses. "Or maybe between black and white is color. I think I like that metaphor better."

Elena was certainly colorful. She was vibrant with it.

"He hasn't spoken to me in months," she said, the words carefully casual. Adam looked at her as he plated their dinner, but she was too good an actress. He couldn't see any trace of her real feelings on her face. "My mother would never go against his wishes in any way, so I've been cut off from the entire family, lest I sully them with my sinful ways. I have younger siblings, you see. Wouldn't want to corrupt them with my unholy influence."

He carried the plates to the breakfast bar, setting them down and pouring the wine. "I have a younger sister too."

"And how does she feel about having a hero for a brother?" She took a bite of the Madeira and closed her eyes, seeming to savor the taste with her entire body. "My God, that's good. You're wasted as a bodyguard."

"I'm glad you like it." It was almost sexual, watching her eat, knowing he'd given her that pleasure. He shifted uncomfortably in his chair.

"*Like* is too mild a word."

Taking a bite of his own dinner, he tried to remember

what they'd been talking about before she had a food orgasm. Diana. Right. He sipped the wine, tasting none of it. "My sister doesn't really care about the heroism stuff. She just wants to know when she can meet Sandy Newton."

"How old is she?"

"Seventeen. Same age as Cassie."

Elena nodded. "My brother is seventeen. My sisters are twenty and twenty-one."

"And none of them have reached out to you?"

She shrugged. "Hard to think outside your own perspective at that age. Though somehow I bet you were thinking only of others and saving kittens from burning buildings when you were still in diapers."

"I think you have a distorted idea of me."

"Maybe." She paused for a few more bites of the Madeira, chewing contemplatively. "I've never been in a burning building, but I bet I would have run. No way am I going back to carry anyone out."

"You're tiny." She couldn't be more than five two. "Who would you be able to carry?"

"Small children? But even then, they're on their own." She laughed. "Can you imagine me as a mother? 'The house is going up in flames, kids! Save yourselves! It's every toddler for himself!'"

"I'm sure you'll be a great mother." It was an automatic platitude and her snort said she knew it.

"The Slutty Suitorette? Hardly. Can you see me in the PTA?"

He could, actually. She wasn't the kind of woman a man looked at and immediately envisioned with a baby on her lap, but he could see her taking no prisoners as a mom. Moving mountains for her kids. Confidently snarking her way into getting her way and driving the other PTA moms crazy. But somehow he didn't think she'd appreciate hearing that. "Don't read too much into your press clippings. God knows mine defy belief."

"Yeah, but yours are *good*. It's a little different. Women probably throw themselves at you whenever you go out in public, eager to have the babies of the most heroic man in America."

His neck heated. "There's plenty of time for that." Right now he was just trying to find his feet again—and figure out how he was going to pay sixty thousand dollars of property tax every year.

"Not according to my parents. That's one of the things they're most pissed at me about. Daniel asked me on one of the episodes if I wanted kids and I told him they were kind of smelly and annoying. America loved that. *Slutty Suitorette hates children!*"

"You aren't required to want children just because you're female."

"Try telling that to my parents. But the truth is I never really gave any thought to whether or not I would have kids. They aren't a priority for me. I might want them someday. But not until I know who I am without them. My mother never figured that out. I want to be me first, before I'm half of a couple or somebody's mother, but being me's not going so well at the moment."

He knew that feeling, better than he wanted to admit. The feeling that his life had gone off the tracks and he needed to find his center again. His sense of self—as cheesy and new wave as that sounded. He wanted to be him again. But how did he get back to that version of him that'd had everything in front of him—including a glowing career protecting the President—when his career was over and he was sliding into debt to pay for a house he didn't feel like he deserved?

He lifted his glass, waiting until she raised hers as well and clinking them together. His words were as much a hope as a toast. "To being us again."

"Here here."

# CHAPTER TEN

Elena was not cut out for hiding out.

Even in the world's most beautiful house, she only lasted an hour before she started to go stir crazy. Adam had needed to go to work. He'd offered to drive her by her place to pick up her car, but she hadn't wanted to make him late for his job—especially not when he was already bending over backwards to help her out.

So here she was. Trapped in the kind of house she'd always dreamed of, slowly going crazy.

She'd discovered when the sun rose that there was no beach in this part of Malibu. The house was built into a bluff, with the cantilevered deck thrust out directly over the water and the waves breaking beneath her feet. Each of the tightly packed houses on the bluff was angled to provide unobstructed views and the illusion of privacy, so Elena couldn't even people-watch the rich folks in the neighboring houses. She wanted to enjoy the luxury, wanted to bask in how the other half lived, but she'd never been good at being idle. Elena had never known when to stop pushing.

Thank God for cell phones.

She called her agent first.

Dale Reese was a little slimy, but he'd landed her a commercial the first month she'd been with him and gotten her a slew of auditions for shows like *NCSI* and

*Law & Order: SUV*—which had all turned her down, citing that she was "distractingly attractive". But he'd gotten her seen at least, and he'd never once hit on her. That kind of thing went far in Elena's book. It was vaguely comforting knowing that she had a morality-free shark on her side—a shark who was way more turned on by the idea of the money she could make him than he was by the idea of getting her into bed.

*Marrying Mister Perfect* had been his idea. He'd coached her through the audition, since she'd never seen the show and didn't know any of the favorite catch phrases. But he had her swearing she was *in it for the right reasons* and *ready for this incredible journey* until it became apparent they really wanted her as a villainess and then he coached her on how to be memorable. She wasn't *in it to make friends*. The other girls were just *jealous of her connection*.

Then she'd drunk the kool-aid.

She hadn't meant to fall for Daniel. She'd meant to be memorable. But she'd trusted him. She'd bought into the Mister Perfect hype. She'd thrown herself into her relationship with him, and now she was the Slutty Suitorette.

Dale loved the hashtag. *"No one will forget you now!"* he'd crowed.

But no one remembered her as Elena either. She would live forever as a punch line.

The auditions had dried up after the show aired. Apparently directors of crime dramas didn't want their faceless victims to be more noticeable than the storylines.

"Elena!" Dale cooed warmly when his secretary finally put her call through. "How's my little Suitorette?"

*Broke and receiving death threats on my door. How do you think I am?* "Eager to get back to work. Are you sure you don't have anything new for me? Maybe some indie movie that wants the free publicity of having me on set? I don't care if I'm someone's promo stunt, I just want a chance to show America I'm more than the Slutty Suitorette."

"I know you do, hon, but you need to be patient."

*Tell that to my landlord.* "I need this, Dale. Send me to a cattle call. I'll take anything."

"The Playboy offer is still on the table. I know you've been resistant to doing it, but I don't think it's a bad idea. We have to think about your brand. You're selling sex appeal. Which are you going to get more mileage out of? A Playboy feature that gets everyone's attention or a grungy little indie film where you hide your trademark sexuality and the serious critics delight in mocking your attempt to show you're a real actress?"

"Maybe they wouldn't mock. It could be my come back, my redemption. Hollywood loves those stories."

"They love them for drug addicted child stars. Everyone roots against reality TV stars."

His cynicism sent her hackles up. "Maybe you should have thought of that before you sent me on the show."

"Elena. Honey. I know this is a hard time for you, but you have to think long run. You're gorgeous. Smoldering. You made those other Suitorettes look like frigid hags. America knows you now. You just need to give them time to cool off a bit and then hit them with your heat again." He paused to let that sink in then added, "The director of that horror movie is still very interested in you."

He was, but Elena had met him once and was reasonably certain he only wanted her in the Oscar worthy role of Topless Co-Ed Victim #2 so he could try to get her topless—and bottomless—in his trailer on set.

"Just think about it," Dale said, with a finality that let her know the conversation was over as far as he was concerned.

"I want real roles, Dale," she argued. "I'm an actress, not a pair of boobs."

"You're both," he insisted. "Which is why you're going to be a star. Just be patient. I'll be in touch."

He hung up and she flopped down onto the couch in Adam's gorgeous sunken living room, gazing out over the sparkling ocean view that was just as breathtaking as she'd imagined it would be when she first saw the windows last night. Here she was in heaven and she couldn't even be happy because she was an interloper. This wasn't her paradise. She hadn't earned it.

She could call a friend to take her to pick up her car— but where would she go once she had it? And who would she call? She wasn't long on friends. Not real ones.

She'd lost touch with most of her friends from Albuquerque and all her LA friends were actors—which meant they were more competitors and step-on-you-to-get-ahead rivals than trusted confidantes. In her recent brush with infamy, most of her acquaintances had either distanced themselves, sold stories of her to the tabloids, or tried to manipulate her into being seen in public with them so they could get their faces on the tabloids themselves.

The only ones she felt like she could trust were the other Suitorettes. And most of them lived half a continent away.

She checked the clock before dialing Sam. Noon central time. Sam was probably at work, but she could leave a message—

"Elena?"

"Hey. I wasn't sure I'd catch you."

"I'm having lunch with Jase, but when I saw it was you I decided it was worth it to ignore him. What's up?"

And suddenly Elena didn't know what to say. Sam was in the love bubble in Michigan, busy planning her wedding with the man of her dreams. The last thing she needed was to be burdened by Elena's bullshit. "Nothing urgent. I should let you get back to Jase. We can talk later."

"Don't worry about Jase. He's using this opportunity to check his email when I can't give him shit for being a compulsive workaholic. You'd think moving back to White Falls would have slowed down the work obsession, but apparently you can take the boy out of the eighty-hour-a-week job but you can't take the eighty-hour-a-week job out of the boy. Anyway he's happy that I'm not making him pay attention to me when his email is singing its siren song. How are you? You were awfully quiet at the wedding. I'm not used to you and quiet in the same zip code, let alone the same sentence."

The wedding felt like a million years ago, rather than the few days it had been. She didn't want to bother Sam with the truth, so she just said, "I'm good. I think the LA grind is getting to me lately is all."

"Come to White Falls! Oh, E! You have to come. You'll love it. Summer up here is so gorgeous and peaceful. Promise me you'll come."

"I'd love to," she said automatically, hedging, "but I don't know when I'll be able to get away."

"Whenever you like. You're always welcome. I'll make Jase clean his work crap out of the guest room."

"Thank you. I may take you up on that," Elena said,

even as she realized she was lying. She didn't have the money, and even if she had, she wouldn't bring her drama to Sam's doorstep.

Elena didn't unload her problems on other people. No one needed to know about the handsy asshole from the wedding or the whore-on-the-door note.

Though there was a certain comfort in having Adam know. She wasn't in the habit of sharing her troubles, but he'd slid into her life so naturally she hadn't even realized he was past all her boundaries until now. It was strange, feeling like she knew him so well—and scarier still, that he knew her—after only a matter of days. There was unfamiliar intimacy there. The intimacy of a friend she truly trusted—as terrifying as that trust was.

She couldn't imagine not trusting him. But God knew she'd made mistakes in the past. "Do you remember the security guys from the wedding? The clean-cut one with the brown hair? Adam Dylan? The guy we ran into in the hall?"

"Sure. He was cute."

Elena heard Jase rumbling in the background, asking who was cute.

"Did you recognize him? Did you know who he was?"

"Adam Dylan? No, why? Is he famous?" More indistinct commentary from the other end of the line. "Hang on, Jase has heard of him. Some hero who saved kids from a burning building or something?"

"That's him."

"Okay, got it. Now why do I need to know who the hot bodyguard is?"

"I'm sort of staying at his place."

Sam squealed. "You're shacking up with all those muscles?" Jase complained on the other end—doubtless defending his own muscle-bound physique—and Sam shushed him. "Quiet, this is just getting good." Then, to Elena, "When did this happen? How long have you known him?"

"We met at the wedding."

"See? This is why I love you. You know what you want and you go after it."

"Yeah, but the last thing I thought I wanted was Daniel, and look how that turned out."

It wasn't until the words were out that she realized she was voicing her deepest fear. That her insta-trust with Adam was as misplaced as her feelings for Daniel had been.

He wasn't settled in this life. Just looking around his house she could see he hadn't made it his home—like he already had one foot out the door, ready to bolt if the Secret Service called him back. A man whose life was in a temporary holding pattern was not a good gamble—no matter how hot he was.

"Hey. Just because Daniel turned out to be a dud doesn't mean all men are lost causes. You're wiser now. You learned from the Daniel experience."

"That sounds like a ride at Epcot Center. The Daniel Experience."

"Not a popular ride. You'd only ride it once before you learned it was a total waste of time, no matter how shiny it looks or how much hype surrounds it."

"Do you ever feel like an idiot? Because we were sucked in by him?"

"I feel like an idiot because I was trying so hard to get over Jase I almost convinced myself I was in love with him, but he played his role well. He said all the right things."

"And we believed them." Elena didn't even have the

excuse that she'd wanted to fall in love. She'd just wanted to win and then she'd somehow convinced herself that he would be the prize that would make winning worthwhile.

"Don't beat yourself up. You aren't the first woman to be suckered by a man and sadly you won't be the last. I'm just excited you're seeing this new guy! Don't let Daniel make you gun shy about throwing yourself into it. You're *Elena*. You aren't you if you're being cautious and taking it slow."

She'd always loved that side of her too—the impulsive, wild side. She *missed* Old Elena, but she was so damn scared of letting it out again after the way the last few months had bitch-slapped her for her previous indiscretions. And letting it out with Adam, who had said he just wanted to be friends... out of the question.

No. Cautious and slow was the way to go. Even if the wrongness of it wrapped around her, smothering her. She'd always been the girl who was begging forgiveness rather than asking permission—when she bothered with forgiveness at all—and she'd liked it that way, but she'd learned her lesson. She would restrain herself. And the vindication of her eventual come back would be worth it.

It had to be.

# CHAPTER ELEVEN

He'd worried about her all day.

Adam was good at his job. He'd flawlessly executed all his duties on the afternoon protection detail watching over a pair of kids with overprotective celebrity parents, but he couldn't seem to stop wondering how Elena was faring.

As soon as he dropped off the celebrities' precious darlings, he headed back to the Elite Protection offices, using his Bluetooth to call the detective working Elena's case. He knew better than to think they would have already had any breaks in the case, but he'd needed to hear it all the same.

There had been DNA on the envelope. It was being analyzed. That sort of thing took time. The fingerprints were being run. Which also took time—despite what cop shows would have people believe.

And no matter how high a priority it was to Adam, the threat against Elena wasn't urgent enough to merit special treatment—which meant she would get the results when she got the results and there was nothing he could do about it.

The one positive thing that came from the conversation was the tidbit that their linguists had analyzed the note and suspected the threat might have come from a woman. It wasn't much, but it was something.

Adam pulled into the employee lot behind Elite Protection, squeezing his Jeep into the space between Candy's Tesla and Tank's Escalade. On the surface, the Beverly Hills offices of Elite Protection were all understated class. A client entering through the street entrance might think they had wandered into a high end Rodeo Drive boutique, if not for the complete lack of anything resembling clothing. The public areas were designed to create an atmosphere of luxury, giving the impression that the clients weren't just hiring bodyguards, they were purchasing status.

The staff areas were a different story. Everything was still top of the line—Max Dewitt didn't cut corners—but the offices on the floor above and the training rooms in the basement below had been designed to spoil the guards not the clients. There were even rooms for them to crash overnight if they needed it. Which he might if he couldn't pay his freaking property taxes.

Adam let himself in through the side door and jogged down the stairs to the lower level. Traffic had put him behind schedule, so he was a few minutes late to meet Tank in the gym. He was supposed to lift weights today with the former NFL lineman. Every EP employee needed to remain in peak physical condition—and standing around babysitting celebrities didn't usually satisfy the cardio requirements.

He stowed his gear in the equipment room, relocking it behind him, changed in the locker room and moved quickly past the gun range to the gym, not wanting to keep Tank waiting. He needn't have hurried.

As soon as he stepped into the gym's main room, he saw two figures grappling on the training mat spread over the center of the space. Tank and Pretty Boy stood to one side of the mat, watching the show with arms folded.

On the mat, Cross and Candy were locked in combat—and Cross was getting his ass handed to him. He might have been a professional athlete, but Candy danced around him, moving with a fluid, confident economy of motion that made him look like a toddler learning to walk in comparison.

Adam moved to stand next to Tank, nodding toward the mat. "What's this?"

"Candy's giving Cross his weekly badass lesson," Tank commented, never taking his eyes from the action.

Cross's body flew through the air to land hard, flat on his back on the mat.

"Ooh!" Tank and Pretty Boy chorused—half sympathy, half cheering section for the slender ninja schooling Cross on the mat.

"They do this every week?"

"When schedules allow. Usually in the mornings before the rest of us get in."

Cross was back on his feet without hesitation, charging at Candy. She ducked under his arm and in a move so fast Adam could barely follow it she was on his back, her legs locked around his waist, her arms in a choke hold around his neck. Cross twisted, trying to get a grip on her or shake her loose, but Candy was on him like a burr. He tucked his chin against the curve of her elbow, gaining himself a little breathing room, but Candy adjusted her grip, taking it away again.

Tank grinned. "I love this part."

Pretty Boy just glowered, like the entire scene annoyed him.

Cross threw himself down on the mat, clearly meaning to shake Candy's grip by slamming his weight down on top of her, but she anticipated the tactic, moving mongoose-fast so Cross only managed to knock the wind out of himself and wind up with a slim woman in bright blue lycra perched with a knee across his throat.

His hand smacked the mat at his side, tapping out.

Candy climbed off him. "You're still telegraphing everything you do. Think of it more like a football play. You have to fake out your blocker."

Cross took the hand she offered to help him up. "I was a defensive back. My job was to make sure no one could fake *me* out. Not the other way around."

"Okay, so don't think of it like that. Just try to be less obvious."

Cross grunted something vaguely affirmative and headed toward the showers, moving stiffly as Candy strolled over to where her audience waited. She snagged a towel from the bench beside Pretty Boy and patted at the light sheen of sweat on her skin.

"He almost had you with that leg sweep," Pretty Boy commented.

"He's improving." She batted her eyelashes. "You sure you don't want to try to take me? I promise to go easy on you."

Pretty Boy just glared.

Adam had a feeling he was missing something there, but he had something else he was dying to ask. "Why aren't you ever in the field? You're incredible."

She stopped eyeing Pretty Boy like a cat with a mouse and turned to Adam with a smile. "Thank you. But, as you know, being a bodyguard is partially about image. You boys are excellent at intimidating people into backing the fuck off because you *look* like big hunks of badass. There's a reason why most Secret Service protective details are comprised of dudes, even if there is the occasional nod toward gender equality. Most men don't want to challenge Tank, but men underestimate me. Which is kinda awesome in its own way, but it makes me less effective as a deterrent. So I hang around here, play with my toys and rule the world from my digital lair while you guys get to play with the celebrities. But fair warning, if we ever get hired to guard Ryan Reynolds, I am taking each one of you out if that's what it takes to get that contract."

Pretty Boy—usually the most easy-going of them—snorted and Candy turned her attention back to him with a purr.

"Don't be jealous, Pretty Boy. I'll still let you join my man harem."

The door at the far end of the gym opened and Max stepped through. "Dylan. Got a minute?"

Adam looked questioningly at Tank who waved him toward their boss. "Go on. I'll get the weights set up."

Adam followed Max out of the room, expecting his boss to lead the way upstairs to his office, but instead Max stepped into the long, narrow room that served as their gun range. He stopped beside one of the shooting stations and picked up a piece of the dismantled gun waiting there, keeping his hands busy cleaning it as he turned to Adam.

"Sandy Newton is still pushing me to find a space in your schedule for her. I'm not asking you to work for them, but it would make my life easier if I could give her an excuse besides you being booked for the rest of your life. I can make something up if that's what you want, but I'd rather tell her the truth. I try to have a policy of not lying to megastars unless absolutely necessary. It's your call, but I think she'll understand why you're uncomfortable. She's not unreasonable. Or I can keep it vague. Tell her it's for personal reasons."

"She'll think I have a problem with them. I don't want her to think I'm ungrateful."

"So I tell her you're too close. I can say you feel too emotionally attached to her family to be effective as a security guard."

He couldn't think of a better excuse since I'm-booked-forever wasn't holding up. "Yeah. That works."

"Great." Max finished polishing the piece in his hands and reached for another. "Did Murkowski work out on Monday?"

Murkowski. The detective Max had recommended for discreetly investigating the threat to Elena. "He was great. They don't have anything yet, but I know it means a lot that the papers haven't got anything on it." Adam shifted from one foot to the other. "Elena's staying in my guest room. Until we know that her place is safe."

Max nodded as if he'd expected as much, reassembling the gun. "I'm glad you're looking out for her. You know she's friends with my little sister, right?"

The wedding planner Suitorette. "I know."

"Good." He chambered a bullet with an ominous click.

His boss was warning him away from Elena. Subtle. "I'd better get back to my workout. Tank's probably adding another twenty reps for every minute I'm late."

Max snorted. "Remind him that I need you to be able to lift your arms tomorrow."

"Will do."

He made his escape before his boss decided he would make a good target. Message received. He'd keep his hands to himself where Elena was concerned.

But when he walked through his front door that

evening and saw her bent over in a yoga pose in the middle of his living room, he knew he was a goner.

# CHAPTER TWELVE

"What are you doing?"

Elena straightened, whipping toward the sound of his voice. "Oh, thank God, you're back. I freaking hate yoga, but I'm trying to be Zen here. You're lucky I didn't feng shui your furniture and alphabetize your socks."

Adam's eyebrows flew up as he grinned. "My socks?"

She found her lips curving, grinning back at him of their own volition. "I don't do well when I'm penned in."

Understatement of the century.

It might have been different if she'd had her car. If she'd known that she *could* leave if she wanted to, perhaps she wouldn't have felt this crazy itch beneath her skin, the incessant drive to move. She'd tried to read and watch TV, but she couldn't sit still. Then she'd caught a few minutes of a talk show and heard her hashtag used as a punch line—again. She'd snapped off the television in disgust and prowled his place.

Maybe she wouldn't have been so restless if it hadn't been his place. If she hadn't been so aware that these were his things.

She didn't want to get too comfortable here, hyper aware that she wouldn't be able to stay. Last night he'd cooked for her and it had been wonderful, peaceful and calming and everything she needed in that moment. But she couldn't stay in with him tonight, not with this pulse of restlessness in her blood, not if she wanted to keep the Just Friends illusion going.

And it was an illusion.

That much was obvious by the kick of attraction that hit her the second he walked through the door. He was hotter than she'd remembered. Somehow since that morning she'd managed to forget the way her mouth would go dry just watching him move. Or smile. Or breathe.

*Shit.*

She didn't want to be just friends. She wanted impulse and heat and the press of skin against skin. She wanted *him*.

And he wanted to be friends. How long would their "friendship" last before she pushed him and he walked away?

"So I see," he said, but she'd lost track of the conversation and wasn't in the mood to even try to figure out what he was responding to. Everything in her was moving forward, not back.

"Can we go out? I will go stir crazy if I have to stay in this house another second."

"Then I guess we'd better go out. If only to save my socks. Where did you have mind?"

"I need my car. And a drink. Not necessarily in that order." She was talking too fast, but the speed felt good. She reached up and snagged her hair tie, tugging it loose so her hair fell down around her shoulders. "You're not on the clock now. Have you been to Seven?"

"The club?"

"I know it's pretentious as hell, but the music is amazing and the bartender wants to sleep with me so he gives me these spicy pomegranate martinis for practically nothing. Do you like to dance?"

He was starting to look dazed, but he nodded. "Sure."

"Great. We'll go there." She'd said last night that she needed to feel like herself again and she could only think of one way to do that. "I need to dance. Then we can get my car. You hungry? We can hit In N' Out on the way. Give me ten minutes to get ready."

"Ten?"

He called the word after her, but she was already bolting up the stairs.

\* \* \* \* \*

Adam was tempted to check the house for cocaine, but he was reasonably certain Elena's manic mood was all natural. He wasn't accustomed to going clubbing—at least not as a partier rather than a guard—so he wasn't entirely sure what to wear, but Elena's little purr of approval when she met him back downstairs twenty minutes later told him he'd chosen well with dark slacks and a dark button-down open at the collar.

"Look at you."

His neck heated. "You look nice too."

She arched an eyebrow, as if she could hear the ridiculous understatement in his words. "Thank you."

She looked like twenty-seven different kinds of sin in her skyscraper heels and tight little yellow dress—the bright color contrasting incredibly against her darker skin. Her hair had gotten poofier somehow and she'd added smoky darkness around her eyes and shocking scarlet lipstick that made him want to smear it all to hell.

Which would get him fired. And probably beaten to

a bloody pulp by Tank. Or Candy.

So Adam averted his eyes and held the door for her. "Shall we?"

She waited in the vestibule as he reset the security system and locked the door. When he turned, she took his arm to steady herself on the ridiculously high heels as they walked to the car. He opened her door, trying not to look at her legs as she swung them in.

He closed her door and rounded the hood, trying to think chaste thoughts. He climbed in and avoided looking in the passenger seat as he pointed the car south toward Seven and hit the button to close the gate behind them.

He was acutely aware of the sound of fabric rustling as Elena crossed one leg over the other, shifting toward him.

"Do you think men and women can be friends without sex becoming an issue?"

Adam's neck heated. "Of course."

"But only when one or both of them are unattractive, right?"

"No."

"Huh. Maybe it's just me."

"You can't be friends with attractive men?"

She snorted. "I can't even be friends with women when they have boyfriends or husbands. You would not believe how many of my female friends will cut me off when they get involved with a guy. They don't want my temptation around them. As if I would ever."

"No," he agreed. Elena wasn't a cheater. She had too strong a sense of fairness. But he wasn't surprised other women felt threatened by her. It couldn't be easy to be friends with the woman who would draw the eye of every straight male in the room. But it had to take a toll on Elena too. "Any idiot can see that isn't your style. You need smarter friends."

He was rewarded with a low, breathy laugh. "That must be my problem."

To get her off the topic of sexual attraction between would-be friends, he pretended to be reminded of an anecdote by a building they were passing and launched into a story to distract her, keeping it up through the In N' Out drive through and all the way until they were pulling up in front of Seven.

The trendy club had its usual line wrapping around the side of the building, as well as a small cluster of bored looking paparazzi lurking in case anyone famous dropped by. Adam stopped directly in front of the door and threw the car into park.

He looked over at Elena in time to see the change as her public face fell into place. The wild, almost frantic look in her eyes faded to indolent ennui. She'd been bursting with emotion only moments before, radiating restless energy, but she reeled it all in until the real Elena was contained, playing her role seamlessly.

"Don't let the paparazzi shoot up my skirt as I'm getting out," she said as he reached for the door handle. "I'm not wearing underwear."

All the blood rushed away from his brain, but he managed not to react. He stepped out, handing the keys to the valet, and rounded the rear of the car to open the door for Elena, blocking the view of the paparazzi who went on high alert at the scent of fame.

She took his arm, sex on four inch heels as she strutted toward the door. Most celebrities traveled with an entourage—the publicist would go first and make sure everyone knew they were coming, smoothing the way to VIP lounges. The rest of the party would arrive with the star, orbiting around her like lesser planets, completely dependent on her light.

It was all but unheard of for a celebrity to arrive alone—or with just a bodyguard as company—but Elena made it look natural. She smiled at the bouncer—the kind of wicked, I-aim-to-misbehave smile Adam had never seen on her face before, but desperately wanted to see again. In bed.

The rope moved out of their way without hesitation and Elena released Adam's arm, but hooked a finger in his belt loop, tugging him after her through the tall, arched door that was the portal into the throbbing beat of Seven.

Inside, she released him and Adam submitted to a security pat down while Elena waited, examining her nails. The elevator arrived and they stepped inside, the operator pushing the button for the fourth floor without needing to be told.

Seven's gimmick was that each floor of the seven floor club was more exclusive than the last. In the status-obsessed world of Tinseltown, everyone was trying to level up and the club's owners had decided to profit from it. Commoners could "level up" by paying increasingly exorbitant cover charges and membership fees—but only as high as level five.

Adam had guarded celebs on every level from three to six, but even he had never been up to seven. Four was an impressive level of fame for a reality television star, considering the heroic Adam Dylan probably couldn't even have gotten in the door on one without Elena tugging at his belt loop.

Someone must have called up, because by the time the elevator doors opened on the fourth floor, the bartender had a purple martini waiting for Elena. She purred her thanks and took a long drink before turning to Adam with another of those wicked Public Elena smiles.

"What'll you have, Stud Muffin?"

"I'm not drinking." Even if he hadn't been driving, he was looking out for Elena tonight and he didn't need his senses dulled when he did it.

"You aren't on duty." She was shouting to be heard over the pounding bass, but somehow she managed to infuse sultriness into the yelling. "Come on. I insist you loosen up. One drink." She thrust her glass at him. "Here, try mine. You might like it."

"One drink and you'll let it go?"

"Deal."

He took a large swallow of her purple martini, expecting a fruity drink and nearly choking when the liquid that hit the back of his throat was almost pure vodka. "Christ," he wheezed.

"Yeah. Eddie makes 'em strong."

He tried to hand the glass back to her. "I did it. One drink."

"That was one swallow." She tapped the glass with her nail. "*This* is one drink. You finish it and I'll get another from Eddie boy."

He would have protested, but Elena was already moving toward the bar. She was a force of nature, all fire and will, and he was out of his depth with her. Especially here, where she had home field advantage.

He sipped more cautiously at the purple vodka, finding it had a hint of fruity sweetness and a zing of spice that built the more he drank. When Elena returned, cradling a new full glass in both hands, he leaned close to shout, "Is that cayenne?"

"Mm-hmm," she hummed affirmatively, taking a

hefty swallow of her own drink. "Isn't it divine?"

He met her eyes over the rim of her glass, taking in the wicked glint in them and her wide, inviting smile. The thoughts running through his brain were about as far from divinity as they could get. His fingers itched to touch her smooth skin, glinting copper in the flicking orange lights that added a sense of warmth to this level of the club—or a sense that he was immersing himself in the flames of Hell.

The music was too loud for conversation and he found himself falling into the guard role—even with a drink in his hand. He scanned the crowd for possible threats, using his body to shield Elena when someone would have bumped up against her.

She scanned the crowd as well for reasons of her own as she sipped her martini. "No one's here," she leaned toward his ear to comment.

The dance floor was packed and every table around the edges reserved for bottle service was full, but he knew what she meant. No one famous had decided to come out and play this Tuesday night. Elena was probably the most recognizable face in the crowd. But the paying customers were enjoying the thrill of their Level Four status.

He started to suggest that they could get out of here—she'd had her drink, she'd been seen, usually that was all the celebrities wanted when they came out—but then the music shifted to a faster, more recognizable beat and Elena squealed. "I love this song! Come on!"

She downed the rest of her drink and handed the empty glass to him to dispose of as she raised her hands above her head and danced toward the crowded dance floor. Adam cursed under his breath, ditching their empty glasses on the bar and moving quickly to keep her in sight. The dancers made space for her as they recognized her, smiling and waving, welcoming her to their bobbing, grinding world and then whipping out their cell phones to snag a discreet pic as she passed.

Elena made her way to the heart of the dance floor and Adam plowed in her wake. He stopped when he had her at a safe distance—close enough to protect, but far enough that his brain didn't shut down from lack of blood. She moved with sinuous grace, head thrown back, eyes half-closed, arms above her head as her hips wove patterns in time to the music. He could see her lips moving, singing along, but the pounding music was too loud for him to hear her voice.

Those dance shows didn't know what they were missing. She would have won for sure. He couldn't take his eyes off her.

And she wasn't wearing underwear. Christ.

Her skyscraper heels were no impediment here. She moved on them as gracefully as he'd seen her sashay barefoot across his living room. He'd seen her on the dance floor at the wedding, but she'd been more restrained then—this was pure abandon, and he had a front row seat.

The song segued seamlessly into another and Elena's hypnotic communion with the music became less complete. She looked at him and made her eyes wide as a little smile curved her lips. She shouted something.

Adam shook his head. "I can't hear you!"

She danced closer, until she was in his space, her body a fraction of an inch from his, tipping her face until he could feel her breath against the side of his neck. "You're a good dancer!"

He yelled, "You too!" His awareness of her a kick in his gut, he bopped backward in time with the music until the same three foot gap fit between them. His hands might itch with the desire to touch her, to grip her hips, pull her close, feel that weaving movement beneath his palms—but he wasn't an animal. He could restrain the urge.

A hand brushed his arm and his attention snapped down to see a petite girl with a round sweet face beaming up at him. "Hero cop! Would you... selfie?"

Half of her question was lost in the thrum of the music, but he got the gist when she lifted her cell phone and gestured at him and herself. Adam looked to Elena for an excuse to say no, but she was already giving her permission with a wave and turning away, dancing off in her own little world.

He didn't like taking his eyes off her even for a second, not when this club was part of her usual routine and the memory of that note loomed large in his thoughts, but he bent down and smiled for the camera. He started to straighten away, but the girl yelled something, grabbing his arm and tugging him back for a second shot.

It had only taken a few seconds, but by the time he turned back to Elena it felt like a lifetime. Especially when he didn't see her immediately. She'd danced farther away, the crowd filling in the space between them. He could see over almost everyone, but Elena was small enough—even in those insane heels—that she disappeared easily.

He caught sight of her several feet away, no longer communing with the music, but standing still as the crowd danced around her. Adam began to push toward her—getting a better angle and realizing she was frowning and shaking her head as a tall man with greased up hair bent close to her ear to talk to her. She started to move away and the man put his hand on her arm.

He saw red.

# CHAPTER THIRTEEN

Elena was busy worshipping at the altar of Rhianna's genius so it wasn't until the douchebag planted himself in front of her and shoved his face into her personal space to yell into her ear that she realized he was trying to talk to her.

"Huh?" she shouted, giving up any attempt to dance until she had shaken him off.

"I said my friends and I would love for you to join us for some Cristal!" He waved to a table where four other trust fund twenty-somethings were crowded around a trio of bottles that must have cost as much as her car.

She made it a policy not to alienate strangers in clubs—you never knew who was influential in this town—but part of the appeal of Seven was the knowledge that if these guys had really been important, they would have been upstairs. These boys were garden-variety rich dicks, paying ten times what a bottle of vodka was worth so they could impress women with how much money they threw around and lure them to their table with their baller ways.

"Sorry. Just dancing tonight."

She tried to step away, but he caught her arm, his grip hard. "You can dance for us."

She snorted. "Sorry. I'm not that kind of dancer."

Something hard and mocking flashed on his face.

"What? You only take your clothes off for champagne when there are cameras around? Because I can take my cell phone out and we can make that shit happen."

"What did you just say to her?" Adam loomed out of nowhere—and Elena had an inappropriate thought that she was impressed he could hear the Bottle-Service Dickhead over the music. Then Dickhead released her arm and puffed himself up to face the new threat to his masculinity.

"None of your business, asshole."

"Apologize."

The growled command was really very sweet. Delusional. But sweet. There was no way the Bottle-Service Dickhead was going to apologize to her and insisting on it was only going to escalate the situation. Adam was good enough at his job he had to know that, but he didn't appear to be able to connect with the rational part of his brain at the moment. He was too busy being the Big Bad Alpha.

"Adam, it's fine," Elena said, moving around Dickhead to take her hero's arm.

"No. It isn't."

"He's just a bottle service douchebag who thinks he can buy women with a bottle of Cristal." And the truly depressing part was that he probably could. He just couldn't buy her. "He isn't worth it."

Adam looked at her and she could see the testosterone rage seeping out of his eyes. Then Dickhead, who had evidently only heard a few stray words of what she'd said to Adam, had to pipe up.

"Yeah. Listen to your bitch. She isn't worth it."

Adam turned suddenly, as if bumped from behind though she couldn't see anyone there, his elbow lifted— at exactly the right angle to slam into Dickhead's nose.

Adam jerked back, his eyes huge—the man was a terrible actor. "Oh, man! I'm so sorry. Someone shoved me. You know how it is."

Dickhead snarled something she couldn't hear over the music as blood seeped through the hands cupping his nose. Over his shoulder, Elena could see his friends standing up from their table.

She wrapped both hands around Adam's arm and tugged. It was like trying to move the National Monument—a strength that would have been hot as hell if it wasn't remarkably inconvenient. "Let's go."

Adam looked down at her blankly.

"Dickhead has buddies and while I'm confident you are badass enough to take them all down, I doubt you can make beating *all* of them up look accidental and who's going to drive me home if you're arrested for pummeling them all to a bloody pulp?"

He followed her gaze to where Dickhead's pals were now pushing their way onto the edge of the dance floor. He nodded once, kicking into badass bodyguard mode. His arm looped around her waist and he hustled her toward the nearest exit, scanning the crowd for threats and never pausing until they were inside the elevator and headed down the stairs.

The elevator operator called ahead and the valet was pulling up front with his Jeep. Adam moved her quickly to the vehicle, glaring down a paparazzo who tried to jump in her path for a better shot. He opened the door and tucked her inside with a precise efficiency of motion before shutting the door and rounding the hood to climb into the driver's seat.

The entire extraction had taken under four minutes— and she'd never felt so protected.

It had been months since she'd felt one hundred

percent safe, but she did with him. It was a feeling she couldn't afford to get used to.

"You're pretty badass, you know that?" she commented, trying to get them back to a comfortable emotional place. A place where she didn't feel the waves of intensity from him in the driver's seat or her own answering awareness. An awareness that made her feel vulnerable and feminine in a way she liked far more than she wanted to admit.

Adam spun the wheel, taking them into the empty parking lot in front of a closed pastry shop. Elena concentrated on the elaborate delicacies in the window display so she wouldn't have to look at the man beside her as he turned off the engine and twisted toward her, unbuckling his seat belt when it hindered the motion.

"Are you okay?" he asked.

"I'm great. Clubs like that have security, you know. It's not like he could have sold me into human trafficking or anything."

Her hero's granite jaw worked. "I just didn't like…"

He trailed off, looking at her, the weight of his eyes making her shift in her seat. What hadn't he liked? Seeing her bothered? Seeing her with another man?

Then his eyes dropped to her lips and she stopped caring. Her breath stopped.

Shit.

She'd wanted this. She'd wanted it like crazy and every naughty impulse she possessed—which was a lot of them—still wanted it. But she was trouble and he deserved better than to get sucked into her drama.

She stared at him, hypnotized by his intense focus. "Don't get involved with me, Stud Muffin," she warned. "I'm bad news. You're too righteous and wonderful. You'd want to fight all my battles for me and you'd spend all your time fighting."

She wet her lips and his gaze tracked the movement.

"Some things are worth fighting for."

His voice was gravelly low and hit her right where she was already wet for him. He closed the distance between them, cupping her jaw with one hand, zeroing in on her lips—and the first touch of his mouth hit her *everywhere*. It shuddered through her on a roaring wave of need as goosebumps raced down her arms and her entire body clenched with want.

*This.* This was what she felt like she'd been reaching toward, what that frantic restless need had been driving her toward all her life. This feeling. God, it was perfect. *He* was perfect.

His mouth moved over hers, coaxing, luring. Men always kissed her like they owned her, but his mouth— Christ, it *worshipped* her. Every resistance she'd ever considered having liquefied into a puddle of *yes, please* and *more*.

His free hand went to her waist, sliding up beneath the curve of her breast. He cupped her, his thumb sliding over her nipple, and Elena moaned into his mouth, silently cursing the fact that she'd worn such a tight dress and she couldn't just yank down the top to give him access.

His mouth moved from hers, finding the sweet spot on the line of her neck. She gripped his shoulders, marveling at the solid feel of him. Her seatbelt cut into her chest, but she ignored it—ignoring everything that wasn't him. She wanted to crawl into his lap and wrap herself around him. She wanted his weight pinning her down with hard, hot pressure everywhere she needed it most. She wanted—

Headlights panned over them as another car pulled

into the parking lot.

"Shit." Adam jerked, throwing himself back into his own seat.

Elena panted, watching the car—paparazzi? How had they been found? Had someone followed them from the club? How much had they seen?—but it just executed a tight turn and pulled back onto the street, heading in the opposite direction. Just some random lost person turning around.

Adam gripped the steering wheel at ten and two. "I shouldn't have done that."

"No," Elena whispered, though she didn't know whether she was agreeing or protesting.

"We're… Anyone could have seen us."

She nodded numbly. And if they'd been seen someone would undoubtedly have taken a picture and they'd be in the tabloids tomorrow, Adam's good name forever tarred by her reputation.

"I apologize," he said, rigidly formal.

He reclicked his seatbelt and shifted uncomfortably. Her gaze fell automatically to his lap until the harsh grate of his voice commanded, "Don't."

She snapped her chin around, staring out the passenger side window, uncomfortable and tense and still wanting him so badly it felt like her clothes were two sizes too tight.

"I'm sorry," he reiterated. "It won't happen again."

*What if I want it to?*

The words hovered on the tip of her tongue—but he was her friend. Maybe the only one she had. And he didn't deserve to get sucked into the bullshit drama of her life. She'd already caused him too much trouble. The last thing he needed was more. So she bit her lip and looked outside, nodding once. *Never again*.

Adam put the car into drive. "Let's go get your car."

# CHAPTER FOURTEEN

Elena had learned to read paparazzi swarms like tea leaves. She could tell at a glance how big the star—or the scandal—they were stalking was. The crowd outside her apartment was too big. Like movie-star-screwing-his-nanny-and-being-chased-down-the-street-with-a-golf-club-by-his-supermodel-wife big. She had never merited that big a horde, not even when the infamous Jacuzzi episode first aired and she claimed the title of the Slutty Suitorette.

Something was very, very wrong.

"Drive on by." She doubled over so it looked like Adam was just driving along by himself. If they saw her, she'd never shake them. This crowd wasn't just looking for a good shot to sell, they were looking for a story. She would be peppered with shouted questions as soon as they saw her and they wouldn't be polite about stepping out of the way as long as she gave them a pose before getting into her car. Normally she could pay her toll with a smile, but the mob staking out her apartment had caught the scent of something big.

What had she done lately that could be considered big? Nothing. But that didn't mean there wasn't a story out there about her.

People lied. The Dickhead at the club tonight, Purple Tie, Daniel—any of them could have thrown her under the bus for free publicity. It was a lot harder to avoid the minefields in her life when she could get into as much trouble for fiction as for fact.

She'd turned off her cell phone and she didn't want to turn it back on and see what this new crisis was. She'd reached her saturation point on frustration tonight. All she wanted was to go home and curl up in bed—preferably not her own, but that option was apparently no longer on the table.

"We're clear," Adam said, thankfully not offering any additional commentary on her sudden rise in celebrity.

Elena straightened, smoothing out her dress where it had been wrinkled by her contortions—and by his hands.

The more she thought about that crowd of paparazzi as he drove the more she dreaded tomorrow, but if she could just hang onto something good tonight, before the storm broke, maybe it would be okay. He wouldn't have to get sucked into her drama any more than he already was. Inside the privacy of his house, no one had to know that they were together. They could pick up where they left off and it didn't have to damage his reputation.

By the time they arrived at his house, she had talked herself into a one night affair with Adam so thoroughly she was squirming in her seat with anticipation.

He came around to open her door for her and help her inside, always the gentleman, and she took his arm, throwing in a little stumble so her breast brushed him. She heard his breath catch.

He wanted her. She'd seen the proof of that. Now all she had to do was convince a good guy that sometimes being bad was worth it.

"No one would have to know," she said, keeping her

voice low and inviting. "It's none of their business anyway."

Adam looked down at her, frowning. "I'm not ashamed of you, Elena."

"Then what's the problem? You're attracted to me. You aren't seeing anyone." She paused. "Are you?"

"No." He unlocked the front door, holding it open for her, but now irritation was starting to pulse and the courtesy irritated her. He was always so freaking courteous but he wouldn't do her the courtesy of banging her brains out.

"If we can make sure you aren't tainted by my reputation, what's the problem?"

He closed the door, facing it for a moment as if steeling himself before turning. "I'm not in a position to be what you need right now."

She let her gaze drop to his pants. "Wanna bet?"

"It wouldn't just be sex between us."

That brought her eyes up to meet his and cynicism laced her echo. "Wanna bet?"

Irritation flashed briefly behind his eyes, but he reined it in. Always so freaking contained. "Good night, Elena."

His footsteps retreated upstairs and she heard the thud of his bedroom door shutting.

"Shit." She leaned against the foyer wall, reaching down to unbuckle the slinky ankle straps on her stilettos one at a time. Her feet almost sighed with relief when she released them from the torture devices masquerading as footwear. She wiggled her freed toes, dangling the heels from her fingertips and thunked her head back against the wall.

He wasn't in a position.

What the fuck was that supposed to mean?

Was he actually trying to pass off his rejection as some kind of *I'm-not-good-enough-for-you* bullshit? He was so freaking noble it made her want to throw things at his head—like her clothes—and scream at him to just take what he freaking wanted for a change. And he wanted her. She knew he did. But he thought sex with her would be more than carnal satisfaction. He didn't want to be tied to her as a couple—and she couldn't blame him for that—but he was too damn good to use her as a fling.

Didn't it figure that the one guy she wanted was the one too nice to use her like she wanted to use him?

She climbed the stairs barefoot and paused outside her door, staring at his. She could take off her clothes and walk in there—but that was what Old Elena would do and she was being New. Being good. And Adam had already turned her down. She should respect that, or she was just like all the assholes who didn't respect her *no*s.

She opened her door, peeled off her clothes and climbed into bed.

Alone.

\* \* \* \* \*

Morning came too quickly. She'd thought she wouldn't be able to sleep, but she'd been out as soon as her head hit the pillow and the night had gone by too fast.

Now the morning was here and she had to face another day. Elena pulled on yoga pants and a t-shirt, not bothering with a bra. She snagged her hair into a messy ponytail and wandered into the en suite bathroom. Catching sight of herself in the mirror, she cringed in horror.

She'd forgotten to take her make-up off the night before and what had once been a smoky eye was now raccoon circles. Her lipstick had smeared off, leaving her lips bloodless. She could walk onto the set of a zombie movie right now. No additional make-up required.

*Maybe the undead are a turn-on for Adam.*

Not that she needed to be worrying about what turned him on. He'd made his position clear the night before.

She washed off the make-up, leaving her face a blank canvas, and padded barefoot to the top of the stairs. Adam's voice floated up from below. She couldn't make out the words, but something in his tone made her shoulders tense.

Bad news.

She hesitated on the top step. She could turn her phone back on. Then she'd know. Whatever it was, she'd know. But she didn't want to get the news from a voicemail. She wanted to get it from him—like seeing his face would soften the blow.

His voice stopped, staying silent long enough that she decided he must have hung up the phone. Now or never.

She descended the stairs, trying to keep her steps silent, but he must have heard her because he was turned toward her as she entered the kitchen, his phone in one hand, the partially prepared beginnings of breakfast forgotten on the counter behind him.

Elena found herself fixating on the partially scrambled eggs. It was easier than facing him.

His face was like chalk and drawn in hard lines. Jaw clenched. Tension lines bracketing his mouth and eyes.

"What is it?" she forced herself to say. "Did someone get a picture of us in your car last night?"

He shook his head, a single tight shake.

"The fight at Seven? Did someone leak your name?"

"No." His voice was gravelly low. "It isn't me."

She'd known that, but hope sprang eternal. If it was just some gossip about a fight, that was manageable. That was small.

"I know what the paparazzi were doing at your house last night." He struggled for words. "It's bad."

Sympathy shone in his eyes and her brain immediately jumped to the worst possible news.

*Please don't let this be how I find out something happened to my family.*

"It's a sex tape."

"What?"

She was so braced for grief the words didn't even make sense.

And then they did.

# CHAPTER FIFTEEN

"Who?"

He could see the hope in her face that it wasn't real, that it was some kind of promotional hoax, and he wished he could have given her better news, but from what Max had told him when he called the news only got worse.

"Apparently his name is Dermott Kellerman."

She winced, closing her eyes as if the name had struck a physical blow. She nodded, eyes still shut. "It was right after the reunion special," she confirmed. "Just some guy I met in a coffee shop, but he was nice and Daniel had just thrown me to the wolves on national television. I felt like an idiot for ever trusting him and I hated that he was the last guy I'd slept with, so I went home with Dermott just to get the taste of Daniel out of my mouth. He wasn't even that good."

And he'd made a sex tape of them. "Did you know he was filming you?"

She shook her head, opening her eyes though I doubted she was seeing anything. "Why did he wait so long? He must have been sitting on the tape for months."

"The network made the announcement yesterday about dropping *Marrying Mister Perfect* from the fall line-up. Max thinks Kellerman was waiting to see if you'd be picked as the next Miss Right. The video would be worth more if he released it in the middle of the season." Adam grimaced, hating that he had more to tell her. "The clip he released is only a few seconds. A teaser. Enough to confirm it's definitely you. He's auctioning off the full tape to the highest bidder and using the media frenzy to drive the price up."

"Christ." She sank onto one of the stools at the breakfast bar. "I was trying to hit the reset button after one asshole screwed me over and I managed to pick a guy who made a sex tape and held onto it until he could shop it around for maximum impact. Can I pick 'em or what?"

"This isn't your fault."

She didn't look like she'd heard him. "I don't know what to do."

"We stop it. He tipped his hand because he was greedy. We can get an injunction. Make sure he can't sell it or release any more clips."

"I don't know how."

"This is why you have people to protect your career. Call your agent. Make him earn his fifteen percent."

She nodded, paler than he'd ever seen her. Her shock was understandable, but worrisome. He didn't like the way her eyes wouldn't seem to focus.

He grabbed orange juice from the fridge, pouring her a glass and setting it in front of her. "Where's your phone?"

She waved vaguely toward the ceiling.

"Why don't you go get it while I finish making breakfast? Do you like omelets?"

She frowned at him as if confused by the question. "Have you seen it? The teaser?"

"No. Max called me this morning when he heard

about it because I mentioned to him that you were staying in my guest room until the other situation got cleared up."

"The other situation." She snorted. "We're using euphemisms now for the psycho who threatened to kill me because of my slutty ways?"

His helplessness burned. He didn't have a magic button he could push to get rid of the sex tape or the death threat or even the jerks who treated her like she was a prostitute whenever she stepped outside her door. But he could feed her. "Do you like peppers?"

She laughed, a dry, humorless sound. "Yeah. Peppers are great." She slid off her stool. "I'll go get my phone."

\* \* \* \* \*

Maybe it was a joke.

Adam hadn't seen the clip and she didn't know Sidney's brother Max. Maybe he had the worst possible taste and was just winding Adam up. Maybe it wasn't really happening.

But when she turned on her phone there were too many texts and voicemails to support her wishful thinking. Dozens. And only a handful of people had this new number. She pulled up her web browser, typing in her name.

It was the first hit.

She tapped the link to the teaser clip. At the first frame, memory crystallized, bringing her vague memories of that months ago night into sharp focus.

He'd wanted to leave the light on. His bed had been warm from all the lights he'd aimed at it. The asshole. The clip didn't look like a grainy, blurry, night-vision sex tape. It looked like porn. And it was undeniably her.

Jesus.

It was—Thank God—only a few seconds long, but it was long enough to be damning. And tantalizing. The asshole was probably going to make a fortune.

She dialed Dale's number as she descended to the kitchen. Adam was plating an omelet that looked like a work of culinary art, but she didn't have anything resembling an appetite.

Dale picked up on the second ring—no run around with his secretary today. "Elena! I'm glad you got back to me, hon. We have to move fast, strike while the iron is hot—"

"We need to get an injunction," she interrupted before Dale could launch into whatever plan he wanted to pitch. "Stop Dermott from releasing the full tape."

"Smart," Dale agreed instantly. "Playboy won't pay nearly as much if you're already out there. Exclusivity is the name of the game—"

He kept speaking, but her ears didn't seem to be working. All she heard was a high, echoing ringing— like she'd been in a club too long and her hearing had been blown out by the bass.

He didn't want to stop it. He wanted to spin it. Work it into her brand.

Everything in her revolted.

"No."

"Elena?" Dale sounded confused—which wasn't surprising, considering she'd interrupted him mid-sentence with her explosive no.

"I don't think we have the same vision for my career anymore."

"Okay," he backpedaled. "You're upset. That's understandable."

"You're fired."

It felt good. The relief of it was almost sexual it was so acute. She disconnected the call and dropped her phone on the breakfast bar, staring straight ahead as the certainty that she should have done that months ago shivered through her. She felt… *free*.

And alone.

"I just fired my agent," she told Adam.

"I heard. You okay?"

She nodded, a little dazed. "He was worried about exclusivity. Apparently my vagina isn't worth as much to Playboy if everyone has already downloaded it."

Adam swore with a creativity she would have found impressive if she wasn't still shell shocked.

She frowned, trying to make her sluggish thoughts respond. "I don't know what to do now."

"Eat," he commanded, nudging her plate closer to her. "Then we'll find you a lawyer or an agent or someone who can file that injunction for you. The show has teams of lawyers, don't they? Could they help you?"

*Miranda.*

She wasn't with *Marrying Mister Perfect* anymore, but she knew this business and she knew how to manage scandal. She'd probably even smothered a sex tape or two in her day. She would know what to do. And how to do it.

She ignored the omelet, reaching for her cell phone again.

Five minutes later, Elena felt the first flicker of hope she'd had all morning.

"Let me make some calls," Miranda said in her familiar, competent manner. "I'll take care of it."

"Why?" Elena asked, wanting to accept the help, but confused by the offer. "You don't even work for them anymore."

"Honestly, E, if you called them, I doubt they would lift a finger to help you unless it was going to hurt the ratings. But I never felt right about how you were treated Daniel's season. We did this to you. You signed eleven million different kinds of releases when you signed up for the show, so you can't make us help you or come after us for trashing your reputation, but *Marrying Mister Perfect* gleefully encouraged America to pile on with the slut shaming and I owe you. So I want to help."

Elena didn't cry. She reminded herself of that as emotion pressed against the back of her throat. It was the first time anyone affiliated with the show had acknowledged that what had happened to her wasn't entirely her fault. Not the sex tape, but the rest of it. The Slutty Suitorette. Everyone had always implied—either tacitly or outright—that she was only getting what she deserved. She'd encouraged Daniel. She'd flirted and tempted and put out—God forbid—so everyone looked at her as if she deserved what she got. The betrayal by the man she thought she loved. The shaming by the American viewing public.

Miranda had said she was sorry for what had happened to Elena before, but she'd never said the show was to blame. Elena had always assumed the unspoken second half of *I'm sorry it happened* was *but you brought it on yourself*. This was different.

And if she let herself think about it, she was going to cry. "Thank you."

Miranda signed off, on a mission to stop the tape, and Elena set down her phone. It was several moments later before she looked up and found Adam watching her.

"Good news?"

She nodded mutely. Then caught sight of the microwave clock behind his shoulder. "Do you have a job today? I don't want to make you late for work."

"Max and I discussed it when he called this morning. He's reassigning my detail today so I can stay here with you."

Her relief that he wasn't leaving her alone was embarrassingly acute. She didn't want to need him like this. "Why are you so nice to me?"

He met her eyes, his own steady and calm in spite of the blaze of anger banked in them. Anger on her behalf. "You deserve it. And you don't deserve this shit."

She pressed her lips together, nodding her thanks because she couldn't speak or she would cry.

"Eat."

She nodded, digging into the omelet.

Whether she deserved it or not, she was grateful for him and she wasn't too proud to admit she needed him today.

# CHAPTER SIXTEEN

Expensive lawyers apparently made house calls.

Elena sat in Adam's gorgeous sunken living room during the hours which she would later come to think of as the Afternoon of the Lawyers and tried to focus on the meaning behind the legalese flying around her. Miranda had arrived with three lawyers from a Very Respectable Firm and they had introduced themselves with brisk efficiency before ensconcing themselves in the casual luxury of Adam's couches and getting down to business.

She tried to feel comforted rather than intimidated by their aggressive voices spouting complicated legal jargon. They were legal sharks, but they were *her* legal sharks. It was irrational to feel defensive every time they spoke, but she just felt herself getting smaller and smaller as her muscles got tenser and tenser as she sat on the couch facing them with Adam at her side.

"It could be much worse," the older of the two male lawyers said when she finished going into nauseating detail about her relationship—or lack thereof—with the man holding her sex tape for ransom.

Though he hadn't actually demanded ransom—so that was something. Though at this point she wondered if that wouldn't have been preferable. Dermott must have known she didn't have a penny to pay him with.

"Once it's online you can't close Pandora's box again, but this way we have very different options," he continued, discussing her drama in the same coolly analytical way they'd all been talking about it since they arrived. As if it were a particularly complicated puzzle they were solving en masse. He seemed to be the leader of the trio—smooth and slick and polished, like a politician with a haircut that cost more than she spent on groceries in a month.

"Of course we'll start with an injunction, but after that is when it really gets interesting." The female lawyer bounced on her seat, practically getting off on the legal machinations. "We'll essentially be suing for custody of the tape."

"Which is a tenuous claim at best," the younger male argued disapprovingly, speaking around the stick up his ass. He would have been cute—a scaled down version of Idris Elba—if he hadn't looked so constipated.

"What if he releases it?"

"That's what the injunction is designed to prevent," the politician explained with a smarmy smile.

"Does the injunction physically remove it from his possession? What if he's made copies?" Of course he'd made copies. He wasn't a complete moron and he'd had it for months. There could be hundreds, squirreled away all over the globe. Suddenly getting back all the copies of her sex tape seemed more complicated than the plot of Ocean's Eleven.

"He'll go to jail if he violates the injunction," Idris Elba's pissy little brother said with excruciating patience. "And there may be a small fine."

"What if he does it anyway? What if he decides it's worth it?"

Her parents already weren't speaking to her. After

this…

Adam reached over, catching her hand with his. She latched on and squeezed it tight, grateful for the support.

"Revenge porn is illegal in California, so you could file a criminal claim, but you might run into jurisdiction issues since he lives in Nevada where there are no revenge porn laws and you say the tape was made in Las Vegas," the woman explained. "Additionally you'd have to prove his intention was to harass, where it appears to be to make money and he could easily claim that your position as a celebrity who has made a living from displaying your love life has made your sex life newsworthy and therefore claim protection under the first amendment."

"What about invasion of privacy? He's not allowed to film me without my knowledge or consent, is he?"

"He's claiming you did know you were being filmed and apparently he believes the content of the tape backs this up," Elba-mini explained. "We'll get a copy of it during discovery and see what he's referring to, but his lawyers may already argue that your right to privacy is compromised since you willingly participated in a reality show—and your behavior on that show may be a contributing factor."

"Shit."

"That's why we'll be working to establish your ownership of the video," the woman said.

"And if that fails?"

"You'll want to copyright your likeness, so we can go after him for infringement as well if he attempts to profit from it. We'll start on that paperwork right away as well."

She was copyrighting her body. Something she never

thought she'd have to consider.

"That still doesn't answer the question of what happens if he just releases it anyway."

None of them answered. Because they all knew the answer was simple. They could file all the paperwork against him they wanted and levy fines and lawsuits and put him in jail, but if he decided to do it, she couldn't physically stop him.

"We're going to try to make sure that doesn't happen," Miranda said from her position leaning against the French doors, unflappable in her reassurance.

"Then we'd better hope my luck has changed," Elena muttered under her breath.

"This is going to get ugly," warned the younger man.

"Sex tape lawsuits always draw attention and this kind of case hasn't been done in this way before, so it may get even more attention," the woman chimed in and then their boss added his two cents.

"You're going to be discussed, not just on entertainment shows, but on the 24-hour news networks. Some pundits will say that you didn't give your permission to be recorded, but you did consent to the sex. And you are a public figure, so we may face issues of whether normal privacy statues apply to you."

"So women should never have sex if they don't want to be on sex tapes?"

"You just need to be prepared for the kind of arguments we may face," Idris Jr. clarified. "They'll say this wouldn't have happened if you'd been in a serious, committed relationship," he went. "They'll try to blame your lifestyle. To discredit you. And much of that will be done in the most public way possible."

"The Slutty Suitorette got what she deserved," she said sarcastically.

"Precisely."

Adam's free hand fisted on his thigh.

And it went on from there.

\* \* \* \* \*

By the time the lawyers left, the sun had set and Adam had fantasized about throttling each of them at least five times.

He kept reminding himself that they were on Elena's side, they were only trying to prepare her for what she would face so she wouldn't be blindsided by any of it, but as he watched her shrink in on herself, her arms wrapped tight around her middle as she huddled on the couch, none of that seemed to matter as much as the fact that she was hurting.

He'd made baked mac n' cheese for dinner, picking the most comforting food he could think of, and together they'd polished off a bottle of red wine, but it hadn't improved the mood. It wasn't likely that anything would today. He'd found a mindless comedy on TV in an attempt to cheer her up, but she was still too shell-shocked to laugh, staring blankly at the screen.

The movie was only half over when she drifted out to the deck to lean against the rail and stare out at the night-dark water. Adam shut off the TV and followed her out, giving her space but taking up a place a few feet down on the rail in case she wanted to talk.

"You looked like you wanted to punch the three musketeers today," she commented after a moment of silence staring out at the waves.

"I did."

"You might want to keep them on retainer. You're going to have a lot of assault charges to deal with if you go around punching everyone who insults me."

He hated that she was right, that things were only going to get worse before they got better, that she was in this situation at all. He hated *all of it*. And he hated that there was nothing he could do.

He reached out, catching her to him, a little surprised when she nestled against his chest without protest. He wrapped his arms around her shoulders and rested his cheek against the top of her head as she looped her arms around his waist and pressed her cheek to his chest, her face still pointed out toward the water.

As she held on, the tension in her body relaxed—not all the way, but enough that he felt her sigh.

"I really fucked up this time," she whispered.

"*No*." He swore. "*You* didn't."

She sighed again, releasing another notch of tension. "It still doesn't feel real. I didn't know I was famous enough to have a sex tape." She snorted. "Watch out Kim Kardashian. Here I come."

Now she was the one cracking jokes and he was the one who couldn't laugh. He wanted so badly to be able to take it all away. Make it better. And the only thing that would help now was time. And a lot of it.

"It won't last forever. Public memory is shorter than you think."

She breathed out a humorless laugh. "Tell that to Monica Lewinsky."

"Dermott Kellerman isn't Bill Clinton."

"I should be grateful for that, I guess, but I'd almost rather get caught banging the President than some random douchebag with a web cam. Monica had better taste. Though Dermott isn't married—I don't think—so that's a plus."

He tried to think of something else to say, but he'd

pretty much tapped out his comforting homilies with *This too shall pass.*

He held her, listening to the ocean, but she broke the moment, pulling away.

"I'm exhausted." She pushed her hands through her hair, pulling the tie free so her dark hair fell loose around her shoulders. She looked gorgeous—and it was the absolute wrong time for him to notice. "Apparently being auctioned off to the highest bidder is quite tiring. Who knew?"

He leaned back against the railing, gripping it with both hands so he wouldn't be tempted to touch her again. "Get some sleep. I'll see you in the morning."

She nodded. "G'night, Adam. Thanks for everything today."

He shook his head, ready to protest that he hadn't done anything, but she was already slipping through the French doors back into the house. He listened, barely making out the sound of her steps over the lap of the waves. He waited until he thought he heard the click of her door before turning back to face the Pacific.

Tomorrow would be better. It had to be.

# CHAPTER SEVENTEEN

The injunction went through that night—which was a good news/bad news situation. The good news was Dermott couldn't release the tape without going to jail. The bad news was it was all anyone seemed to be talking about on the morning talk shows.

Day Two of Tapegate, as Elena had started calling it in her head, dawned with an almost insultingly gorgeous blue sky. No smog today. Just crystal blue water and enough of a breeze to invite everyone out into the Californian paradise.

Everyone except Elena, who was hiding out at Adam's house and watching her personal drama play out on television.

After a short argument that morning, she'd managed to convince Adam that he would only annoy her by hovering over her all day and he needed to get his ass back to work. He'd gone, under protest, leaving her alone with the blank television screen staring ominously at her. She'd told herself she wasn't going to watch the coverage—but that promise lasted about two seconds after the door shut behind Adam.

She felt strangely at peace with the whole mess this morning. She'd slept off and on for a few hours at a time the night before—certainly not well—but she felt more awake, and more human, than she had all of yesterday.

And then she found herself wondering if it was normal to feel better or if there was something wrong with her because she was actually okay.

Of course, the morning talk show hosts had plenty to say on the question of whether there was something wrong with her or not. After the third rehashing of the MMP Jacuzzi incident—as if getting topless with one man in the controlled environment of reality television had given all of America permission to tape her having sex without her knowledge—she turned off the television.

Then she'd made the mistake of looking up how much the lawyers charged. They weren't so gauche as to post it right on their website, but when she looked up what the kind of legal action she was involved in could cost, she nearly had a heart attack.

Miranda had brought them in to solve the problem, but there had been no discussion of how Elena was supposed to be able to pay them. She didn't have the kind of money to throw around that their usual clients did.

To take her mind off her financial panic, she decided to check in with the dissection of her life on the midday discussion shows.

The narrative was largely more of the same—with the occasional dissenting voice added to the mix, arguing that she wasn't Satan's helper. She was about to turn off the television again, figuring she'd gotten the gist of it, when she saw a teaser for the upcoming episode of TMZ.

A teaser that featured Daniel's reaction to her sex tape.

Her blood went cold.

She froze on the couch, biting her nails until the top

of the hour rolled around and TMZ came on. The Daniel clip was toward the end of the second segment.

A camera crew had cornered him coming out of a restaurant—and the good folks at TMZ had helpfully captioned the shouted questions of the cameraman, in case anyone missed them.

*"Daniel! Daniel! What do you think of the Slutty Suitorette Sex Tape? They say it's gonna go for over a million. As someone who knows, is one night with Elena really worth that much?"*

Elena groaned, pleading with the television, "Take the high road, Daniel. Walk away."

He kept walking, but glanced over his shoulder. "No comment." And he winked.

The asshole *winked*.

And the charmers at TMZ replayed it over and over and over and over again. In slow motion, pausing and rewinding, gleefully commentating.

She stabbed the power button.

So.

Daniel was a dickhead. Nothing new there. Daniel had been a dickhead ever since the day he'd stood across from her on a Tahitian beach, holding her hands, *smiling*, and telling her that she was every man's fantasy, but reality was different and in reality he wanted to marry someone else. When only the night before—and for *months* before—he had been taking every opportunity he had to talk about their incredible chemistry, their incredible connection, the way she made him *feel*.

Lust. It had been lust. But she'd wanted to believe it was more. Wanted it so badly she hadn't even cared what her own emotions were. If he could really love her, that was all she needed.

But he hadn't. She'd just been a shiny toy.

And it wasn't just Daniel. It was *all of them*. All the men who treated her like her cup-size automatically made her a bimbo. All the people who needed her to fit into a nice neat box labeled SLUT and couldn't get their tiny brains around the idea that she could be impulsive and sexy and still a freaking *human being* who deserved to be treated with a shred of respect every now and then.

Her cell rang and she was tempted to ignore it—since in her current mood she was likely to screech at whoever was on the other end of the line—but so few people had that number she checked the caller ID, and then immediately hit the button to accept the call.

"Sam."

"I want to kill him," Samantha said without preamble. "Who is he? Some guy from before the show?"

"Right after, actually. Just a fling to try to get Daniel out of my system."

Sam cursed—the vulgarity of it surprising for the girl who had been portrayed as a sweet Midwestern girl with wholesome family values through the entire show. Her box, in its own way, just as restrictive as Elena's.

"If you need to get away from it, you can come here," Sam said staunchly. "You know that, right? White Falls would rally around you."

"I appreciate the invitation, but I'm going to stick it out here for a few more days. There may be legal proceedings and they're easier to handle if I'm not in hiding in Upper Peninsula Michigan."

"Well, the offer stands. What's happening to you... It makes me want to scream when I think about it. If there's anything I can do, I'll do it. I could get a Twitter account! Some of the girls are already tweeting their support."

"Don't get a Twitter account. Just steer clear. We have an injunction to stop him selling the tape and with any luck things will die down when they realize we've stopped the release of the full version."

"You're so much calmer than I would be."

Elena almost laughed. Calm was not how she would have described her emotional state, but if she could pass for it, she'd take it. "Doesn't do me any good to panic," she said—as if she wasn't freaking out every second of the day.

"How's the new guy handling things?"

Adam. Feeding her. Holding her hand. Hugging her tight on the deck last night, his arms so warm and comforting and right around her even as everything else in her life felt wrong.

"He's a prince." And any second he was going to figure out what a trainwreck she was and throw her out.

"Thank God," Sam breathed, relief thick in her voice. "You need someone with you right now who is good to you."

"He's good to me," she reassured Sam. He was better than she deserved.

Now if only he could want her after all this.

Twenty minutes after she got off the phone with Sam, Sidney called. Elena hesitated before picking up the call. She and Sidney had never really been close. They shared the show and they shared friendships with Caitlyn and Samantha, but the two of them had never really bonded. Now that Caitlyn's wedding was over, she couldn't think of a single reason why Sidney would call her—unless it had to do with Max and Adam. Maybe she was warning Elena to keep her scandal to herself and not drag Elite Protection into it. That made sense.

"Hello?" she answered, evicting any trace of

tentativeness from her voice. Never let them see you tremble.

"Elena? Oh my God, how are you? We've been so worried."

"You have?"

"Of course we have. Josh just showed me that awful clip of Daniel winking. Can I kill him for you? Because I would love to kill him for you. Though I'm not sure how much that would help." Elena heard a voice in the background. "Josh says he'll make a statement of support. I will too. Whatever we can do to help."

"Thanks," Elena said, though she was pretty sure the only people who could help right now had legal degrees. Though a statement of support from the host of the show couldn't hurt. "So you and Josh, huh? I thought that wasn't anything."

"He persuaded me." Elena could hear the blush in her voice. "I'm going to have to get a bigger apartment because he's practically moved in since the wedding."

They chatted about Sidney's glowing happy life for a few minutes—like the friends they might actually become—and Sidney even insisted they had to go out for coffee sometime, since she lived less than an hour north of LA.

"I'd love to, but I have no idea how long it will be before I can go for coffee and not have it be a zoo." And with Sidney she knew the other former-Suitorette wasn't trying to use that media zoo for her own publicity.

"Have you thought of leaving LA until it dies down?" Sidney asked, echoing Samantha's offer to escape to White Falls.

Elena repeated what she'd told Sam, adding, "I tried disappearing to Albuquerque a few months back, just for a few days when the show was airing and the hashtag stuff first happened, and I realized the show is popular *everywhere*."

Things had been going badly with her parents and she'd hoped to patch things up with them, to explain, to hide, but they'd refused to even see her, and if anything the attention had been worse in New Mexico. At least in LA, half the population pretended they were too cool to be interested in celebrity lives. In New Mexico everyone who recognized her seemed to feel like they had the right to touch her.

"Besides," she said to Sidney, "running away lets them win and that isn't okay. None of this is okay."

Not just that it had happened to her, but that it happened. Her injustice button had been pushed and if she skulked off with her tail between her legs, wasn't she admitting that they were right to shun her and treat her like shit? No. It was *not okay*.

"Do you think I'm crazy to stick it out? Crazy to think I can still make a living as an actress after all this?"

"A little crazy never hurt anyone," Sidney said. "But that isn't the important question."

"No? Then what is?"

"Is it still what you want?"

"Yes." Her answer was immediate and absolute.

She'd never wanted anything the way she wanted to make it as an actress. Not to be one of the glamorous people with their glamorous lives, but because when she disappeared into a role it was like something clicked into place inside her and she *knew* down to the pit of her soul that this was what she was meant to do. She had a calling and that wasn't something you just walked away from. Even when it felt impossible.

She'd had an acting teacher in college who told her the business was hard. *"If you can give up acting, do it,"* he'd said, *"because this business isn't worth the pain."* She'd thought he was being melodramatic at the time, but now she understood his words in a way she never had before. She *couldn't* give it up. Not and still feel like herself, anyway. It had become too much a piece of who she was.

So she would stick it out.

This was still the beginning of her story. She would look back on this with Barbara Walters some day and laugh, damn it.

After the call from Sidney, she dared the television again.

The networks had a rare window where none of the shows were talk shows or entertainment gossip, so she flipped over to the twenty-four hour news channels. The first few were talking about politics and the stock market. Her name didn't even appear in the ticker scrolling across the bottom. Maybe that was it. Maybe the worst was over.

She clicked to the last news channel—and her tiny flicker of hope coughed and died. The pretty blonde pundit spoke forcefully into the camera, emphasizing her words with a pen she pointed at the home audience. *"Ashamed—"* Point. *"—of herself. I normally try to take the female side, but women like this set the fight for true gender equality back *fifty years*.*" Point. *"Stay tuned. After the break we'll speak to Dale Reese, a spokesperson for Dermott Kellerman, the man selling the tape."*

Elena's heart thudded hard. *No.* It had to be a mistake. Dale Reese wasn't a spokesperson for Dermott. He was *her agent*. Or he had been before she fired him yesterday morning. She'd trusted him. He wouldn't just turn around and work for the enemy, would he?

He would. She knew he would.

Her agent had the ethics of a rabid mongoose, of course he'd jumped camps. Former agent. She was lucky to be rid of him.

Oh yeah. Her life was all about the luck these days. And she couldn't even call in to the show he was on and scream at him for betraying her—though, *God,* that would feel good—because it would be replayed on every news show for the next week, feeding the flames with her harpy tirade.

She couldn't *do* anything but watch her life implode. Trapped in this house for the third straight day, going crazy and thinking every day, *This. This has to be rock bottom.* Even as she had a sinking feeling she hadn't hit it yet. And all she could do was brace for impact and wait.

## CHAPTER EIGHTEEN

"How is she?"

Adam suppressed his impatience to get back to Elena, answering Max as he stowed his equipment from the day. "Better than I'd be."

His job today had been for one of his regulars, escorting her around town as she ran the usual rounds for a pre-release press junket for the movie about to release. He was just glad this particular actress was a new mother with a baby at home who didn't want to hit the club circuit and be seen until two in the morning. His wasn't the kind of job where he could just clock out at five and head home. If the celebrity was still out, he was still out—which often led to late nights with after parties and after-the-after parties.

But this week, Max appeared to have reworked his schedule so he didn't have as many late night red carpets. So maybe he owed Max a little more information.

"She's hating every second of it, but she's tough. She was trying to crack jokes last night—" When he'd had her in his arms on the deck and she'd felt so incredibly right there. "I hate this. I hate that there's nothing I can do."

"Comes with the territory."

Adam's hackles rose. "It shouldn't."

"No," Max agreed. "It shouldn't." His boss shifted and Adam could feel the change of topic before Max said, "I talked to Sandy Newton. Gave her the too-close-to-be-effective excuse."

"And?"

"She seemed satisfied. I assigned Tank to that premiere her daughter wanted you for. Just wanted to let you know we're good on that front."

"Good."

"I'll let you get back to Elena." Max started to leave and Adam turned, calling after him.

"Max? Thanks."

His boss nodded. "You're one of us now, Dylan. Someday you'll accept that."

Then he was gone—and Adam had other things on his mind besides figuring out what that last cryptic remark was supposed to mean. Things like getting home to Elena.

He wasn't sure what he expected—maybe more of the dazed denial or cynical depression he'd witnessed yesterday and this morning before he left—but when he walked in the door, he was once again confronted by Elena with a manic gleam in her eye. She must have heard the car pull up because she was leaning against the wall in the front hall waiting when he opened the door.

"Honey! You're home!"

She'd changed out of the yoga pants and t-shirt she'd worn all day yesterday and slept in last night. She was back in her tight jeans and a bright aqua off-the-shoulder shirt that draped loosely over her curves. Her hair was clean and swept back from her face in a tidy ponytail, her face free of make-up. She was At-Home Elena, but At-Home Elena with a ferocious intensity on her face.

"How are you doing?" he asked as he set down his keys and relocked the door behind him.

"Oh, you know. My former agent is representing the asshole trying to sell my body on eBay, Daniel is winking at the press every time they ask him how much they should pay to watch me have sex, and I have no idea how I'm going to begin to pay all the legal bills that I'm sure are already stacking up, but enough about me. Let's talk about you. How was *your* day?"

Indignant rage surfaced. "Your agent is representing that asshole?"

"Yep. When it rains, it… you know, I'm not sure there's even a word for this kind of torrential shitstorm."

He gave in to the need to touch her, stepping forward and cupping the side of her neck, his thumb along her jaw. "Are you okay?"

"I'm *pissed*." She pushed away from the wall—and from him in the process—stalking back into the main part of the house. He trailed behind her, pausing at the edge of the living room as she began to pace in front of the windows.

"I've been on my best behavior lately. New Elena. And look where that got me? No one even noticed. I can be a saint for the rest of my life and all anyone will see when they look at me is the Slutty Suitorette. Well, fuck them. Yes, I took off my top with Daniel in the Jacuzzi! Yes, I slept with him on the two-day dates! Yes, I have had sex with other men! And now the entire world gets an all access pass to my sex life." She flung out her arms, nearly taking out one of the sculptures Sandy's decorator had placed around the room.

"I just want to scream because no guy ever gets targeted like this. They take pictures of their dicks and text them to dozens of women, *begging* people to look at their junk, but I can't even get naked in my own bedroom without worrying about whether some asshole hacker has accessed the webcam on my laptop."

Adam's chest constricted.

"What the fuck did I ever do that was so wrong?" she demanded. "I didn't use anyone for sex on national television. Yes, I was a smart ass and said some un-PC shit for the cameras so I could get more air time. I played up the villainess role when it became obvious that was how they were going to portray me. I bragged about my connection with Daniel, but I was never intentionally cruel to any of the girls. A bunch of them called and texted and tweeted me today—they *like* me, if you can believe it. And they *detest* Daniel, but Daniel is a guy so he's the stud and I'm the slut as far as society is concerned. He did every single thing that I did, but I'm being punished because I *let* him. Because I *tempted* him. Because I was Eve with the goddamn apple, but I am sick of that shit. Who made that okay?"

"It isn't."

"I've been watching TV off and on all day. You know the stages of grief? I'm discovering the stages of sex tapes. So far I've covered Denial and Depression and this afternoon I achieved Anger. I like Anger the best so far, but it's probably a good thing I don't know where you keep your guns."

"Maybe no more TV?"

"No one is outraged for me. They're gleeful. Because they disapprove of me, they feel like they're allowed to pile on. Hell, it's *encouraged*. Like I deserve the shame. My punishment for being a slut." She spun toward him, thrusting a finger in his direction. "It would be different if the girl being attacked was pure. Of course if it's a sex tape then she must have had sex and any female who has consensual sex is voluntarily giving up their purity and therefore fair game. She was *asking for it*."

"That's bullshit."

"It's how they think!"

"Who?"

"Everyone! Like it's my own fault this is happening to me because I wasn't perfect. If you'd saved me from a burning building, it wouldn't make news, but little miss perfect Cassie *deserved* to be saved." She stopped pacing, throwing back her head. "*God,* I hate that word. They talk a lot about who deserves love on the show. And only the nice girls who are sweet and demure and never put a foot wrong or their tongue down anyone's throat *deserve* love. Like there's a scale. Single moms and widows are at the top. They *deserve* love the most. My season it was Sam with her broken heart and Caitlyn with her difficult childhood who *deserved* love—even if they deserved better than a self-absorbed dipshit like Daniel. They *deserved* happiness. And I was the slut. Always the slut."

"Stop it. That isn't who you are."

"But I can't get away from it! I'm marked. I might as well wear a freaking scarlet A on all my clothes."

"I can think of worse fashion statements."

Elena waved away his comment. "It's been done. That cute Emma Stone movie. But see—she can be sexy and cute at the same time. What am I doing wrong?" She flopped onto the couch and he decided the first manic rush had passed enough for him to approach without getting elbowed by one of her flailing arms.

"You aren't doing anything wrong. You're human." He sat down beside her, not quite close enough for their legs to touch. "And so are those jerks indulging in a schadenfreude orgy at your expense."

She breathed out a soft, scoffing huff and he took her hand, lacing their fingers together.

"No one's perfect," he said. "Certainly not Cassie Newton."

"If her only flaw is having a huge crush on the man who saved her life, I think America will empathize," she said dryly, but she didn't take her hand away.

He shouldn't tell her. He'd promised Sandy Newton that he would keep his mouth shut, but this was Elena and he wanted her to know the truth. "I'm going to tell you something, but you can't tell another soul."

She turned toward him, dark eyes curious in spite of herself. "You trusting me with your secrets now?"

He'd trusted her down to his core since the day they met. As if something in him had recognized something in her, a vein of integrity that ran deep. But she'd only make a joke if he told her that.

"Cassie Newton isn't perfect."

Elena arched a brow questioningly, waiting for him to go on.

He hesitated, feeling like he was betraying Cassie's trust, but that was ridiculous. This was Elena. "Everyone believes that Cassie was passed out behind the couch because of smoke inhalation."

Elena nodded.

"Well. She was. But it was a different kind of smoke."

"You're kidding. With her goodie-goodie image?"

"I thought you didn't know who she was."

"I've been trapped in your house for three days with nothing to do. Did you think I wasn't going to read every scrap of news I could find online about your heroic deed and the precious little princess you saved?"

"Well, don't believe everything you read."

"She really was high?"

"And drunk. And underage at a party she shouldn't have gone to in the first place."

"Damn," Elena marveled.

"She's reformed now—"

"And everyone loves a reformed sinner."

"But her parents kept the truth out of the press. They made the story about my heroics, rather than the fact that Cassie had misbehaved."

"I need a better PR team." Elena's eyes grew distant. "Though I guess I don't have one anymore since I fired Dale and he took care of all that." She frowned. "I wonder who's running my Twitter now."

"You're missing the point."

"That Cassie Newton is a bad girl and America still loves her because her PR people are amazing?"

"Everyone deserves to be saved."

# CHAPTER NINETEEN

Elena stared into the hazel eyes so close to hers, noting all the tiny differentiations of color there. Gold. Brown. Yellow. Green. He genuinely believed everyone deserved to be saved.

, "That's why you're the hero," she said. "Because you really believe that."

"You believe it too."

"Do I?"

A stern frown pulled down his brow. "You deserve to be saved, Elena," he insisted.

Did she? Did she deserve to be fished out of the quagmire of her own life? Today it felt like he was the only person in the world who believed that. Well, maybe not the only one. Sam. And Sidney. And Josh. And Miranda. She had support. She had people who cared.

But he was the one sitting next to her on this couch, still holding her hand though it had started to feel awkward several minutes ago, her awareness of him so acute it made even small things like his fingertips threaded alongside hers feel bigger than they were.

What was he doing here with her?

"You're too good for me." The words were soft. A simple statement of fact.

"Stop it." Harsh. Frustrated. "You're good." He shook his head, his gaze boring into hers. "You're better than good. You're *you*. Everyone wants to be as strong as you are. As secure in who they are as you are. As confident as you can be when you aren't listening to their crap. Don't lose that because they're trying to beat it out of you. Be Elena. You're better than all that bullshit."

She'd forgotten how to breathe. Eyes wide, she whispered, "Do you really think that?"

"Yes."

Yes. Just that. So simple.

*So fucking hot.*

"Damn," she whispered. There went her self-control. "That might be the hottest thing anyone's ever said to me."

He wasn't far. She had her lips on his before he could say another word.

His shock lasted only a second before he was kissing her back, cupping the back of her neck. *Please don't let him decide this is a bad idea.* She couldn't handle it if he pushed her away tonight. He lifted his head from hers— *No, please don't pull back*—his hazel eyes stunned and black with want. "Please," she whispered, hoarse.

He groaned, "*Elena*," hauling her back to him. Then she was in his lap and he was making a sound that definitely didn't sound like *stop* and his hands were sliding over her. Hips, thighs, indent of her waist, small of her back. He hadn't even gotten to the good stuff yet and already she was putty.

When he broke the kiss to pull her top off over her head, she had a momentary flicker of thought that this wasn't what New Elena would do, but that thought was quickly overruled by *Fuck New Elena* and the feel of his mouth on the side of her neck.

*Yes.*

All her anger, all her frustration, all her impotent, directionless emotion now coalesced into a single driving thought—*Adam.* He was her center, her rock, and she clung to him, trying to get closer, wanting to crawl inside him until the rest of the world disappeared.

More. She needed more.

His shirt came undone beneath her hands and when she spread her hands over his chest her mind went a little fuzzy. He was beautiful, all sleek muscle and just enough hair to remind her that he was a man—not a boy or a grizzly bear. Her bra came loose and he stripped it away, swearing worshipfully under his breath. He put his hands and mouth on her and her thoughts misted again.

*Okay.* This was good. This was better than good. This was better than she'd had in a year and he hadn't even gotten her jeans off yet. She tried to work up the concentration to reciprocate, to make him feel as good as he was making her feel, but then he got her zipper down and his *hands*—

She'd reciprocate later. When she wasn't rocking into his touch and trying to hang onto the good and—*Holy Hell, where had he learned to do that?* She was jolted back to reality briefly by the thought of other women he'd touched, but then he twisted them around so her back was on the couch and he was pressing down into her and she was back in that mindless place where nothing existed but the way he was touching her and if he stopped she was going to *kill him*, which made sense since she was chanting, "*Don't stop, don't stop, don't stop,*" and then she was screaming, shudders ripping hard through her and yanking her roughly from one peak into the next.

"Holy crap." Her body was boneless. If she tried, she

might be able to summon the concentration to move her little finger, but it wasn't a good bet.

"Was that English?" Adam asked, kissing his way across her stomach. Her jeans had vanished somehow, along with her underwear, and her hair had come loose. She was completely naked and must look debauched, spread out on his couch, but he still had his pants on. They would have to fix that. Just as soon as she could move again.

She thought back and vaguely recalled shouting something toward the end there. "Spanish. My father will be so proud that I'm using the language of my ancestors. It always annoyed him that I didn't speak it more often."

Adam chuckled against her skin. "Maybe we won't tell him about the circumstances around your newfound fondness for your ancestral tongue."

"Probably wise." She reached for him, energy returning to her limbs. "Speaking of tongues..." She kissed him, long and deep, and his response was tinged by the impatience of a man who was ready for the main event. She pulled back, smiling her most tantalizing smile. "You've been such a good boy," she purred, "letting me go first. I think you've earned a reward."

Her hands were on the fastenings of his slacks, then they were on him and his eyes were blank with want above her as he panted softly in time to her touch. "Condom?"

"Upstairs."

"Very poor planning, Mr. Dylan."

He groaned as she twisted her wrist to apply pressure just so. Then he grabbed her hands, pulling them away from him and pinning them to the couch on either side of her head. She pushed against his hold, arching a little beneath him just to feel the pressure of his strength. *This could be interesting.* But the condoms were upstairs. And the frustration in his eyes said he knew it.

"Come here." He hooked one arm behind her back and the other under her knee, holding her to him as he stood in a single, fluid motion. She wound her arms and legs around him and he swore under his breath, trying to kick off the slacks that had fallen to tangle around his ankles. She pressed her face against the curve of his shoulder to hide her smile, irrationally delighted by his impatience.

Then his shoulder was right there, so she bit it gently, testing the muscle with her teeth.

"Hey." He smacked her ass, the sound more surprising than the contact—and startlingly erotic. She'd never been into that sort of thing before, but she wanted to play with him. To explore. To test the boundaries of what made them feel good. Because right now everything about Adam made her feel good.

Freed of his pants, he carried her toward the stairs—and he wasn't even winded when they got to the top. You had to appreciate a man with conditioning.

He opened the door to the master bedroom and she twisted around, trying to get a glimpse of his lair—the one room of the house she hadn't explored—but he didn't turn on the light and she didn't have time to think more than *It's bigger than I thought it would be* before he was dropping her on the bed, reaching for a condom and suddenly she was thinking the same thought again for entirely different reasons.

She grinned at the thought—feeling so incredibly *happy* it was strange to also be so turned on—and then he was back, hands and mouth and just *Adam*, driving her out of her mind with everything he did. Undoing her with the way his hands shook when he touched her, the taut way his body coiled above her, trying to hold back, to give her time to get back up to speed, but she was already there, racing up, heart pounding and then he was inside her and she was digging her heels into his ass, everything in her focused on that spot, that feeling, the look in his eyes, right above hers, *Adam*, so freaking close and so damn hot she split into pieces again with a jerk, tightening down on him so he lost his rhythm and lost his mind in her, groaning her name, collapsing hard over her, the weight of him heaven, imprinting him on her until the memory of his skin would be stamped on hers forever.

"Christ," he groaned. "We've gotta do that again."

She laughed, pressing her face against the sweaty shoulder in front of her as her hands roamed his back. "You think?"

"Yeah." He disengaged, rolling onto his back. "Just give me two or three years to remember how to walk and then I'm all yours."

She felt the dippy smile on her face, knew she looked besotted and was grateful for the darkness that meant he couldn't see it. "I have faith in you. You'll be on your feet again in a week. Two tops."

He rolled to his side, reaching for a tissue on the bedside table to dispose of the condom. Then he was back, pulling her against him, tucking her into the curve of his body. One hand stroked the curve of her waist as his other arm served as her pillow. "I do have strong motivation to recover," he whispered against the back of her neck, his breath making her entire body shiver with want—as if she hadn't just had two wringing orgasms in the last half hour.

He kissed down the side of her neck and Elena sighed, closing her eyes. Trying to hang onto this feeling. Trying not to spoil it. But experience was a bitch. And she loomed up, casting a shadow over Elena's happy place.

She'd been here before. In bed with a man she was crazy about. Admittedly, none of them had made her feel *this*, but she'd been here. And it had always gone bad. She'd always been wrong. And she'd always gotten hurt. So even as she squeezed her eyes shut tight and tried to enjoy his hands and his mouth and the press of him "recovering" against her backside, fear slithered in, whispering through the back of her mind, reminding her that this didn't last. That once they had her, once the chase was over, they stopped wanting her. Maybe not right away, but soon. And then all this lovely peace and warmth and security that she felt was pulled out from under her.

Best not to get used to it.

Enjoy it. But don't bask in it. Because no one stayed with the Slutty Suitorette. Not even a hero with a savior complex who had found a mission in her.

Fairy tales were for the sweet Cinderellas. Sexy women were the villainesses, victims and femme fatales. And none of them ever got the guy for long. But she could enjoy him while she had him.

Elena turned toward him, into his touch, taking his mouth with her own, taking this moment and as many more as she could get before it all went away.

# CHAPTER TWENTY

Adam woke up feeling inexplicably amazing—then he rolled over and saw the explanation, sprawled out on her stomach, one arm hanging loosely over the side of the bed, the sun from the skylight painting her skin a rich golden hue.

Gorgeous.

Who wouldn't want to wake up to that for the rest of his life?

Not that he was going to. Her life was in uproar at the moment. He represented comfort and safety to her. A temporary sanctuary. He knew better than to expect anything more from her right now. And even if he had wanted something real and permanent, something more than just coming together in the night, he didn't have anything to offer her at the moment. His life wasn't stable. His future, when he looked into it, was still murky. The job with Elite Protection was a temporary measure. Something to keep him afloat until he figured out who the hell he was now that all his goals had been stripped away.

He wasn't in a position to make promises that lasted. But for now he could be here for her. Make her life easier any way he could.

He saw the moment she woke up. He tended to come awake all at once—like being shot out of a cannon, one of his non-morning-person exes had grumbled—but Elena's waking was a slow, inch-by-inch process. Her shoulders tensed, her hands spasming as she fought to stay asleep. Then the muscles along her spine clenched, one by one, as consciousness invaded and her troubles returned. She released a soft, disgruntled sigh and he knew she was truly awake, though her eyes stayed squeezed closed.

Unable to resist, he leaned over her, pressing a kiss to her bare shoulder blade. "Good morning."

She released an irritable grumble and opened one eye—and he was gratified to see her irritation melt away. Her face was pointed away from him, toward the view out the windows. He'd woken up to this for the last several months, but it still startled him sometimes, the ocean right outside the glass.

He tried to see it through her eyes—the same long bank of windows like the living room below, but brighter here, blazing with light from the pale hardwood floors to the giant gleaming skylight. The room seemed to have been designed to bring the sea closer and accent the light on the water. The bed was a large four-poster, sturdy and massive, like something that had been taken from an old sailing ship—or made out of one. From her position she wouldn't be able to see the fireplace or the reading nook, nor the walk in closets and luxurious master bath that jutted off this room—but the view was enough.

He'd never felt like it was his, sleeping in this bed, living in this room. He'd never fit. But with her here… It still didn't feel like his, but he felt right being here somehow. Like an expensive hotel room he could indulge in for a few nights before returning to reality. The kind of hotel room he would want to get for Elena, to spoil her. To see her smile and sigh as she gazed out over the view.

"Wow," she murmured.

He hummed against her skin, kissing along her spine now, his hands sliding over her silky smoothness. Her muscles slowly began to unknot.

"That is some view to wake up to."

"I couldn't agree more."

She turned her head enough to see his face, realized he was ignoring the view outside in favor of the one in his bed and rolled her eyes. "Don't be cliché."

He shrugged—it had been a cheesy line—and went back to saying good morning to every inch of her gorgeous self.

She sighed, going loose-limbed beneath him. "Can I just stay in this bed and never leave? Pretend nothing else exists?"

"I certainly wouldn't mind," he said. "I have a job tonight, but I'm yours until three."

"Oh?" She twisted, stretching beneath him, all lovely soft limbs and sweet curves.

"Mm." He bent his head to kiss her—and her stomach rumbled loudly. Adam lifted his head. "We need fuel."

Only when he said the words did he become aware of his own stomach's complaints. They'd never gotten to dinner the night before and by the angle of the light, they'd already missed his normal breakfast hour this morning. And after their marathon last night...

"Sadly, mankind cannot live on sex alone," he declared, already rolling out of bed. "How do you feel about pancakes?"

\* \* \* \* \*

172

Elena sank deeper into the plush covers on the massive bed, watching Adam's world-class ass disappear into the bathroom. Moments later she heard the water running, but before she could work up the energy to decide whether she wanted to join him in the shower it shut off again and Adam came out, wearing a pair of dark blue cotton pajama pants and rubbing a towel over his wet hair.

"That might be the fastest shower I've ever seen," she commented, still without moving from her cozy nest on the bed.

"I was motivated by starvation," Adam said, moving to the bed to drop a smacking kiss on her mouth. "Gotta keep my woman fed."

He straightened and headed for the bedroom door, tossing the towel back into the bathroom as he passed it.

She shouldn't like being called his woman. Especially considering she couldn't keep him. They were just playing. Enjoying the moment. But it was a good moment. One worth enjoying. So she let herself bask in the feeling the words conjured.

That would be her motto today. Live in the moment. The sensory. Enjoy the scents and sights and not think about anything outside this room.

She heard him banging around in the kitchen below, whistling little snatches of an old Otis Redding song, and she smiled to herself, dragging herself out of the most comfortable bed on the planet to go investigate the shower.

It was—unsurprisingly—glorious. Cassandra Newton the Elder had excellent taste in everything, and that included walk-in showers with half a dozen adjustable shower heads and automated temperature controls. Elena rinsed off the sweat and scent of sex from the night before, quickly washing her hair before adjusting the massage settings to pound the kinks out of her shoulders.

She could get used to this. Nothing like a zillion dollar showerhead to deal with the effects of having your life shredded by the press.

Apparently the moral of the story was if your life is going to hell, make sure the amenities are top notch.

She found a hair-dryer wedged all the way at the back in the cabinet beneath the second of the two vanities in the spacious master bath. The other vanity held Adam's toothbrush, deodorant, comb and shaving detritus, but this one looked abandoned. Like it hadn't been used since he moved in.

She didn't care to examine the thrill of possessive pleasure that he'd never had anyone else use this vanity. Instead, she dried her hair and found the top half of the pajamas he'd been wearing sitting neatly folded on a shelf to one side of his laundry hamper.

She buttoned the top, picturing him carefully laying out his pajamas the morning before in preparation for his evening routine. Dirty clothes off and in the hamper, quick shower, clean pajamas folded and waiting.

He was so organized. So disciplined.

So unlike her.

She took another look around the bathroom and bedroom, noting how tidy everything was. A peek in the closet revealed the same ruthless order. It looked like a catalogue. Whereas the guest room she'd only been in for three days looked... well, she'd just choose to think of it as thoroughly lived in.

It was a good thing they were just temporary. She'd drive him crazy with her mess in under a week if they were really a couple.

Elena padded barefoot down the risers. Adam was humming now, slightly off-key, and cooking merrily away, but she couldn't escape the feeling that reality was waiting for her in the kitchen.

Her phone was down there.

"Smells good." She walked into the kitchen, inhaling the inviting scent of bacon, and boosted herself up onto one of the breakfast bar stools, grateful his shirt was long enough to keep her bare ass from touching the chilly stool. And on the topic of underwear... "I'm running out of clothes."

She hadn't been thinking long term when she packed her bag. She'd brought a variety of items, but only enough to last a couple of days.

Adam glanced up from the skillet, pausing in his pancake flipping. "You're welcome to the washer and dryer. Or we'll buy more."

She was glad he hadn't suggested braving the paparazzi at her place to get to her clothes, but it still felt cowardly. "I hate the idea of leaving LA to get away from the drama—like it's letting them win. But is hiding out here any better than that? If I really want to show them I don't care, don't I have to face them?"

Adam ignored her questions, asking instead, "Do you want to face them?"

"Not today."

He shrugged as if that said it all and turned back to the pancakes. "We'll swing by a store after breakfast."

She studied his bare shoulders, marveling at him— and not just his physique. He was so different than anyone she'd ever met. Whatever she felt, he accepted it. If she wanted to hide, he didn't think less of her. If she was feeling wild and manic, he didn't shy away from her. He just let her be… *herself*. And he seemed to like it. Had anyone ever done that before?

She was good at shoving who she was down people's throats—because she had to. Because everyone seemed to be trying to fix her. But Adam… he was built differently.

"Syrup?" He set a plate of pancakes in front of her, still holding the spatula with his other hand.

She caught his bicep before he could turn back to the stove to load up the other plate. She stood on the rung of the stool, balancing with her free hand on the breakfast bar, and kissed him.

It wasn't fast and lusty and open-mouthed. It wasn't urgent and pleading and needy. It was simple. It was brief. It was all she could do to thank him.

She fell back onto the stool as he blinked at her. She could feel herself blushing, squirming under his gaze, inexplicably more exposed now than she had been last night laid out naked on his bed. She focused on the plate. "Syrup would be great. Thanks."

Adam shook himself and turned away, returning moments later with his own plate and the syrup. He took the seat beside her, diving into his own pile of pancakes with gusto.

They sat side by side, having breakfast. Such a normal domestic scene for distinctly non-domestic people.

"I should check my messages," she commented when the silence began to get to her. "See if there's anything new from the lawyers."

Adam nodded. "I'll call Max's detective again. See if there've been any developments there." He forked in another bite of pancake. "I was serious about not having to work until three today. If there's nothing more we need to do for your case, how do you feel about a field trip?"

"To get clothes?"

"That, too, but I had another idea. A surprise."

Elena was not a fan of surprises—they always seemed to backfire and disappoint—but there was something about the glint in his eyes that appealed to her. "All right. Surprise me."

# CHAPTER TWENTY-ONE

The Elite Protection offices in Beverly Hills were not what Elena had been expecting when Adam had said he had a surprise for her. Typically when men said those words to her they were followed up by some hackneyed romance-by-the-book date. Generic red roses. An overpriced restaurant. Tickets to an opera she'd never heard of.

Adam had brought her to his office, as if it was Take-Your-Live-In-Friend-With-Benefits-to-Work Day.

She climbed out of his Jeep, eyeing the motorcycle in the next space as he rounded the hood. "Clearly I'm shacking up with the wrong bodyguard. Who's the biker?"

"My most repellent coworker," Adam joked. "Lucky for you, he's offered to let me borrow it whenever I want. Play your cards right and I'll even teach you to drive it. Come on." He took her hand, tugging her toward the building.

She was tempted to pull back, to argue that she knew how drive it, to beg him to jump on that bike with her and just go, but she let him guide her in through the back employee entrance and down the stairs into the basement. He didn't stop until they reached a large open room with weight equipment and a central ring of padded mats.

"If this were a movie, we'd have a training montage right now," she commented, eyeing the hanging punching bag in the corner dubiously.

Adam grinned. "That's exactly what we're going to do."

She transferred her doubt from the punching bag to her lover. "I think you've mistaken me for someone else. I only sweat when I'm naked or there's a really good song playing so loud I can't hear myself speak. I pretended to jog while I was at the Suitorette Mansion so I would have an excuse to sneak over to Daniel's mansion on the other side of the wall, but even pretending to be a runner was miserable. I have no idea why people do that voluntarily." She waved a hand at the training room. "This isn't happening."

He caught her with one arm when she tried to bolt. "Aren't you even curious why I brought you here?"

"To *exercise* apparently," Elena said, making the words sound like *to get a root canal.* She should have known something was up when he told her to bring a yoga outfit, but she'd been secretly hoping their destination was a day spa.

"Not to exercise. To teach you how to kick ass."

The first little glimmer of interest flickered in the back of her mind, quickly quashed by reality. "I'm five-one and I weigh one hundred and four pounds. Whose ass am I going to kick? Minnie Mouse?"

"Size helps, I'm not gonna lie, but you don't have to be huge to be a badass. There's a woman upstairs who can probably take me to the cleaners if she ever decides she wants to and she's only a few inches taller than you."

"If you teach me to kick ass, what will I need you for?"

"I don't want you to need me. I want to know you can get out of any situation you don't want to be in. And I want you to know it too."

Another glimmer of interest kindled.

"Come on," he cajoled, seeing an opening. "You can take out all your aggressions on me. I'm volunteering to be the whipping boy for every guy you'd like to beat senseless."

"Funny. Because you're the one guy I've never wanted to beat senseless."

"Is that a yes?"

"Sure. Fine."

He grinned and pointed her toward a closed door. "Changing rooms are through there. Suit up, killer."

* * * * *

Two hours later, Elena sank down onto the mats, sweaty, sore and feeling ever-so-slightly badass, though she still complained, "This training montage sucks. Aren't I supposed to be Bruce Lee by now?"

"You're getting it," Adam encouraged. He'd been unfailingly encouraging all morning as he showed her pressure points and weaknesses in various holds so she could get the most impact with the least force. "You were able to get away from me a couple times—now you just need to work on it until it becomes natural and instinctive."

He was a good teacher, patient and clear, explaining repeatedly that the best way for her to end a fight was to escape it and tailoring the moves to someone her size— and it hadn't hurt that she was rolling around with someone ridiculously hot who turned her crank big time. Though he'd been nothing but professional as they grappled—even when his hands had been all over her body and she'd been twisting and pressing against him.

She watched the bend and shift of his body as he pulled two water bottles out of a mini-fridge. No wonder Cassie Newton had a thing for him. "You know, if you wanted to grope me all morning, you could have just said. This elaborate set-up was entirely unnecessary."

"You found me out. All this so I can cop a feel." He tossed her a water bottle and she caught it, pressing the coolness against her forehead. Adam settled down beside her, everything about him graceful and contained. He'd barely broken a sweat, the jerk.

She cracked open her water and drained a third of it in one go, eyeing him. "You're good at this. The teaching stuff." Of course, she'd yet to find something he *wasn't* good at. "Have you ever considered offering your celebrity clients self-defense courses?"

He cocked his head. "That's not a bad idea. Max has probably already thought of it as part of his master plan for this place, but it wouldn't hurt to mention it to him."

"Just be sure you give me credit. If he makes millions off making celebrity chicks feel badass, I want a cut. I'm too broke to be generous with my genius."

"Deal."

She recapped her water and flopped onto her back on the mats, resting the bottle on her stomach beneath her sports bra, idly rolling it back and forth. "You'd think with all my dance training I'd be better at this."

"Different kind of movement. How do you feel?" The question was cautious enough she knew he wasn't asking about the muscles that would be sore tomorrow.

"Badass. Thought I'd go pick a fight with a biker gang tonight."

Adam sighed his irritation, but didn't rise to the bait.

Lesson One—as he'd drummed it into her head—was don't get cocky. Apparently the worst thing about having a little training was thinking you were tougher than you were. Elena wasn't in danger of that. She'd managed to twist out of a few holds and learned a lot about where to squeeze to get the most impact, but she didn't fool herself that she was a ninja after two hours.

But it was nice in a way. The little knowledge she had now. The way it gave her a feeling that she wasn't *completely* helpless. She'd always had one option before this—talk her way out of situations—but now if a man grabbed her wrist in a bar she knew how to twist away, suddenly so she could surprise him and putting all her limited force against the weakest part of his grip, where his thumb and fingertips met. And then run. Don't give him a chance to get his hands on her again.

It was a small thing, but it was an option she hadn't had before.

"I hate that this is necessary."

Adam was silent, but then that wasn't unusual. And she could feel his attention on her, knew he was listening.

"It's *wrong*." And the injustice of it burned beneath her skin. "It's wrong that women have to learn how to kick ass so they won't be date raped. That we have to guard our drinks so we don't get roofied and have a designated friend we check in with when we're going out with someone new or going home alone late at night. *If I don't check in, call the police.* It's not just that it's happened to me. It's that it happens to *anyone.* How can this be a thing? How is it okay that we live in a society where those kinds of precautionary measures are necessary?" She sat up abruptly, squeezing the water bottle between her hands. "And then if we aren't cautious enough and some predatory dick takes advantage, we get assaulted again by public opinion because our lifestyle allowed it to happen. It's *wrong*."

She catapulted to her feet, flinging the half-empty water bottle. It smacked into the wall with a satisfying thud. She should throw things more often.

"Men are animals and we should know that and take appropriate measures. God forbid they should be held responsible for their actions." She pivoted, looking for something else to throw and Adam extended his water bottle. He watched her calmly, making no move to interrupt, always so tuned in to her, always knowing when she just needed to rant and throw things. She snatched the bottle out of his hand. "Dermott planned this." She wound up and fired, the plastic thwack of the second bottle hitting the wall echoing startlingly loud. "The lighting was perfectly set—he was practically *directing* me. Which made it look like I knew I was being filmed. He *set me up*." She needed something to throw. "Of course, that's what you do with a sex tape, isn't it? It's not exactly spontaneous. He's a predator and he should be in jail, not potentially making millions if the decision goes against me and he gets custody of that damn tape. It was freaking entrapment. I should be able to sue him."

"Maybe you can," Adam said and she looked at him sharply.

"What?"

"Maybe you can. I don't know. I'm not a lawyer."

God, how good would that feel? To punish the asshole for everything he was doing. "I need to call my lawyers."

LIZZIE SHANE

\* \* \* \* \*

Adam sat on the mats, watching Hurricane Elena charge off to call her lawyers and wreak justice. He knew shit about the law, but he hoped she could sue. She deserved a win. And that asshole deserved to be behind bars.

Adam couldn't think about the tape without his vision going red. He wanted to pummel the asshole who had betrayed Elena's trust to within an inch of his life, but she was right. He was going to end up in jail himself if he kept trying to fight her battles. But he hated that there was nothing he could do.

Something needed to happen to Dermott Kellerman. Something painful and lasting.

Elena returned a few minutes later, frowning at the cell phone in her hand. He didn't have to ask what her lawyers had said—Elena was never shy about volunteering things.

"Apparently it's not entrapment—that's something else—and he still thinks the invasion of privacy thing will be a hard sell because of who I am—which is idiotic, but I get it—but he says if we prove premeditation it could help us with public opinion, but hurt our claim to ownership. He wants me to focus on being happy that the injunction is working and they're building a case for my custody of the video. He says they feel good about getting a hearing soon so things don't drag on—and then I practically hung up on him because I remembered phone calls count as billable hours and I could feel my bank account emptying the longer he talked." She glared at her phone. "I hate this."

An idea whispered in the back of his mind—a way he could finally do something to help. He couldn't really afford to keep the house anyway... he'd have to sell it eventually. And if he did it now, there would be plenty left over to pay legal fees. He wouldn't have to work for Elite Protection anymore if he didn't want to. His life could go from being a temporary measure designed to keep from losing the house to being about the kind of man he wanted to be again. Not just babysitting celebrities, but doing something meaningful. He could call a real estate agent today, get the ball rolling...

"I'm making a resolution," Elena declared with dramatic flair and he brought his focus back to the present.

"What's that?" he prompted when she didn't immediately go on.

"I'm not going to let them change me." She turned to him with a blend of triumph and stubbornness blazing in her eyes. "I tried to be good, but I am sick of playing by their rules. Fuck that. I want to be me again."

He felt his lips curve. "Good."

Her answering smile was full of wicked intent. "Wanna get into trouble?"

He wanted her to be happy. Whatever it took. "With you? Always."

Her grin broadened until it was wild and blinding. "Let's get out of here.

He was with her until they changed and hit the parking lot—and the searching mischief in Elena's eyes found a target.

"Hello, gorgeous."

She approached the gleaming black and silver Yamaha like it was a puppy at an animal fair, both hands outstretched to pet with a covetous affection in her eyes. She stroked her hands along the lines of the motorcycle. "Can we keep her?"

"She isn't mine."

"I know."

He unlocked the Jeep, tossing in both of their bags. When he shut the rear door and turned back to her, she was still paying homage to the bike. "Pretty Boy might be easy-going, but I think he'd draw the line at me stealing his motorcycle."

"We aren't stealing. We're borrowing. Didn't he say we could?"

"I think he meant at a pre-arranged time."

"So arrange it now." She swung a leg over the bike and petted the leather seat. "Just a little ride? I'll even let you come along."

"Do you even know how to drive one?" He wasn't even sure she was serious, but he pulled out his phone and shot a quick text to Pretty Boy asking permission to "steal" the bike.

"I dated a guy who had one once. He never let me drive it—just liked having me hang onto the back of it like a trophy—but he was also a deep sleeper and had a tendency to leave his keys out." She turned a smile on him that would have tempted an angel. "Come on. I thought you wanted to get into trouble."

"I wasn't expecting to start with grand theft auto."

"Nonsense. What's a little joyride between friends? I bet he won't even press charges. But if he did, wouldn't it be worth it?" She popped open the back compartment. "Oh look, there's even a helmet for you." She fished out the spare, waving it tantalizingly at him. "You know you're going to say yes. The sooner you do, the sooner we can have your friend's bike back where it belongs."

"He may not even have left the keys here."

"You mean the keys hanging on a hook in the locker room where anyone could swipe them? I think that proves your friend wants us to steal his bike."

He'd known he was going to give in as soon as he saw the look in her eyes when she looked at the bike, but he tried to keep his expression stern as he started back inside. "Don't move. And if the keys aren't there, we go rent one or something. I draw the line at hot-wiring."

"Where's your sense of adventure?" she pouted, but she was still straddling the bike and petting it lovingly when he emerged five minutes later with the keys and a text message from Pretty Boy telling him to go for it, but buy him gas while he was at it.

"Fifteen minutes." He tried to sound firm, but he had a feeling the impact was lessened by the grin he couldn't help when her face split into a smile.

"You've ridden one of these before, right?" She asked him as he clipped the helmet on, climbed on behind her and tried to adjust his long limbs on the high pinion seat so he wouldn't hinder her movement—he'd driven a bike, but he'd never ridden on the back.

"It's just like sex. Don't fight the movement. Lean into it when you want to go faster and don't let go." She strapped on the sleek black helmet that had been left hooked over the handlebars and flipped down the visor. "You ready, Stud Muffin?" She didn't wait for an answer, firing the engine to life. She grabbed his hands and placed them around her waist. "Hold on tight."

The crotch rocket leapt forward, jumping off the kickstand, and his hands tightened spasmodically around her waist to keep himself from falling off the back. She spun the bike, gunned it and leaned into the turn out of the parking lot. He thought he heard a shout of laughter over the engine noise, bright and wild, but then they were flying and it was all he could do to hang on for the ride.

# CHAPTER TWENTY-TWO

"I *need* to get one of these."

Elena pulled off the motorcycle helmet and tipped her face up to the sun, feeling exhilarated and free and horny as hell.

She didn't know where they were—and she didn't care. She'd pointed the bike east and left the city behind, driving into the hills on increasingly winding roads until she didn't recognize anything. They'd stopped seeing other vehicles a few minutes ago and then she'd seen the turn-off for a scenic overlook and here they were. Middle of nowhere. An abandoned viewpoint on some random hill, looking out over a bunch of other unnamed hills covered in the brown scrub that covered everything since the drought had gotten bad.

God, she felt good.

She felt like *her*. Impulsive. Daring. Leaping into life with both feet.

Adam had braced his feet on either side of the bike, holding them upright, so she lifted hers up, spinning around on the seat so she was facing him, sitting backwards. He'd taken off his helmet as well, resting it against one knee. She grabbed the waistband of his jeans and yanked, jerking his hips toward her so they slid off the high rear seat and down into the saddle.

He grunted at the movement, the bike wobbling

before he found his balance again. "We should head back," he said, as she draped her legs over his, scooting forward so she was straddling him as well as the bike, the two of them tucked tight together hip to hip.

"Should we?" She unzipped her hoodie, letting it drop behind her. "You sure about that?" Her tank top came off over her head next, and Adam's gaze dropped down to her breasts as if he couldn't help it.

"Don't you want to know why I want to get one of these?" she purred, reaching down to grab the hem of his t-shirt and lifting it slowly, her mouth going dry at the tightly clenched abs she revealed.

"Why's that?" he asked, hypnotized by her body.

She leaned in until her breasts brushed his chest and her smile brushed his lips. "Straddling this big hunk of machinery… the vibrations are like foreplay."

Adam groaned and took her mouth with savage enthusiasm.

\* \* \* \* \*

Two hours later, when Adam had dropped Elena back at his house and returned to EP to get ready for his evening detail, he ran into Pretty Boy in the employee lounge.

The model-slash-bodyguard looked up from the X-Box with a single black brow arched. "You fill 'er up?"

"Yeah." Adam tossed him the keys, unable to keep a grin from his face. "Thanks. Elena wanted a ride."

"Sure, no problem. Of course you realize if you put so much as a scratch on her, I'll murder you and stash your corpse somewhere no one will ever find you."

"And it would have been worth it."

"Ah crap." Pretty Boy straightened from his slouch,

his expression darkening. "You had sex on it, didn't you? Dude. Not cool. No one is allowed to get off on my bike but me."

"And I'm sure your dates appreciate that." Candy swanned into the room, grabbing a soda from the fridge and turning to Adam before Pretty Boy could come up with a suitably stinging reply. "So you and Elena, huh?"

Adam felt heat spreading across his cheekbones and down his neck. "She's a client."

"Not really." Candy cocked her head, eyeing him speculatively as she popped the top on her Mountain Dew. "Good luck, champ. I have a feeling you're going to need it." She made her exit before he could protest again.

"What the hell was that?" Adam muttered.

Pretty Boy's narrowed gaze was fixed on the doorway she'd vacated. "That woman is a menace."

"I thought you two were..."

"Candy?" Pretty Boy looked insulted by the implication. "No. No. *No*. Definitely not. She's insane."

"Right," Adam agreed. "A hot tech genius who can kick your ass. Who would want that?"

"Exactly." Pretty Boy rocked back, returning his attention to the X-Box. He snorted. "Me and Candy."

Adam moved to the door to make his escape. He'd thought he'd gotten away clean when Pretty Boy yelled after him. "You owe me, Dylan! And you better have disinfected the hell out of that seat!"

He knew it was wrong, but as he jogged down to grab his gear for the night, Adam couldn't keep a grin off his face.

\* \* \* \* \*

Elena stood in the center of Adam's sunken living room in a Wonder Woman pose and decided it was time to take back her life.

Step one had been "borrowing" a Yamaha V-Max for a few hours. Step two should probably be something slightly more legal.

Like getting a new agent.

Someone she could trust. Someone who would share her vision for her career. Someone who would be turned-on by the challenge of plotting a course from the Slutty Suitorette to Meryl Streep accepting her gajillionth Academy Award.

Now all she had to do was figure out who that was.

She fished her phone out of her pocket—not even sure who she would call for a referral but certain there was someone in there who could help—and noticed the voicemail notification blinking. It must have rung while they were on the bike. Elena grinned at the memory, hitting the button to play the message.

*"Elena, hi. My name is Ashley Kenner and I'm a reality television producer. I hope you don't mind me calling you out of the blue like this. I got your number from Dale Reese, who said he wasn't representing you anymore, but didn't know who your new representation was. If you or your new agent could call me back, I'd love to talk to you about working on a new project with us. It's reality television, but not the way you've done it before. No competition angle. More of a Kardashians type thing. We're thinking of calling it My So-Called Slutty Life or something like that. Just you being you. Think of it as a chance to really tell your side of the story. My number is—"*

Elena tuned the numbers out, her thoughts racing.

A chance to tell her side of the story. That was what she wanted, wasn't it? It sounded too good to be true—

but then devil's bargains always did. And she knew better than anyone that getting involved with reality TV was always a devil's bargain.

But was it one she should take? God knew she needed the money.

Yes, she wanted to be a real actress, but even before the sex tape those offers hadn't exactly been thick on the ground. Maybe this could open more doors for her.

It wasn't her dream—but she'd been fighting for her dream for three years now and she wasn't any closer to it. She'd been failing as an aspiring actress. Sure, they said the only people who failed were the ones who gave up on their dreams, but they also said insanity was doing the same thing over and over again and expecting a different result.

She couldn't live with Adam forever. Someday she would have to go back to the real world. And maybe that meant reality TV.

Her stomach turned at the thought. A few weeks ago she'd been so sure getting back on TV would be her redemption, but now everything felt different.

There was still the whore-on-the-door to consider. And the sex tape.

Maybe all she was good for was reality TV. But when she thought about giving up acting, really thought about it, it felt like something inside her screamed. A Munch painting in her soul at the idea of walking away from her dream.

She couldn't do it.

She might have to go back to reality TV. She might have to become a "personality" before anyone would look at her as an actress. But not yet. Not today.

Today she was a woman on a mission and she was going to get a new agent.

# CHAPTER TWENTY-THREE

"So 'Tank' is short for James Tancredo and he was a five time Pro-Bowl offensive lineman who left the NFL when he met his wife because she was worried about concussions, but now she has no problem with him jumping in front of bullets to protect celebrities?"

Elena sat on the kitchen counter, eating a yogurt and swinging her bare legs as she watched Adam cook dinner. Her skirt was bunched up around her thighs and by the glances he kept throwing her direction he appreciated the view.

"The odds of a bodyguard getting shot at even once in his career are far lower than the odds of a lineman taking a blow to the head at least once in every game. Shareen plays the odds. And it helps that Tank tends to refer to his job as 'overpaid bouncer' rather than 'bodyguard.'"

"You like him," she observed.

He shrugged, attention on the mushrooms he was dicing. "He's a good guy."

"And Max?"

"Also a good guy."

She rolled her eyes at his typically cryptic answer.

They'd spent at least part of each of the last three days at the Elite Protection offices, so she figured it was about time she knew a little more about it. Life had calmed down in the last few days. The worst of the paparazzi frenzy had moved on, thanks to a bigger celebrity creating an even bigger scandal. Part of her felt guilty that her reprieve was at someone else's expense, but mostly she was just relieved not to be on every broadcast of the day.

There hadn't been any more news on the whore-on-the-door front, but Adam assured her it wasn't unusual for a busy crime lab to take weeks to process DNA or run a set of fingerprints.

Whenever he worked, she would do research on agents online, occasionally calling them and pretending to be her own manager in an attempt to set up a meeting—but the agents she wanted wouldn't take her calls and the ones who would weren't the kind of representation she needed. So far her search had been an exercise in frustration.

She hadn't called the reality show people back—she still didn't know what she would say to them if she did. It felt like the only choice she had—for the money and a chance to tell her side of things—but she wasn't ready to make it. She hadn't even told anyone about the offer, not even Adam, as if talking about it made it a fait accompli.

But other than that and the twin guillotines of the sex tape and death threat hanging over her head, things were… good.

Really good.

The good was making her nervous, but she was making a concerted effort not to question it. So she was questioning him instead.

"If everyone is so great, why don't you like working there?"

His hands stilled on the cutting board. "What makes you think I don't?"

"The way you talk about it. Like it's a necessary evil. Like you're biding your time."

His brow furrowed into a frown, but his hands resumed their familiar movements, chopping and slicing.

"Why do you work there?"

"I needed something and it came around at the right moment."

"What would you rather be doing? Besides guarding the President."

He shrugged. So forthcoming, her lover.

"What about your coworkers? You like Tank and Max is 'a good guy'—"

"You know Max. You're friends with his sister."

"Sidney and I aren't really that close—or we weren't. I don't know. We might be now. But that isn't the point. I want to know what *you* think of him."

Adam shrugged again—and she thought that might be all the answer she was going to get out of him but then he added, "He's a Dewitt—which means he was born with a silver spoon and everything he touches turns to gold—but in spite of that he's actually, I don't know. Real. Down to earth. Treats you like an equal. Has your back."

"So he's a badass bodyguard in addition to owning the business?"

"He doesn't do a lot of field work. He takes care of the business side. And the networking and marketing crap. But I've seen him train. He's not someone I would fuck with."

"Good to know." She tossed her empty yogurt container in the trash for a three-pointer and snagged an olive off the cutting board. "And the others?"

"Cross was in the NFL too. Defensive back. He and

195

Tank have been friends since they played together in college. When he blew out his knee, he was looking for something else to do and Tank vouched for him so Max brought him in even though he's still training on the security side."

"Helps that he's pretty."

Adam scowled. "He is not pretty."

Elena snorted. "Trust me, Stud Muffin. Every man in that building is a certifiable hunk because Max knows image matters in Hollywood and he can charge more for you if you're gorgeous. Take it as a compliment. Whose bike did we borrow?"

He hesitated before finally admitting, "Pretty Boy's."

She laughed, almost slipping off the counter before she caught herself. "I rest my case. What's his real name?"

"I have no idea. I've never heard anyone call him anything else."

"Is he the one who looks mixed race—dark hair, insanely gorgeous eyes?"

"That's him."

"I swear I've seen him in a magazine somewhere."

"He models on the side. As a hobby."

"And the female magazine-readers of America thank him."

He scowled again. "He's not that attractive."

"Honey. You don't know his name because everyone calls him Pretty Boy. He is that attractive."

"Candy doesn't seem to think so."

It was her turn to frown, jealousy spiking. "Who's Candy?"

"Our tech wizard. She doesn't do any field work that I know of, but she designs security systems, that sort of thing, and I've seen her take a man twice her size to the cleaners on the training mat."

"I didn't realize you worked with any women."

Adam shrugged. "I don't work with her much."

"Anyone else I should know about?"

"Nope. That's it. It's a small crew. Max has this whole philosophy about exclusivity and selectivity. Only invites people with very specific credentials to join."

"There goes my dream of being Elite Protection's next hot shot bodyguard."

"I don't know." Adam grinned at her. "You're a pretty good shot. And god knows you're hot enough. He might consider you."

She smiled, ridiculously pleased—more by the good shot comment than the nod to her hotness.

He'd taken her to the EP range and taught her how to fire a gun today. It was satisfying to know how to use a weapon, but she hadn't gotten anywhere near the rush she got from the motorcycle—mostly it was just loud. She had no idea why so many people found it empowering to fire projectiles at paper targets.

Now if they'd been firing at bottles and could watch them explode that might have been different. Sadly, this wasn't the Wild West. Though if it had been, Adam would undoubtedly have been the sheriff in the white hat. And she probably would have been the saloon girl with a sordid secret who turned out to be his downfall.

He knew she was trouble.

She just couldn't figure out why he was still with her.

The sex was good—okay, better than good—but he seemed to really like *her* not just what he could do to her body when they got naked.

She was used to guys liking her body and liking the adventure of being with her as long as it meant they were getting laid, but the rest of it confused her.

"Why do you like me?"

The question popped out without her permission. She felt her face heating and tried to think of a smooth way to backpedal, but Adam was already answering— utterly unflustered, as if it were the sort of question that always came up in pre-dinner conversation.

"You're free. And fierce. And strong. Like a lioness." He looked up from the cutting board then and the look in his eyes was enough to melt her panties.

Her breath went out in a whoosh and didn't come back in again.

"And I never know what you're going to do, but I have never felt as alive as I do when I'm with you."

And just when she started to think he had nothing to say...

Elena reached out and hooked a finger in the waistband of his pants. "Come here."

He set down the knife, sliding over to notch his hips between her knees, his palms braced flat on the counter on either side of her. "If you distract me, you won't get dinner," he warned, bending to take her mouth in a quick kiss—or a kiss he doubtless intended to be quick.

"Dinner can wait," she murmured when they came up for air. Hooking her ankles behind his back, she wound her arms around his neck. "Ever had sex on a kitchen counter?"

"I'm all for new experiences." He smiled against her mouth, his clever hands already sneaking beneath her skirt to hook onto her panties and drag them down. She lifted her hips to help him, forced to unlock her legs from behind his back to kick them off. When he swooped to kiss her again, her hands fell to the fastening of his trousers, impatient to feel him.

She wasn't used to this—it wasn't just lust. There was

something else driving her need to drag him inside her and never let go.

*Connection.*

It was another of those idiotic *Marrying Mister Perfect* catch-phrases that got thrown around every season. Everyone competing to see who had the best connection with Mister Perfect. But that was what this was.

Adam knew her. He understood her. He *saw* her. And he liked her anyway. When she was with him, she never felt that alone-in-a-crowded-room feeling that had defined her life for years. Whatever came at them, they were in it together. Connected.

She could barely breathe for wanting him so badly in this moment. "Hurry," she whispered against his lips.

He sank his fingers into the flesh of her hips and yanked her forward on the counter until she would've fallen off the edge without him there to stop her. He shoved her skirt out of the way, fumbling with the condom as she thanked the gods of spontaneous sex that he'd started carrying them in his pockets—

"Adam?" A light voice called from the front hall.

"*Shit.*" Adam leapt away and Elena slipped from the edge of counter, catching herself with one hand when her knees threatened to buckle.

"Who—?"

He shook his head, frantically fastening his pants, shoving the unused condom into his pocket as the answer to her question came around the corner to the kitchen. A young girl with long, ironing-board-straight sandy brown hair and unusual bone-structure— distinctive, but just a shade less attractive than her famous mother's. Layers of make-up accented her giant doe eyes and made her broad mouth glisten with shiny peach gloss. She looked dressed for a date—everything about her shiny and glowing with youth—but the light in her eyes dimmed as she looked between Adam and Elena.

"Cassie, what are you doing here?"

Thanks to Adam's leap they were several feet apart and Elena's skirt had fallen back down around her thighs when she fell off the counter—thank God—but they both looked disheveled and guilty. The truth of what Cassie had interrupted was obvious.

She might be seventeen, but she wasn't naïve. She looked back and forth between them, and Elena could see the effort in her face as she fought not to show her hurt.

*Shit. She really is in love with him.* Elena had teased him about it, had seen the hero worship on the girl's face when he saved her, but she hadn't realized how true the words were until this moment.

Cassie's gaze fell to the floor and she went white, looking queasy. Elena followed her gaze—and flushed guiltily. *If it hadn't been obvious before...*

On the floor several feet away, half-hidden beneath the edge of the cabinet, lay Elena's blue lace panties.

# CHAPTER TWENTY-FOUR

"Cassie?" Adam tried to sound authoritative and firm—not like a teenage boy caught necking with his girlfriend by his parents. He was a grown man. Elena was a consenting adult. They were allowed to have sex in his kitchen, damn it.

Except it had never felt like his kitchen. It felt like Sandy's. And Sandy's daughter had just walked in on them and was now staring at Elena like she was the Antichrist.

"Adam," Elena said with a forced smile. "Aren't you going to introduce me to your friend?"

"I know who you are."

The words were coated in acid and Adam felt his hackles rise. "Elena is my guest."

Cassie finally looked at him then, something unreadable in her huge brown eyes. "I needed to talk to you."

"I'll just get some fresh air. Let you two—"

Elena made to move past Cassie out of the kitchen, but Adam caught her elbow. "No. You're fine."

Cassie shot him a look redolent with betrayal, but something about Cassie's appearance was unsettling him. He hadn't been trained to notice details for nothing. The clothes. The heels. The make-up. She was trying to look older. And succeeding. He didn't know what she was up to, but he had a feeling being alone with her was a very bad idea.

But since he evidently wasn't going to get her out of here until she'd had a private word with him...

"Why don't we talk in the living room?"

It was open to the kitchen, private without being private. Elena wouldn't be able to hear every word—but she would be close enough to be a viable chaperone.

Cassie sulked, but descended into the living room without a verbal protest. Elena arched her brows at him—trying to convey some message he couldn't read. He shrugged and followed the teenager. When he got to the base of the steps, she was facing him, not sitting, her back to the windows with her arms wrapped around herself as she glared toward the kitchen.

"Cassie?"

Her gaze swiveled to lock on him. "My mother told me you won't be doing any more security for us."

"That's right."

"She said you care too much about me to be impartial."

The way she said it. The way she looked at him, steady and hopeful.

*Fuck.* She thought he was refusing to work for her because he was fighting an attraction. She'd gotten all dressed up and come over here—

He stopped that thought right there. He did *not* want to consider what she had hoped would happen.

"Cassie..." he said, low and careful, and just the tone of his voice made her expression tighten. "You're very special—"

"Are you fucking her?" She flung the sentence like a projectile.

He froze. "Excuse me?"

"I'm not an idiot. You were fucking her when I walked in, weren't you?"

He fought to keep hold of his temper. She was a kid. She was hurting. "That's none of your business."

"That's what you like? You'd rather be with some trashy slut from a reality TV show—"

"*Cassie*. You can't come here and insult my guest."

Her eyes were bright, glistening with anger. "Everyone has had her. You have to know that. *Everyone* knows that."

"Cassandra, stop."

"Why? Because she can hear me? Let her. She's just some skank—"

"*Cassandra!*"

Her mouth snapped shut with a click at his roar.

He swallowed, forcibly reining in his temper. "Get out."

Betrayal flashed in her eyes. Then her chin quivered and she hissed in a rush, "She's dirty and everyone will think you're dirty because you're with her. I hope that makes you happy."

She ran out of the room toward the front door, one hand raised to cover her face. He didn't try to stop her. Her heels thwacked loudly down the hall and then he heard the door open and slam.

He scrubbed both hands down his face. "Shit."

"That seemed to go well."

He looked up, remembering Elena's presence, and saw her watching him from the top step leading to the kitchen. "Sorry about that."

She shook her head, coming down into the living room. "You don't have to apologize to me. She was upset. You realize she's completely in love with you."

He cringed. "It's a crush. I was hoping it would fade

on its own."

"I think you're underestimating the teenage capacity for obsessive adoration. Look at One Direction. Hell, look at the Beatles. This isn't new."

"At least I'm not special."

She didn't try to touch him. "You okay?"

"This was probably for the best. She was going to have to figure out that there was nothing between us at some point." Though he might have preferred she not walk in on him when he had Elena pinned against a counter.

*Shit*. If she told Sandy...

Not that it mattered, he tried to convince himself. This was his house—even if it didn't always feel like it. He had a right to have sex on the kitchen counters if he wanted to.

"She has a key?" Elena perched on the arm of the sofa.

"Keypad lock."

"Ah. Right." She smoothed down her skirt, drawing his eyes to her legs. "And you never changed it?"

He shrugged. "They gave me the house. I didn't want them to think they weren't welcome here."

"And little Cassie is in the habit of just dropping by unannounced?"

"Now and then," he admitted.

"I see. And you haven't said anything."

"It's her house."

"No. It isn't. And I somehow doubt this is what her mother had in mind when she gave you the place."

Irritation flashed. "Just leave it alone."

He turned away from her, climbing the steps to the kitchen to resume their interrupted dinner preparations, no longer in the mood to dwell on what had initially interrupted them.

He heard her follow him but didn't turn, adjusting the burners and taking stock of which part of the meal would have to be tossed. The sauce had burned onto the skillet—lost cause—but he hadn't put in the chicken or vegetables yet, so he could modify his plans and whip up a quick stir fry without having to redo much work.

"Adam."

"I should call her mother," he commented as he got out the wok. "Make sure she got home okay. She was upset when she left here and you know teenage drivers."

"It's not your fault—"

He cut her off. "How do you feel about peppers in your stir fry?"

"Fine."

She didn't try to bring it up again as he cooked. She set the breakfast bar and poured the wine without comment. He was silent as he made inroads through his food, which wasn't unusual, but Elena was as well. Which was a relief. It gave him time to think.

Not that it helped. He still felt like an ass.

He'd been careful never to lead Cassie on—she was like a little sister to him—but even if she hadn't needed much encouragement, he couldn't help feeling that he could have done something to prevent tonight's mess. He should have talked to her sooner, but he hadn't wanted to embarrass her by confronting the crush.

He excused himself as soon as they were done eating, slipping away to call Sandy. He got her assistant instead and left a message letting her know Cassie had seemed upset and he'd just wanted to make sure she was all right. Leaving comforting Cassie to her mother, he returned to the kitchen to find Elena rinsing the dishes.

"I can get those."

A glance over her shoulder before she dismissed his help. "They're almost done."

She was gorgeous. Standing there in his kitchen. A thousand types of fantasy in a flimsy pink skirt.

And he felt guilty just looking at her.

When she set the last dish in the drying rack and turned to face him, he averted his eyes.

And Elena went off like a bottle rocket.

\* \* \* \* \*

"All right. *What*? Which one of us are you pissed at? Her for walking in or me for seducing you in your kitchen?"

"Neither."

"Do you want me to go?"

"No. It isn't you."

"Then what is it? What's wrong?"

His face closed down and he seemed fixated on the floor to her left. She'd already collected her panties so she knew that wasn't his fixation. Elena wanted to shake him until answers came out.

"Nothing."

He was shutting her out. Maybe it wouldn't have bothered her so much if she hadn't believed, not two hours earlier, that they were really connected. It was like he'd dangled everything she wanted in front of her only to yank it away and Elena was not the kind of woman who passively accepted that sort of bait and switch.

She planted her hands on her hips, squaring off against him. "I tell you everything."

"We're different like that."

"I'm getting that," she snarled.

He held out his hands like a lion tamer. "Look, let's just table this for the night—"

"What exactly are we tabling? Because I'm having a hard time figuring out why one minute you want me naked on the counter and the next you won't even look at me. Are you ashamed to be with me? Ashamed that someone knows?"

That brought his eyes up, flashing with anger. "Don't be ridiculous. Lots of people know. All of my coworkers—"

"Know that I've been staying in your guest room. Know that you're being a really great guy and looking after me while there's some psycho asshole leaving notes on my door. They don't know that you're lowering yourself to fuck me—"

"Goddamn it, Elena." He prowled toward her and she stopped him with a hand on his chest, straight-arming him.

"What else am I supposed to think? Cassie caught us and you just shut down. If it's not me, what is it? Are you worried about her?"

"Of course I am."

"But that's not it. Something else is making you crazy—"

"I can't fucking *win*."

The words burst out of him and Elena froze. "Okay…"

"I tried to do the right thing and I lost my job, but it wasn't just my job it was my fucking *identity*. It was everything I wanted to be and everything I knew about myself. I was the Secret Service golden boy. I did everything right until I had to choose between doing my job and doing what was right and then poof. It was all gone. And I can't complain because look at my consolation prize." He waved a hand at the house. "But this life doesn't feel like mine. Sandy's house. Max's job. My life is being handed to me and I can't complain because it's more than I've earned, but I feel like I'm not choosing anything anymore, it's all just happening to me and I'm a passenger in my own life."

"And I just happened to you too. You didn't choose to get stuck with—"

"Elena." He cupped the nape of her neck, his longer reach letting him hold her even with her arm still extended between them. He lowered his head, as if he would have touched his forehead to hers if not for the distance. "You are the one thing I've chosen in the last six months. The one thing that I want for myself. You make me feel like me again."

She fisted her hand in his shirt and bent her elbow, dragging him in for a kiss. "Me too."

But it wasn't just that. She'd never been afraid to be herself, but he made her feel like it was okay. Or better than okay. Amazing. She wasn't just her, she was the best, purest, most undiluted version of her because he could take it. He *liked* it. And she wanted to be that for him too.

She pulled away enough to meet his eyes. "You can still be you with that job. In this house."

"It doesn't matter anymore. When I found out about your legal bills, I called a realtor about putting the house on the market."

"You *what*?"

## CHAPTER TWENTY-FIVE

"You're selling your house to pay my legal fees and it didn't occur to you to tell me?" Irritation surged— counterbalanced by a matched set of awe and terror that he would consider doing that for her.

"I'm telling you now."

She pushed away from him, resisting the urge to slug him—and not even one hundred percent sure *why* she wanted to slug him, but certain it was a good idea. What had he been thinking? But then she knew.

He was trying to save her. Just like he tried to save everyone. Another rung on the ladder to sainthood. Always so damn *selfless*.

"I didn't ask you to do that. I don't want you to sell this house."

"You didn't have to ask."

"Because you're the hero and no one ever has to ask the hero to swoop in and save them?"

"Why are you pissed at me?"

"Because you can't just fix my life without my permission!"

And she was scared. Scared she was just another project for him. Another damsel in distress.

If that was all this was—another chance for Adam to play the hero—what would happen when he succeeded? When he'd found her stalker and paid the legal bills to keep her sex tape out of the public eye, when he'd saved the day, what then? Did he just walk away? The thought of him leaving shuddered through her like a cold wind.

"I don't want to be another Cassie to you, Adam. Just another girl you need to save."

"You aren't."

"Are you sure? I don't want you to be with me because it satisfies your hero complex."

"I'm not. I don't want that either."

"Then what do you want?" She needed him to say her. She needed him to say forever. Even as the thought of it terrified her. But he was so distant, so uncharacteristically closed off.

He shook his head, running a hand through his hair as he turned, walking out of the kitchen.

"Adam?"

"It just seemed like selling the house would be the solution to a lot of problems," he said over his shoulder as he descended to the living room. He threw himself onto one of the couches and she moved to join him, but kept her distance, curling up on the opposite end with her back braced against the arm.

"I thought it would give me distance from Sandy and Cassie. Like if I didn't have the house anymore, I would regain the ability to say no to them. I wouldn't have to worry about paying property taxes and utility bills, so I wouldn't have to work for Max anymore if I didn't want to. I could decide for myself what kind of job I wanted to do without the desperate need to pay my bills any way I can. And I could have helped you. But it wasn't about saving you, Elena. It was about the fact that I *hate* that I can't do anything for you. Like you said, I can't fight your battles without being drawn up on assault charges. I just wanted to be able to do something and this was something."

He grimaced. "I probably couldn't have done it anyway. How would I have faced Sandy after selling her gift? Would've been a cop out. Just a way to get away from everything that's happened in the last six months rather than owning it."

"And now?" She hated the softness in her voice. The vulnerability. But for once he didn't seem to hear it. His gaze didn't pierce right through all her defenses.

He rubbed a hand across his face. "I don't know." Weariness made his voice hoarse. "Can we think about it later? Right now can you just kiss me?"

Relief she couldn't explain rushed through her. One more night in his arms. It would be okay. She was already crawling along the couch toward him before he finished speaking. "That I can do."

\* \* \* \* \*

Elena woke up alone the next morning, certain Adam wasn't in the room even before she rolled over or opened her eyes. The entire house felt different without him in it. It was still Fort Knox, but the bright, airy rooms were cool when he was gone, lacking the warmth of his presence.

Crap. She had it bad.

She needed to lock down this infatuation fast before it got out of control.

She heard the front door open and shut downstairs and suddenly the house felt warmer. Alive.

*Crap.*

Elena rolled out of bed, showered quickly and dressed with less care than she usually took with her appearance, oddly impatient to get downstairs. It wasn't as if he was going to evaporate if she didn't rush right down there, but she hurried nonetheless.

Last night seemed to linger in the air as she padded rapidly down the stairs, back to the scene of the crimes. The kitchen where Cassie had nearly walked in on them. The living room where Adam had broken her seventeen-year-old heart. The same kitchen and living room where she and Adam had had their first fight.

At least it felt like a fight. Him boxing her out until she wanted to throw things. And then the make-up sex. Though it hadn't really been make-up sex so much as distraction sex. But that was what they were good at, right? Avoidance sex.

Another excellent reason why she shouldn't get too carried away with him. They weren't a couple. They were a coping mechanism. If he wanted to sell his house, it was none of her damn business.

She found him in the kitchen, his back to her, an unopened bag with the logo of a local bakery bulging on the counter beside him.

"Hey," she began, preparing to launch into her it's-none-of-my-damn-business apology, but Adam held up a finger, turning toward her, and she realized he was on his phone.

"No, I appreciate the call. Thanks, Murkowski. We'll be in touch."

The name rang a distant bell, but she didn't place it until Adam disconnected the call and tucked his cell back into his pocket. "There's movement on your stalker case."

Murkowski. The detective. "They called you?"

"I've been nagging him," he admitted, sheepish. "Apparently he called you first, but when he got your voicemail he tried me."

"I almost forgot about that part of the shit storm," she muttered, more to herself than to him. "So what is it? What's the big news?"

"The fingerprints had a match in the system and when they confronted the suspect, they got a confession within five minutes."

Elena blinked. "You're kidding." It couldn't be that easy, could it? "Who was it?"

"Do you know a woman named Mary-Kate Kenton?"

She started to shake her head, but a memory swam up from the back of her mind. The mailboxes in the lobby of her building where all the tenants picked up their mail. The one next to hers reading Kenton/Bryce. The little red-haired girl with paint under her fingernails who would smile at Elena when they bumped into one another in the hall. "My neighbor?"

She tried to reconcile the girl with the earnest blue eyes with the death threat and her brain refused to process it. "You can't be serious. I *know* her. We're not friends or anything. It's not like we go out for coffee, but she borrowed a roll of tape last Christmas when she ran out." Why would you borrow tape from someone you wanted to kill?

"Murkowski assures me that the police psychologists don't believe her to be a danger to you or to herself. Apparently it took her weeks to work up the gumption to leave the threatening note and she never had any intention of escalating beyond that. That was her coup de gras."

"Was it some kind of prank?"

Adam hesitated—as if he was considering lying to her, but he was too much of a Boy Scout for the thought to take hold. "No. She admitted she was trying to scare you into moving out."

"Don't tell me this is all about that apartment. It's not even that nice!"

"She felt threatened by you."

"She threatened me because she felt threatened by me? That's her defense?"

"She doesn't seem to care about her defense. Murkowski said she had about as much fortitude as a wet tissue when they brought her in for interrogation."

"But she's saying I threatened her? That is such bullshit—"

"She's not saying you threatened her. She's saying she felt threatened by you. Apparently she lived with someone—" *Bryce.* The other name on the mailbox. "And he was pretty open about talking about how hot you are in front of her. She became convinced that if she could just get you to leave, her relationship would be perfect."

"Hence the whore-on-the-door. Awesome."

She'd been scared shitless, run out of her home, all because some insecure bitch was afraid of losing some asshole Elena couldn't even remember meeting. It made her feel like a fool. Like the girl who cried stalker. But how was she to know it was just garden variety crazy-ass jealousy? She felt weak that she'd been scared by something so inconsequential.

"Murkowski wanted to make sure, since you know one another, that you still want to press charges. We'll need to go in and sign some papers. Do you want to—"

"*Yes.*" Maybe it was feeling like an idiot. Maybe it was the fact that this was one thing she could do to get justice for a change, but… "I absolutely want to press charges."

A new idea sang a siren song in her brain, unspeakably tempting.

"And I want to talk to her."

"I'm not sure that's a good idea."

"Fuck good ideas. Let's go."

# CHAPTER TWENTY-SIX

Her scary nightmare stalker was Bambi.

Elena had remembered the red curls frizzing in every direction and the paint-chipped fingernails, but she had forgotten the big brown doe eyes and the delicate bird-like bone structure. Mary-Kate's features were a little too sharp to actually be beautiful, the angles turning them from pixie-ish to severe, but her eyes were freaking *enormous*, made even more so by the shadows under them from hours of tears.

She didn't look like a villain. She looked like a victim. Which must be why all the detectives seemed so uncomfortable with the idea of actually arresting her precious little self—even though she'd confessed to the death threat.

They'd arrived at the precinct and Elena had insisted on speaking to Mary-Kate. She'd expected resistance, and Adam obviously had as well, but Murkowski almost looked relieved. He thought it was a *great idea* for them to talk, and so did Mary-Kate's lawyer, who kept vehemently protesting how *understandable* everything was.

As the pair of them led Elena to the little office where Mary-Kate was being detained—God forbid her precious self should go in a dirty jail cell—she began to realize Murkowski wanted Elena to let bygones be bygones almost as much as the lawyer did. He felt *bad* for the precious princess. And this from a hardened cop. She'd expected more from him.

"What happens to her when I press charges?" Elena asked, frowning through the frosted glass of the office door at the girl sniffling into a Kleenex.

"She'll be charged. Most likely released on bail. I expect she'll plead guilty. First time offender. No record. Good character references. She'll probably get probation," Murkowski answered.

"But she'll lose her job," the lawyer interjected.

"You can't know—"

"It's inevitable," Murkowski interrupted. "She's a teacher. That's why her prints were in the system."

Ah. That was right. Art teacher. All that paint on her hands.

And a teacher with a stalking record wouldn't go over well with the parents.

"Just give her a chance to tell you her side of it," the lawyer urged.

*She left a note saying DIE WHORE on my door. There's only one side to that*, Elena wanted to argue, but she nodded instead and Murkowski opened the door to the office.

Bambi looked up, blinking tearfully. "*Elena.*" She scrambled to her feet and Elena was instantly snared by irritation that there were no cuffs linking her wrists. This girl had completely snowed the cops.

"Mary-Kate, right?" she said dryly. "I think I lent you some tape once. Though if I'd known at the time you were going to use it to tape death threats to my door, I might have reconsidered."

Mary-Kate sank back into her chair, flushing and tearing and gasping and sniffling all at once in a medley of messy feminine distress. Elena found herself remarkably unmoved by the entire thing, one detached part of her brain analyzing Mary-Kate's performance and wondering if it was genuine or if MK was just acting. She might be an art teacher, but that didn't mean she hadn't come to LA to try to act. Hell, this might be her idea of a fast-pass to celebrity.

Mary-Kate sniffled wetly. "You have to understand."

*No, I don't.*

"After Aidan walked out on me again I heard him in your apartment, heard the two of you through the wall—"

"No, you didn't. He was never in my apartment."

"*I know you slept with him.*"

Elena arched a brow at the intense snarl, keep her expression bland as Bambi's victim act cracked, her crazy showing through.

Mary-Kate flushed, pulling herself back under control and getting back to her script. "I swear I thought I heard him. But I'd been drinking and I was on these really strong allergy meds. I wasn't myself."

"Uh-huh."

"I knew he wanted you. He'd taunt me with you. *Fuckable Elena, right next door.* It just made me so crazy and I knew if you would just leave, everything would be good between us again. So I wrote a note. It was just a note. And I really am sorry. I never meant to hurt anyone. I would never hurt anyone. That isn't me. *This isn't me.*" She dissolved into ugly sobs—either really committing to the role or completely overcome. The detached jury in the back of Elena's mind was still out.

Elena waited for the volume to die down enough for her question to be heard. "If it's not you, why did you do it?"

Bambi's sobs quieted and she looked baffled by the question. "I just explained. It was a mistake. Aidan—"

"Yeah, I get that you were dating an asshole. But what I don't understand is how that was an excuse for making my life hell? Where's the fucking sisterhood? Because nothing you've said has anything to do with me."

"But you were the one he wanted." She waved a hand at Elena, as if that said it all. And maybe it did. "You were like... like candy being waved in front of a dieter."

"Lovely analogy. But unless I'm also the one tackling the dieter, sitting on his chest and forcing candy down his throat, it *isn't my fucking fault he cheats*. I am not responsible for your relationship sucking. I don't even remember what your loser boyfriend looks like."

"He isn't a loser—"

"Yes, he is! Any dipshit who tells his girlfriend that he'd rather be fucking the girl next door is a loser. And that isn't the fault of the girl next door. He isn't the victim of my hotness. And neither are you. *I'm* the victim here, you spineless psycho. And *you're* the bad guy. Take some fucking *ownership*."

Bambi's jaw dropped with shock and before she could gather a response Elena slammed out of the office, feeling winded—and a little guilty about the spineless psycho crack. She really shouldn't have resorted to name calling. But it had felt good to yell.

She didn't delude herself that it would do any good. But maybe community service and a change in career would be a good life lesson for Bambi.

She turned to Murkowski. "Book her, Dan-O."

"You sure?"

"Absolutely."

219

\* \* \* \* \*

"Do you think I'd drop the charges if I were a nicer person?"

They were in Adam's Jeep on the PCH, halfway back to his house when Elena asked the question philosophically from the passenger seat, her bare feet propped up on the dash in what had become her standard pose. Her initial take-no-prisoners mode at the precinct had faded into contemplation as they drove.

"You are a nice person."

"Not really," she said, though she didn't seem bothered by it. "If this goes on her record, it pretty much ruins her life."

"She's being held accountable for threatening your life."

"Yeah, I know. I'm still pressing charges. I feel bad for what's going to happen to her, but not that bad. I just... I don't know. I wonder if I overreacted because I was pissed that the cops seemed to be on her side."

He frowned. "What made you think they were on her side?"

She waved a hand. "You know, the whole thing about hearing her out. How she was a sweet girl with a bright future who was led astray and I should forgive her because she cried and insisted she was sorry." Her brows pulled together. "Maybe that's my problem. I've never been good at feigning contrition. Even when I bitch and whine about the consequences, I own my actions—and people hate that. They would rather I cry and beg forgiveness because if I own my actions then they have to also. Everyone wants a free pass and if you don't ask for one, they don't know what to do with you." She turned to face the passenger window. "But it does suck that Mary-Kate's wrecked her whole life because she freaked out about some guy. I know what that's like. I did it with Daniel."

"You never threatened the other Suitorettes."

"I never saw them as a threat."

"You were gracious in defeat." He hadn't actually seen the episode, but he'd heard from Max—who claimed he had only watched the show for his sister's sake—that Elena had wished Daniel the best as she was led to the Rejection-Mobile.

Elena snorted. "I'm never gracious in defeat. I'm just not going to give them the satisfaction of seeing me cry."

*I thought you didn't cry.* "Did you cry over Daniel?"

"Fuck yes. I believed every word he said. I was *convinced* he was in love with me. Then he yanked that certainty out from under me. That kind of betrayal—I would have cried just from the injustice of it."

"Did you love him?"

"It didn't matter. I never even thought about whether I loved him. I—" She broke off, her feet hitting the floor as she leaned forward and frowned at the congestion ahead. The congestion that seemed to be centered around his house. "What the fuck is that?"

But the question was rhetorical.

The paparazzi had found her.

\* \* \* \* \*

Elena ducked down, shielding her face with both hands, but it wasn't just her name the photographers were shouting as flashes erupted against the glass, trying to penetrate the slight tint of the windows.

"Pull in," she instructed when Adam hesitated at the

edge of his driveway. "They'll just chase us if we drive somewhere else and at least this way we can lock them outside the gate. Private property."

"Right," he grunted, his face severe.

The shouting only got worse as the gate opened, the more daring throwing themselves in front of the vehicle in an attempt to get the best shot. Adam kept the Jeep moving, slowly but steadily into the driveway—slow enough not to run anyone over, but eventually nudging the bodies out of the way. They fell back, even the most eager able to recognize the clearly posted No Trespassing signs.

Adam hit the button to close the gate behind them. "If someone sues me because they are too stupid to get out of the way of the gate, I will not be held responsible for my actions."

At the last minute Elena deemed it safe to look, raising her head and checking the rearview where she could clearly see photographers leaping on top of one another like the world's most feral cheerleading pyramid in an attempt to get the best shot.

"This isn't just the sex tape."

There were too many of them. And they were far too rabid. The sex tape was over a week old and busy being slowly buried under a pile of legalese. This was something else.

"Shit," she whispered, yanking out her phone and Googling her name. The usual hits. She typed in Adam's.

The rescue video was no longer the hottest link.

"Oh God."

"What is it?"

*Hell hath no fury...* "Cassie."

# CHAPTER TWENTY-SEVEN

The article was thick with innuendo. What Cassie hadn't outright implied the tabloid had gleefully speculated. Elena sat on the counter, reading every word, as Adam prowled around the kitchen. It seemed like they always ended up in here. Sad that they now had a routine when it came to dealing with a media crisis.

"I should call Max."

"Good idea. Private property will keep out the smart ones, but I think we're going to want some of your security buddies down here. The ambitious stupid ones won't care about trespassing charges."

Adam swore and pulled out his phone, every movement tight. Restrained. Pretty controlled for a guy who'd just been implicitly accused of statutory rape. Good in a crisis, her Adam.

Not that he was hers.

Though by now half of America thought he was.

She'd given Cassie too much credit. She'd thought the girl was too smart to run her mouth to the tabloids. She should have remembered that Cassie was a seventeen-year-old in love and seventeen-year-olds in love were notoriously idiotic.

The little brat had called it a love triangle. Claimed Adam was her soul mate. Accused Elena of seducing him away from her. The details were vague, but she'd very explicitly recounted walking in on them having sex—embellishing quite a bit and playing the role of the cheated-on lover to the hilt.

Any sympathy Elena might have felt for her last night turned to smoke. Her empathy was broken this morning. She was too busy being pissed on Adam's behalf. The little brat could drag her name through the mud all she wanted, but she'd implied—repeatedly—that she'd had a sexual relationship with Adam, never seeming to realize that it might complicate the problem a bit that she was *seventeen*.

A year shy of California's age of consent.

The fall of a hero—of course the press was rabid. Tie Sandy Newton's name to it and it became national news.

No surprise they were surrounded.

In the house her mother had given him, no less. The press jackals were eating it up.

Adam ended his call and leaned back against the counter opposite her, gripping it with both hands. "Max is going to make some calls. He might know someone who can help with damage control. He called her the Olivia Pope of Hollywood. Whatever that means."

"It means she's a fixer." And right now they needed one. She grabbed her own phone. "I'll call Miranda. She's bound to know someone."

"Elena."

She looked up from dialing Miranda, taking in the stark lines of his face.

"I never touched her."

"I know."

He nodded, some of the tension leaving his face, and Elena turned back to her phone.

Miranda answered on the second ring, forgoing a standard greeting. "You know that old Chinese curse

'May you live in interesting times'? Your life is very interesting, Elena."

"I've noticed. I don't suppose you have any suggestions as to how I can make it less interesting?"

"What's your PR team saying?"

"I don't have one anymore, since I fired my agent last week and he took care of all that."

Miranda cursed. "I was wondering why your team had been so quiet. Okay," she said, regrouping, "You need Kathleen Tao."

"Is she an agent?"

"No. She's sort of a PR consultant slash miracle worker."

Which meant she probably wouldn't be willing to take fifteen percent as payment. "Can I afford her? I'm already wondering how I'm going to pay for the lawyers."

"I thought I told you I was taking care of that. I talked them into taking you on pro-bono. One of the partners is considering a run for political office and needs more cases that make him look sympathetic to women's issues. But you're right. Kathleen Tao doesn't do charity and she doesn't come cheap. And you don't have enough influence for her to trade her services for a favor. Though she may have some ideas about how you can come up with the money—exclusive interview rights can be worth a small fortune. Or you could write a tell-all book." Elena heard the clacking of Miranda's rapid-fire typing. "I would've tried to put you in touch with her last week, but I thought your agent had you covered so I wasn't thinking beyond the direct threat of the tape's release to managing the media." More clacking. "I don't have her number, but Bennett may know how to reach her. Let me see if I can get you a meeting. Hold tight."

Elena hung up and met Adam's eyes.

"What's the verdict?" he asked.

"We're supposed to hold tight. Is Max's fixer Kathleen Tao?"

"He didn't say."

"Miranda seemed to think she was the only name on the list. Hopefully she's as good as they say and she agrees to help us. And then I can sell a kidney to pay for it."

"I was going to sell the house anyway." He cringed. "Fuck. How long before the press finds out I was talking to real estate agents and jumps to some conclusion about it?" He laughed without humor. "And to think just last night I was bitching about my house and my job."

"Max isn't throwing you to the wolves yet and Sandy gave you this house legally, didn't she? She can't just take it back."

"Max didn't hesitate to take my side, but he's selling an image. If people believe I touched Cassie Edwards…"

She suddenly understood how helpless he'd felt for the last week. Wanting so badly to help and knowing it was out of her control. Or maybe…

"What if I issue a statement?" She brightened, warming to the idea. "I can tell them I hired you as a body guard and there's nothing else between us. If I discredit Cassie about that, they may start to question the rest of what she's saying."

"You want to lie to the press. And what happens when someone gets a picture of us together?"

"Well, obviously we'd have to stop this." She waved a hand between them. Whatever *this* was. "With the whore-on-the-door thing resolved I don't really have any reason to stay anyway. I'm not in danger anymore."

Though she'd stopped thinking of his place as a just safe house on day two. She wanted to be here not just because it was safe, but because she wanted to be with him. For the past week she'd been playing house—and falling for him. Which was practically inevitable under the circumstances. It was just like the show. Isolated from reality in a high stress situation with a man you've been conditioned to think is perfect. No wonder she thought she was falling in love with him.

But it was time to get back to reality. Best for both of them. "I really don't have an excuse to be here anymore."

"So we just stop seeing one another?" Anger thrummed in his voice. "I never pegged you for a quitter. Bailing as soon as things get bad."

"I'm not. This is a solution. America *hates* me. The longer I stay, the more I'll drag you down. It will be easier for you without me here."

"No. It won't." He didn't move toward her, didn't reach for her, just met her eyes across the expanse of the kitchen. "Stay."

She ignored the thrill that worked through her at the intensity in that single word. "You could try calling Sandy."

He flinched. "What if she believes Cassie? She could hate me right now. They could be getting ready to have me arrested."

"Cassie didn't actually say you'd slept together. You don't know what she's told her mother—"

His phone rang, cutting her off. He checked the caller-ID and swore. "It's her."

"Cassie?"

"Sandy."

He looked at his phone like it might bite him. "Isn't it

better to know what we're dealing with, one way or the other?"

"You're not the one who has to talk to her."

"Would you like me to?"

He shook his head, tapping to accept the call. "Hello?"

\* \* \* \* \*

Adam felt sick to his stomach as he got off the call with Sandy's people. She hadn't called directly. But at least she wasn't swearing out a warrant for his arrest. Cassie had come clean to her mother, admitting she exaggerated for the press—and then they exaggerated some more for her.

He'd been assured Sandy didn't blame him. He'd been assured her people were on it. He'd been assured they would make it right.

He still felt sick.

He'd wanted to throw up ever since Elena had told him what the tabloids were saying.

"Well?" Elena asked from her perch on the opposite counter.

"They said to sit tight and wait for them to clean up Cassie's mess."

"Do we listen to them?"

He didn't hesitate. "No. They're looking out for Sandy and Cassie. I don't want to be anyone's third or fourth priority right now."

Elena nodded as his phone's text alert went off. He glanced at the screen, frowning at the message.

"Who is it?" Elena asked.

"Candy. She's offering to hack Cassie Newton's phone to get me proof that we were never a couple."

"Aw, that's sweet."

"And illegal," he muttered as his phone rang again, her own buzzing with a text.

This time it was Max.

His boss skipped the preliminaries. "I have someone working the problem. She says not to go anywhere or say anything to anyone. Just hunker down while she defuses the bomb. She'll be in touch in a couple of hours with an update."

Elena frowned when Adam related the instructions to her after getting off the phone with Max. "I'm sensing a theme—Miranda just texted me pretty much the same thing. So what now?"

"I guess now we wait."

# CHAPTER TWENTY-EIGHT

Elena was not, by nature, a patient person.

Sitting around doing nothing while they waited for word on whether or not some faceless stranger had managed to magically erase Cassie Newton's accusations sounded like fresh hell to her.

Miranda had called back, reiterating the sit-tight-and-wait-for-news mantra everyone else had been giving her. It felt like that was all anyone had said to her in months.

Sit back. Take it. Do nothing. Keep quiet.

She wanted to fight back against the unfairness of it. To scream and hit something.

So when Adam suggested they work on her self-defense moves, she leapt at the idea. She changed into yoga pants and a sports bra, then helped him shove the couches in the living room aside to clear a space on the rug.

Adam fell into a ready stance. "The rugs won't have the same give as the mats at the gym, so try not to hurt me."

"No guarantees," she said, though the flirty words lacked their usual lightness. It was hard to feel light when he was threatened. A lot easier when they were throwing stones at her, but Adam didn't deserve this one bit.

Then he lunged at her and all her thoughts faded away into the immediacy of deflecting the attack. It was oddly Zen, sparring with him. Harder to worry when you had to be moving and reacting, ducking and twisting. Though they paused whenever one of their phones beeped with a text notification, just in case there was new news, so the reality of the situation was never far from her mind.

Adam had her pinned on her back on the rug, calmly asking, "Now which pressure points can you reach from this position?" when another text notification bleeped from his phone. He rolled off her and to his feet in a single graceful motion that had her thinking maybe she wouldn't try to get away so hard next time he pinned her—then he frowned at his phone.

"Where did we put the remote?"

"I don't know." Elena came to her feet and scanned the shuffled furniture of the living room. "Is something happening?"

"I'm not sure. This is someone I used to work with in D.C. They say I need to turn on CNN."

Maybe Cassie was issuing a retraction—though Elena didn't dare say that out loud, not wanting to jinx it. She found the remote and tossed it to Adam, who quickly pulled up the news conference in progress.

Not Cassie.

A serious brunette in a very serious suit was standing in front of a bank of microphones, speaking very seriously and deliberately. The caption below read "Agent Michele Lowry, Secret Service."

"—personally vouch for the character and integrity of former-Agent Adam Dylan. I am certain these claims will reveal themselves to be baseless."

She looked too young to be his boss. Maybe a

colleague? Someone who'd worked with him? "Who is she?"

Adam didn't look away from the screen. "My ex."

*His ex.* Damn. She didn't know why the words hit her so hard. He was a gorgeous man. Of course he would have exes. Beautiful—if overly serious—accomplished badass Agent exes, apparently. But she hadn't been braced for it. He never talked about anyone from his past. How well did she really know him?

"She thinks she's helping," Adam muttered at the television, sinking down on the nearest couch. "But she's just feeding the crazy."

On screen, the serious agent with her serious suit and serious hair completed her prepared statement and opened the floor for questions—and the reporters fell on her like wolves.

*"Have you spoken with him?"*

*"No. But I know his character and I was aware of an unhealthy fixation by the Newton girl after the incident in Malibu last year."*

Adam cursed. "Sandy's going to love having that one out in the public."

His text alert sounded and he grabbed his phone to read the message, snorting. "Pretty Boy says the Secret Service chick is hot, but my new partners support me way more than my old partners. Apparently it's a competition." A series of chimes announced a slew of texts. "Tank says press conferences are for pussies and he and Cross are planning to jump out of a plane over the Hollywood sign with a banner reading *DYLAN WRONGFULLY ACCUSED.*"

Elena grinned and settled beside him, but her smile faded when the intense agent on screen once again insisted on Adam's innocence of all charges, fielding all questions with chilly calm. "She doesn't doubt you for a second."

"Neither did you." He lifted his phone, texting back. "Neither did they, apparently."

Elena shrugged. "No one who knows you will. You exude moral fiber." While Elena apparently had a sin tractor beam that sucked in the unsuspecting. "You're the anti-me."

And so was the woman on the screen.

Adam frowned at her, looking up from the text he'd been sending, but before he could speak she nodded to Agent Michele Lowry. "That's your type?"

He hooked his arm around her, dragging her against his side. "You're my type."

They watched the press conference in silence for a few minutes. To an outside eye, it might have looked like they were just cuddling on the couch, watching television. No reason to suspect it was their own drama being dissected for the entertainment of the masses.

"How long were you with her?" Elena asked when she couldn't stand it anymore.

"A couple years."

Jesus. That was forever. She'd never had a relationship last longer than six months. "Pretty serious?"

"Not really." Relief sprang to life—only to be brutally murdered by his next words. "We lived together for about a year, but it was mostly for convenience. Both working our way up through the Service, there's a lot of travel—training, long assignments in other cities. It was efficient to share a place in D.C. when we were both in town."

"Why did you break up?"

"I left the service. The job with Max was here in

California. Sandy was offering me a house in California. It wasn't efficient anymore."

How romantic. "What did she say?"

"She understood our lives were leading us in different directions. Michele was always very practical."

No one had ever called Elena practical.

She heard her name on television and tuned back into the press conference in progress. *"—that's the most ridiculous part. Adam Dylan would never get involved with a woman like that."*

Adam cringed. "Sorry about that."

"Guess she doesn't know you as well as she thinks she does."

His phone rang before he could reply. Elena leaned over to mute the television while he reached for his phone. "Max wants to Facetime."

Elena leaned away from the phone's camera as Adam accepted the call. "Hey, Max. Any news?"

"Some. Is Elena with you?"

Adam waved her over into the shot and Elena waved. "Hey."

On the screen, Max sat beside a petite Asian woman with intense powers of eye-contact. "This is Kathleen Tao. I'll let her fill you in."

"I've been in touch with the Newton camp," Kathleen said, her voice carrying a surprisingly husky rasp. "Cassie will be issuing a statement at two fifteen to get her retraction in before the east coast evening news."

"She's retracting?"

"The Newton camp will clarify there was never a relationship with either Cassie or her mother—"

"People are saying I'm sleeping with Sandy now?"

"Don't worry, we're changing the narrative. Cassie will confess that she was wrong. What we need from you is a statement—preferably written since we don't want them focusing on your part in this, we want her apology to be the sound bite that gets airtime."

"What kind of statement?" Adam asked warily.

"You'll need to confirm that you have only ever had professional feelings for Cassie Newton and that you continue to feel indebted for the generosity of her mother blah-blah-blah. Understand the folly of youth, that sort of thing. And then we'll need you to either confirm or deny the affair with Elena Suarez."

"How is it an affair if neither of us is married?"

Kathleen went on as if he hadn't spoken. "How would you like your relationship characterized in the press? Serious? Just friends?"

"There isn't a middle ground?" Adam asked, but Elena knew what Kathleen was going to say before she spoke.

"Not when it comes to public perception. So you two need to decide if you're in a serious committed relationship, or if you're purely platonic. Right now, those are your options."

Elena didn't hesitate. "Friends." Adam frowned at her, but she just shook her head. "Trust me."

He nodded, the picture of reluctance. "Good friends."

Moments later, Kathleen and Max signed off, promising to call back in ten minutes with a draft of "Adam's" statement. He immediately turned to her, his frown darkening.

"Why are we just friends?"

"It's easier this way." Easier when it was over. Easier when he wanted to distance himself from her.

"How exactly is it easier? I thought we agreed you weren't going anywhere."

"I can still stay here, but it will be a lot easier to rebuild your image if you're the nice guy letting the Slutty Suitorette stay in your guest room rather than the questionable guy with the Slutty Suitorette in your bed."

"I hate that nickname."

She grimaced. "I'm sorry you got pulled into my reputation vortex. None of this would be happening to you if you hadn't taken me in. Cassie wouldn't have seen us together. She wouldn't have lost it and run to the press—"

"She still would have showed up here to profess her love to me. I do *not* want to think how that could have gone without you here as a buffer."

He was so disciplined, so controlled she couldn't always tell what he was feeling. "Are you angry?"

He hooked his arm around her. "Not at you."

She let him pull her against his side, studying his profile from a distance of inches. "You're so contained," she marveled.

"So are you."

She snorted. "Me? The Slutty Suitorette with the impulse control of a cat in heat?"

"You're impulsive," he agreed, turning so he could study her in return. "And you go into these wild, manic modes, but you're also proud and stubborn and you have these walls so no one can ever see when you aren't okay. Your world falls apart and you're cracking jokes so the assholes lashing out at you can't see that their blows are landing. So no one knows you hate being treated like the Slutty Suitorette."

"It's what I deserve, right?" she asked, her voice choked. "I was asking for it."

"Fuck that." Hard. Blunt. "Don't believe that bullshit."

"Women are supposed to be goddesses."

"You are *everything* a woman is supposed to be."

His intensity sent shivers down her back. She tried to think of a comeback. Anything to lighten the mood, but he must have seen right through her so-called walls, because he rumbled, "Don't."

He looked into her eyes, pouring his intensity into her—along with unforgiving honesty. "You're sexy. You're strong. You're sweet. And it pisses me off when I have to keep telling you this." His hands sank into her hair and she forgot how to breathe. "You're funny and fierce and I have never wanted another woman anywhere near as badly as I want you right now. Fuck them if they can't see how incredible you are. What the fuck do they know?"

She didn't have a comeback. She didn't even have *words*. The way he looked at her, the things he said, she was lost. Done for. So freaking turned on she couldn't remember her own name.

Then he kissed her and she didn't need pesky words anymore anyway. All she needed was him.

# CHAPTER TWENTY-NINE

He pulled her down against him, wanting to lose himself and all the stress of the day in her arms—and she seemed just as eager to throw herself against him and forget the world, but they were interrupted five minutes later to review and approve Adam's statement.

*Just friends.*

It bothered the hell out of him. Not lying to the press necessarily, but this particular lie. Because he couldn't get over the feeling that she was trying to protect him by putting distance between them publicly. As if he would be tainted by association.

He was supposed to be her protector. But Elena was adamant, and if she didn't want to publicly acknowledge their relationship, that was her right. So he approved the statement, thanked Max and Kathleen Tao for everything, and settled in at two fifteen to watch the carefully constructed theatre of Cassie's retraction.

She stood next to her mother, surrounded by a small cluster of serious, concerned-looking adults on the lawn of one of Southern California's most exclusive rehab facilities. Pale and trembling, she confessed that the entire thing had been a hoax, fueled by drugs and alcohol.

Adam glowered at the screen. "Why is she saying she was high? She's been sober for months."

Elena sat nearby, leaning forward with her hands clasped, never taking her eyes off the screen, drinking in every detail. "If she admits she lied for spite or jealousy, they all turn on her. If she's an addict, it's a sickness. She's getting help. Makes sense. More sympathy this way."

"So she's going to fake rehab because it looks better?"

"That's pretty much the gist of it, yeah."

They watched the rest of Cassie's statement, including a tearful apology to both of them—and she really did seem sincere when she professed that no one deserved her lies less than the shining example of heroism that was Adam Dylan. He almost gagged. Her apology to Elena seemed a bit more forced, but Elena didn't seem to mind.

When the press conference was over, the on-screen pundit had murmured solemnly about the perils of drugs and alcohol and moved on. Just like that. Adam flicked off the television. "What happens now?"

Elena shrugged. "Now the paparazzi go back to chasing the next scandal—though I'm sure we'll have a few dedicated stragglers. You are redeemed and go back to being the hero, though your shiny image may be a bit tarnished for a while, and I go back to being a punch line."

"And no one knows we're together."

"Better that way."

*Better for who?*

He would have argued, but his phone chose that moment to ring. The caller-ID lit up with his parents' picture and he winced. "Shit. The scandal has made it to Maryland."

"Talk to them. They must be worried." She pushed away from his side, moving toward the open French

239

doors.

He wanted to follow, but she was right. He needed to take this call. "Hello?"

"Adam!" his parents chorused his name, both of them on the line as was their habit.

"We just saw the strangest news story. Something about that Cassie girl going on a drunken rampage and accusing you of paying for hookers with money her mother gave you? What on earth is going on?"

Adam allowed himself only a fraction of a second to marvel that he didn't think he'd ever heard his mother utter the word "hookers" before. "It was a hoax. She was upset and misinterpreted a situation. Everything's fine now."

Except his girlfriend refused to publicly acknowledge him. If she was his girlfriend. They'd never talked about labels.

"I knew something like this would happen," his father intoned darkly. "This is what happens when you get involved with those showbiz people. If you were still in the Service…"

Adam almost laughed. The Secret Service hadn't exactly maintained a spotless record when it came to scandals over the last decade—part of why they'd enjoyed the PR boost of the Cassie rescue, even as they kicked him out.

"I'm sure it's not too late to come back," his father continued, and the truth rolled off Adam's tongue without conscious direction from his brain.

"I doubt it. I was fired."

"What?" Shock reverberated in his parents' voices.

"Or maybe not fired precisely, but I was quietly encouraged to resign. I broke protocol." And that really said it all. "I left Sylas Walker to save Cassie and it cost me my job."

"Adam. Why didn't you say anything?" He could hear the concern in his mother's voice, but his father didn't speak.

"I was afraid to tell you. You were always so proud of me for being in the Secret Service. And then I blew it."

"Are you sure you didn't misunderstand?" his father said finally. "I would expect a reprimand, but to throw out the baby with the bathwater, it just doesn't seem logical."

"I could have stayed," Adam admitted. "But it was made very clear to me that my opportunities would be limited." In other words, nonexistent.

His father spoke government-ese. He didn't need a translation. "I'm sure after the initial furor faded…"

"I could have waited it out, you're right," Adam admitted. "I could have ridden a desk and toed the line and waited for my second chance. Proven my loyalty with years of service. But I didn't want to."

And there was something freeing about admitting that to himself. He'd felt off-balance for months, unsure what the hell to do with his life now that his entire identity had changed, but now when he looked at what had happened he didn't remember being railroaded into leaving, forced out. He remembered his choice.

"I know you would have played by the rules and waited it out," Adam went on, speaking mainly to his father. To his sense of duty. "But I was so angry with them. I did everything they asked for six years and then they didn't have my back." And he knew his father would say it wasn't the Service's job to have his back. It was his duty to his country to be loyal to them. But the truth was pushing its way up from where he had buried it and now it was coming out. "I never loved being in the Service," he confessed. "The politics and the protocol. I never felt the camaraderie and loyalty to the man beside me that you talked about having in the military, Dad. It never felt right. But I think I may have found that here. This bodyguard service is more than that. It's a family. They had my back today." And every other day. "And yes, the stars we're guarding may be vain and entitled, but so are most politicians. Maybe this isn't as noble as guarding the President, but I like it here. And I can have a say in my work."

He'd suggested they offer self-defense training courses and Max had loved the idea—even though he'd joked they'd be putting themselves out of business. He'd said he wasn't comfortable working for the Newtons anymore and Max had listened. Today each of his coworkers had sent him texts in support and it was Max who had located the infamous fixer to handle his statement.

When he wasn't looking, Elite Protection had become his family.

"I'm sorry if you're disappointed—"

"I'm only disappointed you didn't feel you could tell us," his father said gruffly. "If you're happy out there in California, we're happy for you. Your mother has been worrying that you weren't settling in."

Of course. "His mother" was the only one who worried. "I wasn't," he admitted, "but I'm good now." He wanted to add that he was even seeing someone, but he could see Elena at the deck rail and her refusal to take their relationship public still stung.

A few minutes later he ended the call, his father's final words lingering in his ears. *They were fools to lose you, son.*

All this time he hadn't been able to tell them he'd

been encouraged to leave the Service, because all this time he hadn't wanted to admit to himself that he'd really wanted to go. That the ideal of being the man who guarded the President hadn't been worth the reality of the life he was leading.

He had a place with EP—and if he let himself, he could belong there.

Now if only he could convince Elena that he also wanted a place at her side.

He crossed to the open French doors. "Elena?"

She stood at the railing, staring out over the water with her face tipped up to the sun. Gorgeous. "How are your folks?"

"They're good. I told them the truth. About being drummed out of the Service. And the world didn't end."

"Good for you."

He grinned. "The truth shall set you free. We should try it. Tell the world about us."

"Adam." She turned, bracing her back on the railing, the sea a glittering backdrop behind her. He wished for a camera, to capture the moment, but then he saw the expression on her face.

\* \* \* \* \*

He had no idea.

She'd been sitting out here, thinking about breaking up with him for his own good. In her life, the hits just kept on coming, and he deserved better than to spend his days in damage control with her. Hell, *she* deserved better, but he had a better escape strategy. She couldn't get away from her life.

He came to stand close to her, his expression cautious. "You okay?"

"Peachy." She tried to say the words, to tell him they were over, but they wouldn't form in her throat.

"Why don't you want people to know we're together, Elena?" he asked softly.

"Seriously? I'm a trainwreck. And you want to just jump on board?" She pushed away from him, walking down the deck, putting more distance between them. "Think about it for a second. Think about what it means to be tied to me. This morning I pressed charges against a girl who put a death threat on my door because her boyfriend thought I was bangable. At that same exact moment a perfectly nice girl who has hero worshipped you for months is driven so crazy by the thought of you with me that she decides to announce to the entire world that you're a pedophile and I'm a slut—as if we didn't know."

"Elena," he warned. He hated when she called herself names. But it was the only way she knew to take the sting out when other people did.

"I'm being funny. Except it's not funny. None of it is funny. The sex tape and the whore-on-the-door and Cassie and, God, do you even remember that asshole from the wedding? Doesn't that feel like a lifetime ago? Just one giant cavalcade of fuckery that has been chasing me around ever since I *kissed my freaking boyfriend in a Jacuzzi and took off my top*. How *dare* I, right? But it's not just me. Women all over the country have to deal with this shit. Have you heard of revenge porn? Guys putting their exes up online? That shit is *not okay*. None of this is okay."

She gripped the railing with both hands, feeling the anger and futility and the anger *at* the futility pulse through her. This was why she felt like she couldn't be with him. Because of the ominous *them*.

"Why are they so freaking insecure that they have to degrade us or take away our power in order to feel manly? Like we're conspiring with their dicks to remove their impulse control and therefore it's our fault they can't own their own freaking actions. We're all Eve. We're the fucking temptresses. But the men aren't even the worst! Women being catty about women. Jealous of other women. Calling one another slutty or trashy. Fully half the talk shows that degrade me are panels of women. Where is the freaking sisterhood, goddamn it?"

Her shout echoed against the house, but Adam didn't even flinch.

"I seem to have a lot of rage about this issue," she said, trying to pull herself under control.

"I noticed."

"Sorry about the yelling."

"I don't mind. But you're preaching to the choir."

He was right. It didn't do any good to rant at him. He was on her side. He was the one person who was always on her side. It was the rest of the world that needed to learn.

If she broke up with him, she let them win. If she ran, she let them win. If she gave up, she let them win. If she kept her mouth shut, she let them win.

She was tired of letting them win.

"I'm not doing the reality show."

His brow pinched with confusion. "Reality show?"

She brushed away the question. "It's unimportant now. I got offered a show, but I'm not doing it. I'm doing something else."

Miranda's words from that morning reverberated through her mind. A tell-all book. All of it in her own words. But more than that. A *manifesto*.

"I'm going to write a book." The rightness of the

words seemed to reverberate through her. *Yes*, her soul answered. *This*. "And go on the morning shows and stand up for myself. I'm going to be the one to say I have had *enough* of this goddamn sexist bullying."

"Good."

*Good*. It was good. It was amazing. She had a *mission*. A plan. A call to action. She felt invincible. Wonder Woman wasn't this badass.

And Adam was right there beside her, believing she could do it. No doubt. No questions. Good.

So damn good.

High on the wild, powerful sensation, she backed him against the rail. She rested her hands at either side of his waist, gently fisting them in the fabric of the T-shirt he'd been wearing since they sparred earlier. It smelled of him. Spicy, clean and masculine. She tipped her face up to his, falling in love with every line of his face, every single angle and curve of him.

"You're amazing." She put a hand behind his neck to draw him down to her and went up on her tiptoes to kiss him, her white knight. Her hero.

"That's what they tell me," he murmured when she finally released his lips.

"No. You are." He was good in a way she'd never encountered before. Not because he should be. Not because he wanted people to see him that way. But because he was. Down to his core. Such a good man.

He bent his head down until their foreheads touched. "So are you."

And he meant it too. That was what he saw when he looked at her. "Yeah. Maybe I am." She grinned at him. "That must be why you're so nice to me."

"That might not be the only reason."

"Oh?"

He kissed her. Long and sweet and hot, until her every cell was restless with the need to get closer to him.

"Don't tell me you were just being nice to me because you were hoping to get laid," she gasped when he let her come up for air. "Because talk about a wasted effort. I hate to break it to you, buddy, but you were already in. From day one."

"That isn't what I meant," he murmured, voice husky. Then he kissed her again—and this time the kiss was different. Sweeter. Shivers ran across her skin. There was emotion in the kiss. Emotion she was afraid to look at too closely.

She turned her face away, breaking the kiss. "Don't make this emo, champ."

He cupped her chin, bringing her face back around to his. "Elena? Shut up."

The next kiss rolled her under. She was dizzy with want when he finally released her lips to kiss down her throat. "God, Adam, when you have something to say, you don't mess around."

She felt his smile against her skin. Then he kissed her again and the world fell away.

# CHAPTER THIRTY

The next few weeks were a rollercoaster ride for Adam—even more than the previous few had been.

By the time he woke up on the morning after Cassie's hoax, Elena had already packed everything she'd brought over to his place and all the extra clothes they'd bought and was practically bouncing with eagerness to get back to her apartment. Her laptop was there and she couldn't wait to get started on her book, she explained, and they'd told the press they were just friends, hadn't they? And she couldn't very well let Mary-Kate run her off, could she? Never let them see you flinch!

The only way to corral her manic enthusiasm was to help her load up his Jeep and drive her back to her Hollywood apartment. He'd been ready for her to have to duck down to avoid being spotted, but by the time they drove out that morning the paparazzi outside his house had mostly dispersed and those that remained didn't even try to jump in front of his car. They were old news already.

There was no parking near her place when they arrived, so she had him double park as she dragged her bags out of the backseat.

"Will I see you tonight?"

"Hm?" She gazed blankly at him, eyes distant, already lost inside the book in her head. "Oh. Sure! Yes.

Dinner? Probably best that we don't go out—"

"Why don't you come out to the house? I'll make us something."

"Perfect," she agreed, smiling. Then she gave him a little wave, bumped the door shut with her hip and charged toward her apartment. He watched her, feeling oddly bereft that she hadn't even given him a kiss goodbye—not that he'd expected her to when they were playing at just friends—which he still didn't freaking understand—but she could have at least winked at him or *something*.

A car honked behind him and Elena turned to look, shooing him off with another wave as she pulled out her keys.

He consoled himself that he would see her that evening, putting the Jeep in drive.

But that evening when he got home a text message buzzed on his phone. *In the zone. Gonna stay here and fuel my art with ramen. Raincheck?*

He was understanding—of course they could do dinner another time, this was important to her, she was on a mission, he got it—but his house still felt empty without her energy vibrating through every room. The idea of cooking lost its appeal without her there to moan appreciatively over the end result.

He'd known that Elena was a force of nature, filling up all the empty spaces of his house, but he'd lived without her before. He hadn't expected her absence to leave such a massive void.

He accepted her rain check and told himself to get over it. It was one night. But then the next night she canceled again—*Brain dead from binge writing. Gonna crash early. Tomorrow?*

By the third postponement he was sensing a trend,

but even though he missed her he couldn't work up any irritation with her absence when he was also receiving periodic texts proclaiming, *I am a rock star goddess!* and *The world shall tremble in the face of my biting wit and genius prose!* Intermixed with *why did I think I could write a book?* and *this might be the crappiest piece of shit ever to hit the page.*

On day four he arrived unannounced with In N' Out burgers and she groaned, "Oh my God, you're a prince," before dragging him and his takeout bag into her apartment and kissing him ravenously. The kiss turned wild in a rush and before he knew it he had her on the kitchen floor, bracing her hands against the chipped faux-wood laminate cupboards as she screamed his name.

"God, I missed you," she murmured in the afterglow, though the timing made him wonder if he'd misheard her and she'd really said she missed *this*.

"You can always write at the house," he offered, tracing a pattern in the delicate skin at her nape as he lay on his back on the knobby rug with her sprawled over his front.

"You're there. I'd never get any work done."

"I wouldn't distract you," he promised.

"But I would want to keep stopping to tell you things. I need to be focused on telling the world." She pushed off his chest as she sat up, catching her hair up in a ponytail as she searched for the clothes she'd lost. "And I somehow doubt it would be much fun for you to watch me commune with my laptop."

"Even you need breaks." He accepted the shirt she tossed his way, pulling it back on. "You can write while I'm at work and spend the evenings with me. Like regular adults."

"Maybe," she admitted, getting to her feet, but he could hear in her voice that she was just placating him.

She kicked him out shortly thereafter to get back to work. As much as he wanted her to, he wasn't expecting her to come around and move back, so he braced himself for another week of lonely nights—but that Sunday he got another text.

*Still want company?*

He texted back that he always wanted to see her and half an hour later she was buzzing at his gate in her little yellow Beetle.

The last of the paparazzi had given up on him as boring a couple of days earlier, so there was no one there to see him buzz her in, or come out of the front door to greet her.

"I missed you," she said simply, shoving the door of her little yellow Beetle closed. He met her halfway, kissing her senseless. He started to guide her toward the house without breaking the kiss but she pulled back. "Hang on. Before you get to have your way with me, you have to help me carry my stuff inside."

It was then that he saw the suitcase in the backseat and the laptop bag on the passenger side. Relief flooded through him at the sight of her luggage. She was staying. "How about I have my way with you first and we worry about the luggage later?"

\* \* \* \* \*

They fell into a new routine—if there could be anything routine about living with a woman on a mission to change the world through the written word.

"How's your Elena doing?" Tank asked a few days later while he was torturing Adam in the weight room.

"She's writing a book." Which seemed like the only way he could answer the question. Just saying *good* seemed wrong somehow.

"Yeah?" Tank breathed through three more reps then lowered his weights, standing as they rotated so he could spot Adam as he took his turn. "Good for her."

"Yeah. But it means she spends pretty much all of her time hunched over her laptop, glaring at the screen as if it has personally offended her. And when she isn't doing that, she's running around the house shouting, 'I'm taking my power back!' at the top of her lungs."

Tank snorted a laugh and Adam grinned himself.

"She's amazing. But I'm learning to be cautious. If she's staring into space, totally zoned out like no one's home, interrupting her thought process will lead to a scene like that head-spinning one from *The Exorcist*."

"Terrifying."

"Pretty much," Adam agreed.

But he loved it.

He loved her. He just couldn't tell her that because she'd already shown signs of bolting on their relationship—the Just Friends thing still grated under his skin.

She'd only brought a few days' clothes when she came back and every few days she would vanish back to her apartment for a day or two, leaving his house feeling dead without her.

He'd told her he wanted her to stay, told her every way she was willing to hear, but she kept the distance between them as if she was waiting for him to wake up one morning and decide she wasn't good enough for him anymore.

He wanted to punch Daniel. Not to mention her parents. Everyone who had turned her away and made her feel like she wasn't good enough. All those small-minded assholes who hadn't been able to accept her as she was. Who had taught her to be wary. To wait for the other shoe to drop.

The only way Adam knew to prove he wasn't going to stop wanting her was to show her. So he just kept doing it.

He went to work. He came home. He cooked. He kissed her. He danced with her around the living room and curled up with her to watch television and lost his train of thought looking at her, hypnotized by the beauty and wildness and sensuality of her. He dragged her off to bed—and woke up in the middle of the night to find her hunched over her laptop again, her face illuminated by the bluish glow as her hands clattered over the keys. He fell asleep to the sound of her obsession. And then he did it all over again.

And for the first time ever, returning to the house started feeling like coming home. Because she was there.

Though it may also have had something to do with the conversation he had with Sandy when she came by the house two days after what the media had taken to calling The Newton Hoax.

He'd known who it was as soon as he looked out the front window and saw the nondescript SUV with darkly tinted windows pull past his gate. He opened the door as soon as she and her entourage spilled out onto his driveway. Sandy waved the others to stay behind, gliding toward him with the innate elegance and poise that had earned her the nickname the Queen of Hollywood. She'd been an ingénue once, and the beauty that had defined her in her youth was still there in the distinctive bone structure of her face, but the sharp radiance of her had softened over the years as she'd made the transition from rom-com star to serious actress.

"Adam." She paused on his doorstep.

"Sandy. Would you like to come in?"

She nodded, looking about as enthused as if he'd just asked her if she'd like to clean toilets all afternoon. She moved past him into the house and he trailed her down to the sunken living room.

He glanced around automatically for traces of Elena—almost relieved she'd moved out. She wasn't a neat person, always leaving a shoe here and a scarf there—and he found himself looking for that evidence like a teenager who'd had a party when his parents got home. He was too old for that feeling.

"Can I get you something to drink?"

"No, thank you. I won't keep you long." She looked around at the white couches she'd bought when the house was hers, as if unsure where to sit. Adam waved her onto the loveseat, taking the couch opposite.

"How's Cassie doing?" he asked and Sandy's face crumpled.

It was so surprising it took him a moment to realize Sandy Newton was crying in his living room. He looked around helplessly—where was a tissue box when you needed one?—but before he could do more than lurch to his feet, she was pulling a linen handkerchief from her pocket and waving him back to his chair. "I'm sorry. Apparently I'm a mess."

Her voice broke on the last word.

"It's okay."

"No, it isn't. I'm so sorry, Adam. I owe you more than apologies."

*Please, don't give me another house.* "You don't owe me—"

"I'm not a good mother."

"That isn't—"

"I'm not," Sandy insisted. "Cassie's father was my second husband and he's never spent much time with her. He used to take her on an extravagant vacation once a year when she was younger. Disney World if she wanted. The south of France. Skiing in Switzerland. But he was never really a father figure. And then a few years ago he remarried and started a new family. Stopped taking Cassie at all."

Adam sat very still, uncomfortable with her confessional air.

"I didn't know about the drugs and the alcohol," Sandy whispered. "But I think I knew without knowing, if that makes any sense. I knew she was different. I knew things were getting bad between us, but I didn't know what to do so I pretended not to see. I pretended it was normal teenage rebellion and tried to fix it by promising she could come with me the next time I had to shoot on location in Europe—even if it meant taking her out of school. Parent of the year, eh?"

"Teenagers are tough to read. You didn't know."

"Thank you for trying to make me feel better, but the truth was I was a shitty mother. I wasn't even surprised when the police called me the night of the fire. I'd been expecting her to get arrested. I just hadn't been expecting them to call to tell me she'd almost died. It woke me up to how stupid I'd been. I didn't want to let her out of my sight—but I also couldn't bear to punish her for the drinking and the drugs because I was so glad she was all right."

"It's understandable."

"I knew she had a crush on you, but I also knew you'd never look at her that way so it seemed safe.

255

Harmless. And then it started to help. She stopped drinking and cleaned up her act because she wanted to be good enough for you. I had my daughter back and I hadn't even had to be the bad guy. So I encouraged it."

A weight landed in his gut. "And then she saw me with Elena."

Sandy sniffled. "I'm so sorry about the story," she said. "When I saw it…"

"It wouldn't be surprising if you wondered if some part of it was true."

She shook her head. "There were too many discrepancies in her story. I knew you'd been refusing to see her. She'd been complaining to me about how you only saw her as a little girl—and I was so thrilled she was confiding in me at all that I didn't remind her that she still is one in the eyes of the law." She wadded up the handkerchief, grimacing. "And it wasn't the first time she'd made up vicious stories when she was upset. I fired two of her nannies for stealing when she was a child before I realized she was telling tales, trying to get rid of them so I'd be forced to pay more attention to her."

"I saw you checked her into rehab. Did she…?"

"Fall off the wagon? No. Though I'm not sure running to the tabloids with lies about you is much of an improvement. She's in therapy now. We both are. And I backed out of a project that would have taken me away next month. I'm trying to be around more."

Adam nodded, not sure what she wanted him to say.

"I'm sorry," she said again. "You probably didn't want to hear any of this, but I felt you deserved to know why this happened. And that I take responsibility for what Cassie did."

"I appreciate you retracting the story so quickly.

Before it had time to feed on itself."

"It was the least we could do. I wanted to make some public gesture, show the press I still think of you as a hero, but my people think anything like that right now would only bring attention back to the scandal."

"Probably."

"They didn't even want me coming here today. They thought it would be better if I apologized by phone, but this is the kind of thing that needs to be done face to face."

"You didn't have to."

"Yes, I did. But I'm sorry if I've inconvenienced you. I understand if you want to distance yourself from us."

"It isn't that."

She didn't seem to hear him. "Is that why you're selling the house?"

Adam cursed internally. He should have known she would hear about that. "I'm not. I never actually put the house on the market. I was just talking to some real estate agents because I needed the money for a friend who was in trouble."

"The woman? The one from the reality show?"

He nodded. "She wouldn't have accepted the money from me anyway, but I wanted to feel like there was something I could do to help."

"If you need money—"

"Sandy." His voice stopped her. "You can't keep giving me extravagant presents." *Because you feel guilty about your parenting skills.* "The truth is the main reason I was thinking about selling the house is because I really can't afford to live here. The property taxes, the maintenance, the utilities—it's outside my means. I was paying off student loans on a government salary before you gave me a beachfront villa in Malibu."

Her eyes widened, the blithe celebrity naiveté when it came to real life falling away like scales from her eyes. "Oh."

"I'm not going to sell it now—that's the kind of gesture we don't need the press getting a hold of right now—but if I could give it back to you, I would. Maybe we can work out some sort of agreement where you will reclaim ownership after things have died down."

"I want you to have it."

"It isn't mine. It's a wonderful thought and I appreciate it. I do. I don't want you to think I'm not grateful. But it's still your house. And if I hadn't been living here, do you think Cassie would have felt quite so comfortable letting herself in?"

Sandy's eyes widened even farther. "She's been just letting herself in whenever she pleases?"

"I changed the door code after the other night, but that isn't the point. It never felt right for me to have it."

"I just wanted to thank you."

"I know. And it was the most insanely generous gesture I've ever seen, but it was too much."

"You lost your job because you saved my daughter's life. I just wanted to help. I never meant to tie you up so you could never get away from us."

"I didn't want to get away."

Her smile said she heard the lie in the words. "I want to argue with you. To tell you that you need to stay in the house, but that isn't my call. Whatever you want—keep it, sell it, give it back—I'll figure out a way to make it happen without a fuss. But I like thinking of you here. I hope you'll stay."

She'd left soon after that, and Adam had found himself looking around the house with new eyes. It was his choice now, not his obligation, and he still wasn't sure what choice he would make, but he liked being here, now, with Elena making the walls feel alive with her presence. Making it home.

## CHAPTER THIRTY-ONE

The weeks after the Hoax were a blur of words and empowerment for Elena.

Everything that had happened to her in the last year poured onto the page. All her frustrations, all her hopes, every insult and indignity. She released it all into the book with one rule. Honesty. It might not be art, but every word she wrote would be true.

She wouldn't lie or hide her emotions. She wouldn't sugarcoat the facts to try to make herself look innocent. When she'd been a bitch, she would own it. Her book would be biased—everything was—but she would be honest about her bias. About her perspective. For whatever it was worth, the book would be true.

Of course, whenever she thought about letting someone else read it, she felt sick to her stomach. Exposing herself to the degree required to actually publish it was a horror she didn't want to contemplate. So she didn't. What she did with it when she finished was a problem for another day. Today her only job was to write fearlessly. To put the words onto the page without pulling any punches.

Adam was a prince.

He seemed to be capable of handling whatever she threw at him and he proved that again as she fell into the ideas of her book and got lost. He fielded every emotion without flinching—from her despondency when she wrote about her family cutting her off, to her righteous rage when she wrote of Daniel leading her on. He was there through it all. Better than she deserved.

Miranda had called back the day after the Hoax with a short list of agents and instructions to drop her name. Two days later Elena had met with the second woman on the list for coffee, a silver-haired woman with the sculpted arms of a triathlete and a style that ran toward Bettie Page. Elena liked her instantly. And even more so when she dissolved into a rant about agents who typecast their own clients.

Her name was Claudia Frost and when Elena wasn't writing they would discuss possible roles and PR strategies. Ways to transition her from Topless Co-Ed #2 to Sidney Bristow.

She met Adam at the door one night, after a long conversation with her agent and a particularly vehement chapter about roles for women in Hollywood. "Do you think you can make me into an action star?"

He dropped his keys on the side table—she hadn't even given him a chance to take off his coat. "Right now?"

"No time like the present. Knowing all the self-defense stuff is good, but I want to be a ninja. And a marksman. I want to be Michelle Rodriguez meets Gabrielle Anwar. I want people to look at me for the same roles they would give Scarlett Johansen—crazy hot, but capable of choking a guy out with her thighs. Can you make me that badass?"

"Absolutely." Adam grinned. "Can I take my coat off first?"

And so her training had begun.

Most of her days were spent in Adam's living room

or on his bed with her laptop in her lap and the Pacific sprawled in front of her. And most of her nights were spent with him—sex, sparring, sparring that led into sex, dinners where they moved around one another in the kitchen, so easy and comfortable it was like they'd been doing this all their lives.

It was going to be hard to let him go, when the time came. Somehow, without even looking for it, she'd fallen into a life with him that made her happy in ways she'd never been before. And that sort of thing didn't last. But she would enjoy it while she had it. Enjoy every second.

It was coming into the hot part of the summer and a new spate of wildfires near the city would turn the sky grey when the wind shifted the right way, but Elena rolled through the days, measuring them by words as her book grew.

It might be a disjointed mess, but there was something there. Something worthwhile. And it felt amazing to be *doing* something. To finally be saying everything she'd bit her tongue on in the last few months.

The legal wrangling on the sex tape was progressing well, her lawyers assured her, though a date for the custody hearing had not yet been set. She'd copyrighted her naked body—which had been creepily invasive in its own special way. And now she was doing her best to ignore the entire mess and get on with her life... by venting it onto the page.

She was doing a pretty good job of it, too. Until one Tuesday afternoon when Slick the Wonderlawyer, as she'd started thinking of the smarmy elder member of her legal team, called.

"They want to settle."

Elena's heart jumped up into her throat. It could be

over soon. "That's good, isn't it?"

She'd heard too many conversations about the media zoo any kind of hearing or trial would stir up—and how her reputation could negatively sway the result—to think settling out of court would be anything but good.

"It's good and bad," Slick—whose real name was Kevin—cautioned. "The deal is worth considering. Keep in mind it's a sure thing. We can't be sure how a judge will rule."

Her heart dropped from her throat, bypassing her chest and landing with a thud in her stomach. "I'm going to hate the terms, aren't I?"

"Just keep an open mind and really think it through before you react."

"Fine. Just tell me."

"We drop our suit, he drops his countersuit, we lift the injunction, and you agree to allow Kellerman to sell the tape, provided you are consulted regarding the terms of the sale and you split all profits evenly. Essentially he's accepting our claim of joint custody."

He sounded so reasonable. As if her only objection to having the sex tape released was the fact that Dermott hadn't *paid* her for it.

"No."

"Really think about this, Elena. You could fight it all the way and end up with it released to the public and nothing to show for it. At least this way you can have some control. You can make sure it's released in a way that makes you comfortable."

"There is no possible way I'm going to be comfortable having strangers watch me have sex. And for him to profit from tricking me into making a sex tape with him—you have to be crazy if you think that's going to be okay with me."

"I'll give you some time to think about it—"

"No. I'm going to fight him all the way to the end. What he did was wrong."

"But it wasn't illegal. At least not in a way that's clear cut. You could lose."

"If I lose and wind up with nothing, at least I'm not going along with it. That's as bad as saying it's okay. It isn't okay. Don't come to me with any more settlements like this. We're not just doing damage control now. We're going for justice."

She got off the phone and returned to the open file on her computer, but she couldn't seem to focus, words blurring on the page. She'd been in the middle of a rant about the entire Madonna/whore complex, but now she couldn't make her anger coalesce into words. She was so pissed about all the things women dealt with—revenge porn and Monica Lewinsky and all of it. It was *wrong*. She wanted to scream against the injustice of it all and this book was her scream, but suddenly it felt inadequate.

It wasn't *enough*.

She heard the front door close downstairs and shoved her laptop aside. She hadn't made it downstairs today, too wrapped up in the words to bother. She leapt off the bed and ran down the stairs. She found Adam in the kitchen, putting away groceries.

"It isn't enough."

Adam pulled his torso out of the refrigerator and frowned at her. "You wanted more yogurt?"

"The book." She paced in the kitchen, the room tiny and restrictive where she'd always thought it was spacious before. "I'm being pro-active. I'm taking arms against a sea of troubles, but the book isn't enough."

"Was that Hamlet?"

She spoke over him. "I need to help others. A warrior for the slut-shamed! Something good has to come out of this, Adam."

"Okay."

She loved the way he said okay—not like she was a crazy person who needed to be talked down, but like he was recalibrating his life to fit her new plan into his every day. Simple as that. God, she loved him.

Her heart stuttered hard at the thought and she felt her face flushing even as she tried to drown the dangerous emotion in words. "We need a foundation or something," she said in a rush. "A place that will help with legal fees and PR and giving advice on what your legal options are when men are exploiting you because they have tiny little dicks. Not you, of course. Your dick is lovely."

"Thank you."

He stood there, in the opening of the refrigerator, and she didn't think a man had ever been more handsome. Yes, he was a good looking guy, but this was something else. Brad Pitt and Chris Hemsworth could suck it. Adam Dylan was the sexiest man alive.

"Do you think I can do it?"

"I think you can do anything." He closed the fridge. "Just let me know if you ever decide you want to conquer the world so I can get out of the way."

Shit.

Men had been trying to woo her since puberty, but no one had ever made her knees go weak like Adam did when he said things like that. Roses were for suckers.

She reached him in two steps. She jumped and he caught her against his chest. Their faces almost level, she kissed him until they were both breathless. When they finally came up for air, he didn't put her down, so Elena wrapped her legs around his waist, grinning into his eyes from a distance of inches. "Hi."

He grinned back. "Hi."

"It occurred to me that I forgot to welcome you home."

"That is an egregious sin."

"Oh, *egregious*," she agreed, her smile turning wicked against his lips. God bless a man who never treated her like her head was stuffed with fluff just because she was hot. "I love it when you talk dirty to me."

He chuckled and she felt the vibration everywhere they touched. "Bed or couch?"

"Both."

\* \* \* \* \*

So.

Love.

Elena lay in bed, studying the man dozing beside her. She should have known she'd fall in love with him. She didn't deserve him, but why should that stop her?

He stirred, draping an arm over her to fit her against him. "Making plans to conquer the world?" he asked, his breath stirring the fine hairs at the nape of her neck.

"Always."

She felt him smile against her skin.

She'd never thought of herself as a feminist. Never intended to become a feminist icon. Even in the middle of the Slut Storm, she hadn't thought of it that way. She'd just wanted to act. Wanted to *do* something.

"I'm not the ideal poster girl for women's issues," she said into the twilit room, looking out over the darkening water. "They may not want me on their side."

"Then they're idiots," he said without hesitation and

she turned in his arms. His sincerity shone in his eyes.

She didn't deserve him. And karma was a bitch. It was coming for her. Guys like Adam didn't end up with girls like her. It was only a matter of time. But for now she closed her eyes, snuggled in close, and tried to pretend it wasn't going to break her heart when he walked away.

\* \* \* \* \*

She called Miranda as early as was civilized the next morning.

"I'm going to First-Wives-Club this thing. You in?"

Miranda didn't miss a beat. "Hell, yes. Let me make some calls."

# CHAPTER THIRTY-TWO

Adam came home the following Tuesday to find the house eerily silent. Even when Elena was absorbed in her laptop, he wasn't used to it being quite this quiet. Her car was in the driveway, so she must be here, but as he searched from room to room, he found nothing but empty space. He was beginning to think she'd gone wandering down the PCH when it occurred to him to check the tiny, rarely-used balcony off the master suite.

She sat on the weathered wooden slats with her knees drawn up to her chest, staring out at the water through the posts supporting the railing.

"Hey." He dropped down beside her, chest tight. "You okay? Did something happen?"

She turned toward him, looking more puzzled than upset—thank God. "I think I finished my book."

"Okay." Not what he'd been expecting. "That's awesome, isn't it?"

"Yes." But she didn't sound sure. "I know I should be excited or triumphant or feel like I've accomplished something, but I just feel sort of... *lost*."

"Understandable. Writing that book has been driving you all summer."

"Exactly. What do I do now?"

"Now you celebrate. This is big. C'mon. Let's go out. Dinner, dancing, whatever you want. We can call Sidney and Miranda, make it a party."

"Can we go someplace quiet? Just you and me?"

"Absolutely." He took her hand, lacing their fingers together. "I know just the place."

\* \* \* \* \*

Mezzo of Malibu was a modern Mediterranean fusion restaurant which bragged of an exclusive private dining room on the second floor that catered to high profile guests. Unfortunately, the downside of dining someplace known to attract celebrity clientele was the small cluster of paparazzi lying in wait across the street.

Adam handed his keys to the valet and rounded the hood to meet Elena on the curb. He took her arm automatically to help her with her sky-high heels, and she pulled away so quickly she nearly fell into the bushes lining the walk.

"What are you doing?" she hissed under her breath. "We're *friends*."

Irritation kindled. "I wasn't aware *friends* meant I couldn't touch your arm in public."

"Not just public." She cut a speaking glance toward the paparazzi. "I know you saw them too."

She turned to lead the way into the restaurant. He didn't try to touch her again until the door closed behind them. Bending his head close to her ear as the hostess looked up with a smile, he murmured, "So what if they get a picture? Friends go to dinner too."

"And I'm sure that's exactly how the gossip columns would frame it. 'Just friends' out for a romantic dinner at a high end Malibu bistro." Her glance asked him what kind of an idiot he was—and maybe he was being intentionally obtuse, but he was sick of this bullshit sneaking around.

"Mr. Dylan, Ms. Suarez, if you'll follow me." The hostess led the way upstairs and Adam put his hand on the small of Elena's back as he trailed her up the stairs, intentionally goading her with the possessive touch.

"Stop it," she hissed at the top of the stairs.

He pulled his hands back, holding them up innocently—until it came time to hold her chair. The hostess stood back, smiling benignly as Elena shot him a tight-lipped smile and sank into her seat.

When the hostess had handed them both their menus and retreated, Elena gave him a death glare. "She's probably off to sell the story of our romantic dinner to TMZ."

"If the hostess here told tales, no celebrity in their right mind would eat here. I think our secret is safe. Though I don't know why it has to be such a secret. Why is it such a catastrophe for people to suspect we're together?"

"You know why."

"I don't need you to protect me, Elena. I'm a big boy. I think I can handle whatever you're afraid people are going to think of us. And if people think less of me for being with you, why should I give a shit what small-minded assholes like that think?"

"It isn't that."

"Then what is it? Why can't I tell anyone you're mine? Because you're starting to make me wonder if you don't really want to be."

For a moment—a flash so brief he wasn't sure he saw it—she looked stricken. Then her composure returned—along with the first appearance of their waiter. They listened silently to the specials and placed their drink order, and as their waiter was walking away before

Adam could take up the argument again Elena leaned forward and whispered, "Can we just have a nice dinner? I want to celebrate."

She had never looked less celebratory. But this was supposed to be her night. Her triumph. And he was being a dick.

"Of course," he said. "I'm sorry." He reached across the table, placing his hand over hers. She looked around nervously—though the tables had been strategically positioned to allow maximum privacy and they couldn't see any of the other diners.

At least she didn't pull away. Tonight he would take his victories where he could.

\* \* \* \* \*

Dinner was probably delicious. Elena would have loved to be able to actually taste it. Instead, stress seemed to have deadened her taste buds. She sat across from Adam, in an insanely romantic setting, celebrating the one thing she'd actually managed to accomplish in the last year, and all she felt was the slow burn of panic raising bile at the back of her throat.

He was annoyed. Manfully trying to hide it, but obviously annoyed. With her. Because she'd brushed him aside outside. Because she wouldn't tell the world they were together. Because the idea of everyone knowing how much she cared about him made her want to run screaming in the other direction.

When Daniel dumped her, it had sucked. No two ways about that. She'd been sure he loved her. Sure that was all that mattered. And she'd been wrong on both counts. But this time she was the one in love. She was the one vulnerable. And losing him would destroy her.

How much worse would it be if everyone knew? Just like everyone had known with Daniel. There had been no sympathy then. Why should there be any now?

She wasn't good enough for him. Everyone knew that. Even the people who didn't see how much he did for her. And what did she ever do for him?

Besides the sex.

She knew he was happy with the sex.

But how long would that last? When would he get tired of her? How crazy would she make herself waiting for the day when he would decide he was done with her?

No. Better to end things herself. Better to take that control.

But just the idea of ending things, of being the one to walk away, made panic swirl like a tornado through her mind, blitzing all of her thoughts and leaving her emotions a shattered mess.

She was officially freaking out.

She tried to tell herself it was just the book. Just finishing. Just the knowledge that she would have to *do* something with it now. Other people would have to see it. People who would see inside her deepest thoughts and judge her for them.

What had she been thinking? Why had she thought she could do this? Any of it. All of it.

"Elena?"

She looked up, startled to realize the waiter was hovering over them, bearing a pair of dessert menus and an inquisitive expression that matched Adam's.

"No. No dessert. Thank you. Couldn't eat another bite. Delicious." She made herself shut up.

Adam didn't comment on her nervous chatter. He paid the bill, making idle conversation praising the meal she'd barely tasted. She hummed agreeably, trying not to show how she was counting the seconds until she could get away. Would he think it was strange if she wanted to go back to sleep at her own apartment? She needed distance. Space.

She stood before he could hold her chair again, moving ahead of him toward the stairs. She gripped the railing to keep from falling headfirst on top of the host stand as she hurried down the stairs as quickly as her heels would allow. When she reached the bottom, she made a beeline for the door.

"Elena—" Adam began behind her, but she pulled open the door before he could hold it for her.

The warm night air hit her skin as soon as she stepped outside, chasing away the chill left by the restaurant air-conditioning. She looked toward the curb—and the flaw in her headlong rush to the door made itself plain. Adam had given their valet ticket to the waiter when he paid the bill, but she'd taken off in such a hurry they hadn't had time to bring the car around yet.

Which meant they were standing in full view of the paparazzi across the street.

At her side, Adam thrust his hands into the pockets of his trousers and stared straight at the cameras across the way. "Would you be more comfortable waiting inside?"

"I'm fine." She turned her back on the street, for once not trying to make sure the cameras only got her best side.

"Elena?" The voice behind her was rife with surprised pleasure—the voice of a chummy old friend, but she didn't recognize it.

Adam frowned without recognition and removed his

hands from his pockets, falling into what she recognized as his "ready" stance in case he needed to kick some ass in her defense.

Elena turned.

And placed the voice.

Dermott Kellerman. One time lover. Sex Tape Machiavelli.

*Shit.*

"I thought that was you," he said with an easy smile as he approached. "You look fantastic. But then you always do."

Elena froze.

She wanted him to be repulsive. She wanted his smile to be repellent, but he was still an attractive man with a charming, easy-going way about him. The same charismatic aura that had convinced her he would be a harmless one-night stand.

He wasn't as tall as Adam, but he still had a good five inches on Elena, even when she was in heels. His hair was black and styled with a lot of care and product to look like he hadn't bothered to style it. His cheekbones were sharp and his skin-tone almost as dark as hers. He had a lean build, but she remembered him being pleasantly muscled. He was, in appearance, the Anti-Daniel. He had been her antidote—until he became a bigger problem than Daniel had ever been.

This couldn't be a coincidence.

He lived in Vegas. It had been part of the reason he'd seemed so ideal as a one-night stand. Less chance of running into him at an industry party. Less chance that sleeping with him could impact her career in some way.

Little did she know.

What was he doing here?

Even if he'd come to LA for lawsuit crap, why was he

*here*, at this restaurant?

He angled his body and she realized he was framing the shot for the cameras across the street.

The bastard. He must have heard she was here. He'd come here looking for her. Looking for the press being seen with her would garner him. He was trying to hang his bid for celebrity on her star. Or drive up the price of the sex tape with more publicity.

"I heard you turned down the deal. I wish you'd reconsider. This could be—"

She cut him off. "We're only supposed to communicate through our lawyers, Dermott."

"Dermott?" Adam went dangerously still at her side.

The Jeep pulled up at the curve.

Elena sidestepped around Dermott. "Goodbye, Dermott."

"Come on, Elena." He caught her by her upper arm.

Adam bristled. "You have two seconds to get your hands off her."

His fingers were pressing into the flesh of her upper arm. She knew this hold. She and Adam had practiced it. *Element of surprise. Pivot quickly. Thrust heel of her palm directly up into her assailant's nose. Be ready to jerk away when his hold loosens. Follow up by driving her heel into his instep if necessary.*

"Let me go." Her words were calm with the knowledge that she wasn't helpless anymore—not that the techniques Adam taught her would work. She'd only managed them successfully twice, but having *options* was an incredible feeling.

"I know I shouldn't have tried to cut you out of the deal, but this lawsuit crap is ridicu—*fuck!*"

As gratifying as beating him up herself might have been, there was something almost better about watching

Adam's fist snap out, lightning fast, and smash into Dermott's nose with a satisfying crunch.

"You broke my nose!"

The crunch certainly supported that claim. Not to mention the copious amounts of blood gushing between his fingers as he cupped the injured area. Adam didn't seem to care any more than Elena did. "I warned you."

The valet's snickering laugh reminded her where they were—in full view of the paparazzi no less. She grabbed Adam's arm, the muscle flexing under her hands, and tugged him toward his Jeep. "Come on, Rocky. Let's get out of here before we're the lead story on *Inside Edition*."

She hustled him to the car, letting him help her into her seat. He tipped the valet, rounded the hood and hopped in, shooting one more glare to where Dermott was bleeding on the sidewalk before driving away.

"I hope you gave the valet a nice tip since he's probably going to be called as a witness when Dermott files assault charges against you."

"I warned him to get his hands off you."

"And I'm sure the judge will consider that when he's looking at pictures of you kicking the shit out of someone half your size." Even if some primitive part of her had thrilled at seeing him do it. "You can't go beating up everyone who looks at me funny."

Violence wasn't the answer. Even if it sometimes felt like it should be.

"I won't beat up everyone who bothers you, but that was Dermott Kellerman."

"It was."

"He's the exception. He set you up. He's trying to profit from betraying your trust. It was either break his nose or put him in the hospital. I took the high road."

"And if he presses charges? If this were an action movie everyone would be cheering for you, but in real life people tend to get litigious when you punch them."

"It was worth it." He shot her a searing look. "You're worth it."

And all of her objections melted into a gooey chocolate center. "Shit. Don't say things like that."

"Why not?"

"Just don't." She squirmed in her chair.

He hit the gate remote and she realized they were already back at the house, the short drive from the restaurant having passed in a heartbeat. He pulled into the driveway and she was out of the car almost before it stopped moving.

"Elena?"

She kept going. The keypad lock slowed her for only a second, giving him a chance to catch up so he was on her heels as she entered the foyer, her heels echoing on the hardwood floors. "I should go home."

"What are you talking about? Are you seriously that pissed that I punched him?"

"It isn't that."

She took off her heels to climb the stairs more quickly. Most of her things were here now. She'd need to pack a bag to go back to her place tonight. He followed closely behind. "Then what is it?"

How did she tell him it was *everything*? That being with him terrified her because any day he was going to discover she wasn't worth the trouble and leave her. She was worth it now, but how long before it got old? Before she did something to finally turn him away.

"It's easier this way," she said, grabbing her roller bag from under the bed and starting to throw things inside. "I'm trouble. You don't need this."

"Christ. Are we back to this again? Damn it, Elena. What is it going to take for you to trust me?"

"I do trust you."

"Obviously not or we wouldn't be having this conversation again. When are you going to understand that *I love you*?"

## CHAPTER THIRTY-THREE

She looked at him like he'd hit her—wounded and betrayed. Not exactly the reaction he'd been hoping for when he confessed his feelings to her. Of course, this wasn't exactly how he'd anticipated telling her.

She turned her face away and kept packing. "Don't."

"Don't love you?" he asked incredulously.

"*Don't say that.*"

"Why not?" he shouted.

She shook her head and walked into the bathroom, returning a moment later with her curling iron and a bag of toiletries.

"*Elena.*"

"You don't deserve to be tangled up with me," she snapped. "You're a hero."

He snarled a curse, dragging his hands through his hair. "I did *one thing*. Something anyone would have done. I'm not a hero. I'm just a regular guy."

"No. You aren't." She stopped packing, finally looking him in the eye. "I know you hate it when people put you in that box. Saint Adam, American Hero. But you're a better man than anyone I know. Not just because you saved Cassie—and tried to be gentle with her even after she threw you under the bus with the press. You punched Dermott. But more importantly than that you held my hand when he first threatened to release it. You believed in me when I wanted to write a book—even though I didn't have the first clue what I was doing—and you stand up for me whenever anyone says a negative word about me. Even when it's me badmouthing myself. You're *my* hero, Adam Dylan."

"Then why are you running away? What are you so scared of Elena? You say you trust me. So trust me to love you."

"I do," she whispered. "You see me. You don't see the Slutty Suitorette when you look at me. You see *me*. Even before the show, no man ever did that."

"And that's bad?"

She just shook her head. She turned away from him—but at least she wasn't taking the suitcase and walking out the front door. Instead she padded silently toward the small balcony off the master suite.

"Elena?"

\* \* \* \* \*

She gripped the railing, staring out over the ocean without seeing it. If she'd stayed in that room a moment longer she was going to cry, but the fresh air wasn't helping. The salty breeze only seemed to make her eyes water more. She tried to focus on the sound of the surf. The repetitive hush and swish of it, but her heart was beating too hard, drowning it out.

"Elena?" he said again, softly, right behind her. She'd known he would follow her out. After all, he loved her, didn't he?

Which only made the dizzy panic worse. He loved her. He knew her in ways no one else ever had and he still *liked* her. Not just that. Loved her.

Every day he meant more to her. More than anyone

else ever had. She couldn't take it if he left. And to trust that he never would… that wasn't the same as trusting him. She trusted *him* completely. But trusting that he would never leave… that was an entirely different kind of suicide leap.

"I don't trust people," she said finally, so softly the waves could have carried the sound away, but she could tell by the attentive stillness at her side that he heard every word. "They always let me down, but I trust you. I have trusted you completely since day one. I can't love you too. That's too much."

"Okay."

She wanted to scream at him to stop being so damn understanding, but the words were stuck behind the wall of unshed tears clogging her throat.

He brushed her hair back from the side of her face, finishing the move by cupping her jaw, gently turning her toward him. "You don't have to love me. I'll lo—"

"Don't."

"You're worthy of love, Elena. You *deserve* it. Just as much as those other girls on the show."

"Do I?" She tugged out of his hold, crossing to press her back against the opposite rail of the small balcony. "I know I rant and rave about how we all deserve it, but do I really buy that? The world has been telling me I don't for so long—"

"Fuck the world. I love you."

"Shit," she whispered as goose bumps broke out across her arms. Just hearing him say that gave her chills. She pressed her eyes closed, her breath coming short, but he kept talking. Kept *saying it*.

"Not because you're the sexiest thing I've ever seen. Which you are. But because you're *you*. You're so damn smart, but everyone misses it because they're busy drooling. You're strong enough to be impulsive, to own who you are, and you have this powerful sense of justice and morality, which no one gives you credit for. You got a bad deal, but this isn't the end of the story. This is just the part where some loser tells you he loves you. And keeps telling you until you hear it."

He was right up in front of her by the end of his speech and he cupped her face, tipping it up to his. She opened her eyes, pleading with him. "Adam, don't."

"We never really talk about the future. Maybe because the present has plenty for us to deal with. Maybe because both of our plans for the future backfired on us pretty badly in the last year. I'm still not entirely sure I know what I want my future to look like, but I know I want you in it. I would do anything for you." He lowered his head, pressing a kiss to her lips that sealed his promise. "I love you. Do you believe me?"

Shit. It was going to be bad. It was going to be so bad. She was going to lose a piece of her soul if he left, but she couldn't fight it anymore. He was everything.

"Yes."

Adam caught the word on her lips. Never releasing her lips, he lifted her, carrying her over the balcony threshold into the bedroom.

## CHAPTER THIRTY-FOUR

The house hadn't changed much since Christmas.

But then, it hadn't changed much in the twenty-five years before that, so she shouldn't be surprised.

Her childhood home was a taupe stucco ranch style with a bright red tile roof. The neighborhood was modest, but every house was lovingly maintained. People here weren't wealthy, but they took pride in their homes.

Elena parked her Beetle at the curb and started up her parents' tidily landscaped front walk.

She hadn't been back since Christmas. The holiday had fallen during that short window of time between shooting the final episode and airing of the first. She'd known what was coming, but she hadn't been able to warn them.

Only weeks earlier Daniel had come with her to visit her family for the Meet-the-In-Laws episode. She'd been so certain she was winning, she'd told her parents they'd better like Daniel because she was going to be coming back engaged. When he'd picked Caitlyn, she'd felt like a fool. And the confidentiality agreements she'd signed meant she couldn't come clean to her family, lest they leak the results of the show.

So she'd faked it.

Elena was nothing if not an actress.

She'd played the role of the besotted fiancé. Because it had felt like the only thing she could do. Last time she was here, she'd lied.

And then a few weeks later the Jacuzzi episode aired and she became the Slutty Suitorette.

The fights with her father had begun that Tuesday night in January. By the time Daniel dumped her on a Tahitian beach, Juan Suarez had long since declared himself shamed by her immorality and stopped taking her calls.

They hadn't spoken since.

But when she'd woken up beside Adam the morning after his big declaration, she'd lain there watching him sleep and known it was time to face her family. She trusted him with her life—but not to stay. She wanted to trust him with her heart, but she needed to do this first. There were some things she needed to say.

So she'd left a note, grabbed her already packed suitcase off the floor, and left before dawn. She made the twelve-hour drive in ten-and-a-half, arriving just before six in the evening, Mountain Time.

She pushed the doorbell—the sensation weirdly disorienting at her parents' house where she had always just walked right in.

Her mother opened the door.

Elena had thought she was prepared, but her throat still closed for a moment. She swallowed thickly.

Her mother's eyes widened. "Elena."

"Mama."

Her mother still had the round face and well-padded figure, her dark hair dyed even blacker than its natural hue to conceal the slightest hint of grey. Elena favored her father more—his eyes, his cheekbones, his temper—but everyone said she had her mother's smile.

There was no evidence of that smile now.

Her mother blocked the door, glancing past Elena as if to see if anyone could see her on their doorstep. "Your father isn't home yet," she said, her accent thickened by her discomfort.

*Good.* "I was hoping you and I could talk." The main reason she's sped through most of Arizona was so she might have a chance to speak to her mother for a few minutes before her father got home from work.

Rosa Suarez fidgeted with the edge of her blouse, but nodded once, stepping back to allow Elena inside. She led the way to the family room where a giant family portrait hung over the mantle.

At least Elena hadn't been removed from that yet.

"Scott is camping," her mother said, when the silence threatened to stretch between them.

Her parents had given each of their daughters traditional Hispanic names—Elena, Gabriela and Daniela—but when their long-awaited son arrived, they deemed he should have a truly American name. Elena and her sisters still didn't know why they picked Scott. They only knew that with her parents' heavy accents, her little brother spent the first three years of his life thinking his name was "Escot."

Elena mumbled something positive. She wasn't here to talk about her brother's camping trip.

When they were both seated, her mother picked up the mending that always sat next to her chair. In all the years of Elena's life, she'd never seen her mother when her hands were idle for more than two minutes.

She shouldn't feel awkward here, in the house she'd grown up in. Everything was familiar, but she couldn't seem to crack the defensive shell that kept her posture stiff and upright. She wanted to be able to just speak to her mother, but her throat was dry.

"I've missed you, Mama," she whispered. The confession hadn't been part of the script she'd rehearsed on her drive.

Her mother averted her gaze, but Elena could see the glitter of tears there as she gave a little nod of agreement. "I read about you. I worry."

*You could have called*, Elena wanted to argue, but she understood her mother. She was the one who had to live with her husband. She would never leave him while Scott was still at home. If ever. And it wasn't in her to defy his wishes—even when she thought he was being an idiot.

So Elena just said, "I'm okay now. No need to worry." And she found she meant it. She'd turned the corner. She wasn't sure when it had happened, but even within the continued chaos of her life she felt... better. Whole again in some indefinable way.

"He *wants* to talk to you. Your father."

Elena didn't blink at the apparent non sequitur. "He has my number."

"He threw away your new phone number, but I think he regrets it. You know your father. You're so alike. Both of you so stubborn."

Acid burned in her esophagus. "We aren't alike."

Her mother tsked, the needle flying. "*Voluntariosa.*"

"Willful," Elena translated by force of habit.

Her mother nodded and repeated the word. "Willful. Rash."

She said the word rash with particular relish and Elena almost smiled. "I guess that's true." She certainly hadn't gotten her impulsive tendencies from her mother's side. She reached for a pen and paper on the end table next to the phone, writing down her new phone number. "You know, you don't have to tell him you're calling me."

Her mother frowned, as if the very idea of keeping *anything* from her husband confused her. But that was their life. The truth of their relationship and it always had been. Elena tried not to resent it. Tried not to resent the way their partnership had cut her off from both of them.

"Gabi and Dani are good?"

They spoke of her sisters for a few minutes, of the nice young man Gabi was dating, and Elena wondered what her parents would think of Adam. They'd liked Daniel, but at the time so had she. They'd liked *her* back then too.

Chit-chatting with her mother slowly softened her defensive shell. She grew almost comfortable—until they both heard the hum of the garage door lifting.

Her father.

He would have seen her yellow Beetle on the curb. He would know she was here.

Acid churned in Elena's stomach. Whatever she'd been saying died on her tongue, the words forgotten, and her mother fell silent as well.

The kitchen door to the garage squeaked, announcing the arrival of Juan Suarez.

He wasn't a large man, only a few inches taller than Elena, but when she was younger he had always seemed larger than life. A giant with a stern frown and a reluctant smile. But she had always been able to make him smile. And laugh. She could surprise it out of him. His unexpected little Elena.

He didn't like her surprises anymore.

He appeared in the kitchen doorway, aiming an ominous frown at her. "*Que estas haciendo aqui?*" he demanded.

If she'd had to script his welcome, that would have been the exact tone, the exact words she would have predicted. She was ready for this. She'd rehearsed aloud to herself for hours on the interstate, but still her heart beat unnaturally fast as she rose to her feet.

"I brought you something." Her mother hadn't remarked on the manila envelope in her hands, but now Elena lifted it up to show them before setting it on the end table beside the phone and the paper with her new number. "I wrote a book."

"A book?" her mother echoed, as if Elena had just announced she'd decided to become an astronaut.

"You can read it or not read it, but I wanted you to be the first to see it because some of what I wrote was for you."

Her father's frown deepened. "What kind of book?"

"It's my story. The story of the last year through my eyes. Good, bad, and ugly."

"You're going to sell this story?" Disapproval was thick in his voice and vivid on his face.

"I'm going to try. And I'm sorry if you don't approve, but I'm still going to tell my side. I just wanted to come here in person and give you the book and to tell you that I never blamed you for cutting me off. Deep down I thought I deserved it. But I didn't." Her father drew breath to speak, but she plowed on, determined to get through her speech. "Maybe what I did was wrong—I know you think so. I know you're ashamed of me."

She paused for a beat now—hoping they would argue, hoping they would deny it, tell her it was all a misunderstanding, that they really did love her, that they weren't ashamed to be her parents—but her father pressed his lips together in a tight, unforgiving line and her mother averted her eyes.

Something hard and terrible began to build inside her, but she ignored it, speaking over it. "I know you think it was a sin. That I disrespected myself and our family and I'm sorry if you felt disrespected. But what you did was wrong too. You don't turn your back on people you love. You're my parents. You were supposed to support me, not be the ones judging me most harshly."

"It is our job to teach you what's right—"

"I know what's right," she interrupted. "I may not always play by your rules, but I'm true to myself and I stand up for what I believe in. I'm strong and I'm smart and I'm driven. You should be proud of me. And if you aren't…." She waited again—that stupid hope for denial that never came. She swallowed down the hard, terrible thing, thinking of Adam. She was stronger now. "If you aren't… that isn't my problem."

"People who know you are my daughter…" Her father trailed off, shaking his head. "You had so much potential. You were so smart—"

"I'm still smart."

"We sent you to college. You could be so much more than this… this…"

"Slut?"

Her father's mouth pinched at the word. "Your behavior is not what I teach you."

"If you're ashamed of what people will say about you because of me, I understand." *I think you're weak, but I understand. It makes it hard not to hate you, but I understand.* She rubbed her palms over her jeans, irritated with herself for how sweaty they were. "But you're my parents. And I'm your daughter. For better or worse. And I want to know you. I want you to be part of my life, but not if you can't accept me as I am. Because I deserve that. *Everyone* deserves that."

She ran out of words then. That was all she'd practiced. The speech had seemed longer in the car.

She stared at her parents, not sure what kind of reaction she'd been hoping for, but getting nothing. Her father's face was angry and tight. Closed off. Her mother wouldn't meet her eyes, but her needle was still as she stared at her hands.

"Don't you have anything you want to say to me?" She waited again—and realized the hard terrible thing was hope—twisted and bent into disappointment and futility and an anger that wanted to take hold if she let it touch her. She still wanted their acceptance. Their love. Her little speech hadn't changed that. Or the fact that there was nothing she could do to get it if she wasn't willing to play by their rules. And she didn't believe in those rules. She wasn't sure she ever had.

She waited for some sign that they would give. Even an inch. Even the hint that they might *someday* give an inch, but her parents held their silence.

Elena nodded once, letting resignation settle over the broken hope. "Okay. You have my number. If you change your mind."

She hoped they would call her back. Say her name. Move to stop her. She hoped for *anything*, but she made it to her car without a single word or gesture from her parents to stop her.

Six fifteen. She'd been inside the house less than half an hour.

She forced herself to start the car and drive around the block so her parents wouldn't see her lingering outside their house like a stalker. She pulled into the

Walgreens parking lot less than a mile away, turning off the engine and reminding herself to breathe.

She'd hoped to feel vindication. Accomplishment. Closure. Something. Now she just felt stupid. Her parents hadn't changed. Her father disapproved. Her mother would never oppose him. Her father had *thrown out her number*.

She swiped at her face, brushing away the hot moisture stupidly clinging to her cheeks, and grabbed for her phone.

Adam picked up on the second ring. "Elena?"

Her relief at hearing his voice was so acute for a moment all she could get out was, "Hey."

"You okay? Your note didn't say much."

She couldn't even remember what she'd written. Something about having an errand she needed to run. "I'm in New Mexico."

"Is your family okay?" Instant concern.

"I talked to them."

A speaking pause. "Are you okay?" The concern deepened.

She swallowed around the thick block of tears, missing him hard, wanting his arms around her. "It was bad."

The floodgates to all the emotion she'd been holding back opened. Months of frustration and hurt all rushing out at once. All that feeling had been kept at bay by her powerful ability to rationalize. They weren't cutting her off, it was just a really busy time for them. She'd changed her number, perhaps they lost the paper they'd written it on or spilled wine on it so one of the numbers smudged. It wasn't that they were trying to disown her, they just needed some space to process in their own way. They still loved her.

For months she'd told herself those stories. She'd known they were pipe dreams, but you could make yourself believe anything if you wanted to badly enough.

The confirmation that they really didn't want people to know she was their daughter, that her father had intentionally thrown away his one way of contacting her, that her mother had watched him do it—that knowledge broke through her carefully constructed illusions, shattering them into jagged shards waiting to cut her with her own determined naiveté.

And it all came out in a babbling rush over the phone.

"Do you want me to come get you?" Adam asked softly when she wound down.

"In New Mexico?" Her laugh wobbled. "Does Max have a private jet I don't know about?"

"Knowing Max he might, but I was thinking of more the everyman approach of booking the next flight."

"No. No, I'm okay now. I'm glad I talked to them. And knowing they don't—" *don't love me anymore, don't want me anymore…* "—don't have anything to say to me hurt, but I'm glad I know the truth. In the long run, this is better than stretching out the not-knowing and the fantasy hope for years. I said what I needed to say. And now I'm coming home."

"Don't drive when you're upset," he cautioned and she smiled at the worry in his voice. He cared. Even when no one else did.

"I won't. And I promise to stop for the night before I get tired. I'll see you tomorrow night, okay? You'll be there when I get back?"

"Always."

She said goodbye to him and tossed her cell phone

onto the passenger seat, feeling emotionally drained but calm. Like being born, screaming and exhausted and ready for a new beginning.

She looked around the Walgreens parking lot, rolling down her window to breathe in the scents of Albuquerque. She'd faced her past—she should get a freaking gold star—but as much as she loved this town, she was done with it now. Her future was in Malibu.

# CHAPTER THIRTY-FIVE

She had the entire drive back to think about what she would say to Adam when she saw him. For the first few hours, her conversation with her parents kept circling in her mind, but after she stopped at a Holiday Inn Express for the night her thoughts miraculously calmed down and she slept like the dead. The next morning she woke up feeling remarkably good. Refreshed and hopeful in a way she hadn't anticipated.

Her new agent, Claudia, called her when she was halfway through Arizona with good news. The New York based literary agent whom she'd worked with in the past was eager to take a look at Elena's book whenever she was done with it and she had a publicist she wanted Elena to meet who had some excellent ideas about ways to subtly change her public image without losing name recognition.

She also had an audition. It was a smaller film—a political thriller—and Elena's character would be murdered after the first twenty minutes, but her murder was a catalyst for the hero. It was a small but pivotal part. And the character was a reporter. Not a bimbo, but a smart, savvy driven woman who was not afraid to use her sexuality to her advantage in a male dominated industry.

Elena was so excited she had to pull over when

Claudia told her about it. And then all she wanted to do was call Adam. But he was working and she would see him tonight.

She had a lot to tell him.

The traffic around Los Angeles slowed her down, adding an unnecessary hour, but she still beat him to the beach house. She hadn't anticipated arriving first. She showered and changed, taking particular care with her hair and make-up, but still he wasn't home.

She wanted tonight to be special. Important. She needed some kind of big romantic gesture to show him she was all in, that she'd decided to stop being an idiot and go for it, but everything she thought of felt cliché.

She printed out another copy of her book, hand-writing three different versions of a mushy dedication to him before she settled on *For Adam, with all my love*. The paper looked too plain, so she tied it in a red ribbon. Then she felt self-conscious with it sitting there on the kitchen counter so she put it in a box. With wrapping paper and another bow from the craft supplies she tripped across in the laundry room a few weeks ago when she was looking for dryer sheets.

But a book wasn't a gesture. It wasn't enough.

What did he want from her? What could she give him?

The Just Friends thing had bugged him, but she couldn't exactly haul off and kiss him in front of the paparazzi when neither he nor the paparazzi were here to appreciate the gesture.

He wanted her to trust him—but how did she *show* him that? A freaking trust fall? Where was a team-building exercise when you needed one?

The front door opened while she was standing in the middle of the living room dithering.

"Elena?"

His voice broke right through her nerves, changing everything. This was *Adam*. She didn't think—she just ran into his arms, throwing herself against him and planting a kiss on his mouth. "Welcome home."

"Thank you." He grinned down at her, hazel eyes glittering with a thousand spikes of color. "How was your drive?"

"Good. Excellent." She pushed off his chest until she held him at arm's length. She wanted nothing more than to drag him to bed and keep him there for days, but she needed to do this now, say this now, before she lost her nerve. "I had a lot of time to think. Process stuff. I have a lot to tell you."

"Should I be worried?"

"No. But you should sit down. When I pictured talking to you, you were always sitting in the living room."

"Okay." He let her tug him toward the sunken living room, shrugging out of his suit jacket and draping it over the arm of the sofa before he sat down. She watched as he unbuttoned his cuffs and rolled up his sleeves. He looked so serious, so businesslike. Always controlled, her Adam.

She would never be controlled.

"I'm a mess."

He met her eyes, brows arching high. "Is this a new mess or one I already know about?"

She twisted her hands together, letting her nerves show because it was only him there to see them. "Physically and emotionally, I'm always going to be messy. Life with me is never going to be neat and orderly."

His lips quirked in a half-smile. "I think I've figured

that out for myself, but I appreciate the warning."

"I need you to shut up. The imaginary version of you in my car didn't talk back. Or move."

He snorted out a laugh but kept his mouth shut.

"I trust you."

He nodded.

"It's easy to trust you to save my life because you're Superman, but it's a lot harder for me to trust you to stay. Because in my experience, people don't. They judge you and abandon you. They don't stick by you when things go to hell and even though you did, I never trusted it. Even though I knew you were different. But it's scary trying to trust someone not to let you down when it seems like people always do. And I'm normally not afraid to do something crazy—you know that—but this is like jumping off a bridge every day for the rest of my life and just trusting that you're going to be there to catch me. That you aren't going to look at me next week or some day five years from now and be bored or disgusted. That I'm not going to do something stupid to drive you away. But I love you. So I guess I'm going to jump off a bridge every morning for the rest of my life and just hope you're always there to catch me, because if you aren't I don't know what I'll do.

"I never used to think I needed anyone, but I need you. You're my best friend. You're the only one I want to talk to when things go wrong and the only one I want to tell when things go right. You make me feel like I can be better than I ever imagined—and not better by anyone else's rules, but by mine. I'm not going to suddenly be a good cook, or be tidy, or be any less likely to snap at you when you interrupt my train of thought when I'm obsessed with my book, but I promise that I will love you more than anyone else ever could. And I'm not going to stop. That's just who I am now. The girl who loves you whether you want her to or not. So…" She wet her lips. "Did I scare you off?"

"I can talk now?"

"Yeah. Your turn. Go for it."

He was in front of her before she finished the last word, cutting it off with a kiss that seared her senses and sizzled through her all the way down to her toes. *Oh, mercy.* He must have been holding back before, because this was a whole new level.

He lifted his head, arms still wrapped around her. "I think we should get married. How's tomorrow for you?"

"You're not serious." She laughed. Then she saw the look in his eyes, daring her.

"Come on, Elena. Be impulsive. Marry me. Vegas is just a few hours away."

Another laugh burst out of her—as if she was so happy it wouldn't all fit inside her. "You are serious. A runaway marriage? People will say I corrupted you."

"You worry too much about what other people think."

Maybe she did. "You think?"

"Marry me," he coaxed. "You know you want to."

The idea was intoxicating—and irresistible. Impulsive. So very *her.* So very them. Another laugh slipped out. "I think you're going to be good for me, Adam Dylan."

"Good is overrated." He brushed her lips, kissed along her jaw, and then whispered into the hair next to her ear, "Let's be bad."

She held onto him, the star around which all her happiness orbited. "Let's."

# EPILOGUE

"Our guest today has seen more than her share of scandal, but today she's here to talk to us about her new book, her new foundation, and her handsome new husband. Please help me welcome... Elena Dylan!"

The studio audience applauded with genuine enthusiasm as Elena walked out to join the panel of women clustered around a table center stage. They each hugged her in turn, murmuring words of support and Elena beamed and thanked them as if she didn't remember every negative word they'd ever said about her.

"First things first," the hostess to her left began as they all settled back down to begin the interview. "Let's see that rock!"

Elena flashed her ring, grinning widely as they all oohed and aahed.

The rock she'd been showing off on the talk show circuit for the last week was completely fake. Adam had wanted to get her a real one, but she liked flashy bling—and *real* flashy bling came with a flashy price tag. They'd agreed that saving their pennies in the hope that they could afford the beach house a little while longer was a better move for them than blowing thousands on jewelry.

Adam had promised to replace the fake stone with

the real thing if they could ever afford it and Elena had told him the next time he saved a celebrity's life, they were welcome to pay him in diamonds. With the way things were going for them right now, there was a chance they might not have to wait that long, but Elena was sentimental about her fake ring. It was the one Adam had put on her finger during their Vegas wedding. And she absolutely loved the feeling of putting one over on the entire world by flashing her giant fake rock on talk shows like it was Neil Lane.

"I thought you two said you were just friends," another hostess said leadingly.

Elena smiled guiltily. "That was my doing, actually. My reputation was terrible and I didn't want him to be negatively impacted by having his name tied to mine. But my husband is a persuasive man and he talked me into til-death-do-us-part only a few weeks later."

"You're very candid in your book about your relationship with your then-boyfriend and how much his support meant to you throughout the difficulties of the last year. Readers have been so moved by your love story and so many people are seeing you in a new light. How does it feel now that America is falling in love with you two?"

The book hadn't been a hard sell. Morbid curiosity had helped it fly off the shelves, and at first those who read it seemed confused that it actually had substance, but gradually the reactions had shifted and seemingly overnight Elena had become America's sweetheart. Something she knew better than to take to heart.

"It's wonderful to feel that support from the American public." *Fickle though they may be.* "But I think what's been even more valuable to me is the realization that I had a lot more supporters than I realized even when things were at their worst. There were people who were speaking out on my behalf. It may have seemed like they were being drowned out by the voices of those who condemned me, but they were there and one of the goals of our new foundation is going to be to try to give those positive voices a megaphone."

"You're speaking of course of the Minerva Foundation you recently founded with Cassandra Newton to provide support to women in similar situations to those you faced."

"That's right. Cassandra Newton is very passionate about women's issues." Something Elena had only realized when Sandy had insisted on meeting her after she and Adam got back from their whirlwind honeymoon. "As is our other partner Miranda Pierce, the producer of *American Dance Star*."

"Whom you met during your time on *Marrying Mister Perfect*?"

"Yes. And it all comes full circle."

Sandy and Elena had actually become surprisingly good friends as they worked together to form the foundation. Things with Cassie were still a bit strained— but now that she'd started college in Connecticut she seemed to have found her place and was less likely to throw daggers at Elena when their paths crossed.

The hostesses chuckled and chatted. Everyone happy and sociable. As if they hadn't been holding tar and feathers with everyone else just a few months ago.

They talked about her recent performance in *Unreasonable Doubt*—which had surprised the critics even more than her book had—and touched briefly on her upcoming roles.

Then came the question she always asked them not to ask- and they always asked anyway.

"One thing that really touched a lot of readers in your book was your honesty about how your difficulty with your family affected you, but I understand you're on your way to reconciliation. How is that?"

"We're in touch now," Elena admitted—though that was all she was willing to say.

The reconciliation, such as it was, was slow going. Her mother had texted her with congratulations on the day news of her wedding went public. It was a small gesture, but it had been a start. Now they texted, emailed and even spoke on the phone occasionally. It was always very stilted, very cautious and mostly talking about her siblings and their lives—and her father was never mentioned, though she knew he was aware of the communication.

It was something. Her mother never mentioned the book, or her visit to New Mexico. She never admitted that Elena was right and they shouldn't have cut her off—there was no vindication, no satisfaction on that level—but starting toward things being good with her parents again was worth more than being right.

When she didn't elaborate, the hostess to her right took the hint and steered the conversation in a different direction. "You're such a busy woman. Is it true you're also training to get your black belt?"

Elena smiled. "I am. My husband is determined to make a badass out of me yet. Although he still refuses to admit I'm a better shot than he is."

Twenty minutes later, the show's talent liaison escorted her outside—where her husband was leaning against his Jeep. "There she is. America's sweetheart, who is delusional enough to think she can outshoot me."

Elena rolled her eyes at the sweetheart bit. "They ate it up. And it's almost true." She crossed into his arms, going up on her toes to kiss him. "I thought you had to work today."

"Sandy's ribbon cutting thingy was rescheduled. And Max wants me to tell you to start mentioning the Celebrity Self Defense courses EP does in your interviews. He's greedy for the free press."

"I'll see if I can cram it into the conversation on the Late Late Show tonight. You wanna grab lunch before I have to head over to their studio?"

"You didn't think I'd come all this way just to nag you for free press, did you?"

He held the door for her, helping her up into the passenger seat.

"They didn't ask you about the sex tape," he commented as he started the engine.

"They know I can't comment on an ongoing legal clusterfuck. And they were going for cheesy-happy-redemption. It would have brought down the tone."

The legal mess surrounding the tape was still ongoing, but she wasn't going to borrow trouble. Whether they won or lost, whether it came out or not, she had people in her corner and a career that would survive it. And Adam.

She twisted to study the man in the driver's seat, his strong profile, his clean-shaven jaw. She was so damn lucky to have him, but life could so easily have gone another way. For both of them.

"Do you ever think about guarding the President?"

He glanced at her, one brow arched. "Not really. Not anymore. Why?"

"I was just thinking about alternate universes. Where I'm married to Daniel and you're guarding the President."

"And we're both miserable?"

"Probably."

He reached over, catching her hand and bringing it over to rest in his on the center console. "No regrets, Elena mine."

"Not one," she agreed. Her fake ring glittered in the sunlight. He made her feel like she could do anything—even things that had always seemed terrifying and impossible. "We should have a baby."

The car swerved ever so slightly. He shot her a sideways glance, laughing, "Now?"

"Maybe next year. Oscar voters love a pregnancy. And I'm definitely getting nominated for Sylvia. Have you read the script? She's incredible."

"So my job is to give you a nice baby bump for the Oscars next year?"

"Yeah. And, you know, a baby could be nice too."

He grinned at her, understanding her as no one else ever had. "It could." His voice was soft.

She smiled and settled back into her seat, pleased with the plan. Pleased with everything.

Her fake ring. Her real husband. Her dreams coming true. Just another of the glamorous people living her glamorous life.

# ABOUT THE AUTHOR

Lizzie Shane lives in Alaska where she uses the long winter months to cook up happily-ever-afters (and indulge her fascination with the world of reality television). A 2-Time Romance Writers of America® RITA Nominee, she also writes paranormal romance under the pen name Vivi Andrews. Find more about Lizzie's books or sign up to receive her newsletter for updates on upcoming releases at www.lizzieshane.com.

# WANT MORE LIZZIE SHANE?
# DON'T MISS THE REST OF THE SERIES:

### MARRYING MISTER PERFECT
(Reality Romance, Book 1)

### ROMANCING MISS RIGHT
(Reality Romance, Book 2)

### FALLING FOR MISTER WRONG
(Reality Romance, Book 3)

### PLANNING ON PRINCE CHARMING
(Reality Romance, Book 4)

### COURTING TROUBLE
(Reality Romance, Book 5)

And look for Max's story, coming in Fall 2016.

Made in the USA
Charleston, SC
17 November 2016